"As the descendant of seven soldiers who fought in the Revolutionary War, I thoroughly enjoyed every page of *Sparks of the Revolution*. I had heard of James Otis and Mercy Otis Warren before, but somehow I did not know very much about them. Todd Otis has brought these historical people to life as fully developed characters in this novel. We see their motivations, passions, fears, and shortcomings here, making them real people to us. Most importantly, we come to understand the integral role they played in the events leading up to the American Revolution, and we see how closely connected they were to other patriots like James Hancock and Samuel Adams. The inclusion of Crispus Attucks, the first martyr of the Revolution and an African American at that, into the story highlights the book's relevance to today, showing how we must continue to protect the freedom our ancestors achieved."

— Tyler R. Tichelaar, award-winning author of *When Teddy Came to Town* and *Kawbawgam: The Chief, The Legend, The Man*

"As a former history teacher and Superintendent of Boston Public Schools, I know the importance of place and history, and how the intersection can instill in students their sense of identity and the formation of their democratic values. These are fundamental to the function of public education and the creation of an informed citizenry. *Sparks of the Revolution* does that and excites the imagination. It shines light on the leaders who helped lay the foundation of our democratic values. This is the kind of book that should fill our school libraries and elicit classroom discussion and debate, and even inspire students to shape the future for the better."

— Dr. Brenda Casselius, former Superintendent of Boston Public Schools and former Minnesota Commissioner of Education

SPARKS
OF THE
REVOLUTION

James Otis and the Birth of American Democracy

A Novel

TODD OTIS

Modern History Press

Ann Arbor, MI

Sparks of the Revolution: James Otis and the Birth of American Democracy – A Novel

ISBN 978-1-61599-787-9 paperback
ISBN 978-1-61599-788-6 hardcover
ISBN 978-1-61599-789-3 eBook

Modern History Press   www.ModernHistoryPress.com
5145 Pontiac Trail   info@ModernHistoryPress.com
Ann Arbor, MI 48105   888-761-6268

Editor: Tyler Tichelaar, Superior Book Productions

Library of Congress Cataloging-in-Publication Data

Names: Otis, Todd H., author.
Title: Sparks of the revolution : James Otis and the birth of American
    democracy : a novel / Todd Harrison Otis.
Description: Ann Arbor : Modern History Press, 2024. | Summary: "An
    historical novel based on the life of James Otis Jr. (1725 - 1783) an
    American lawyer, political activist, colonial legislator, and early
    supporter of patriotic causes in Massachusetts Bay Colony at the
    beginning of the Revolutionary Era. The narrative weaves in other
    historical figures including Paul Revere, Samuel Adams, Crispus Attucks
    and others primarily in the period from 1760 - 1775"-- Provided by
    publisher.
Identifiers: LCCN 2023054763 (print) | LCCN 2023054764 (ebook) |
    ISBN
    9781615997879 (paperback) | ISBN 9781615997886 (hardcover) |
    ISBN
    9781615997893 (epub)
Subjects: LCSH: Otis, James, 1725-1783--Fiction. | United
    States--History--Revolution, 1775-1783--Fiction. | LCGFT: Novels. |
    Historical fiction.
Classification: LCC PS3615.T897 S63 2024 (print) | LCC PS3615.T897
    (ebook) | DDC 813/.6--dc23/eng/20240228
LC record available at https://lccn.loc.gov/2023054763
LC ebook record available at https://lccn.loc.gov/2023054764

To Ren,

A loving partner through thick and thin

Contents

An Introduction to James Otis the Patriot

Decades after the American Revolution had concluded, and after his Presidency had ended, John Adams wrote the following about James Otis and the Writs of Assistance case that Adams had observed in 1761:

> *Otis was a flame of fire!* With the promptitude of Classical Allusions, a depth of research, a rapid summary of historical events and dates, a profusion of Legal Authorities, a prophetic glance of his eyes into futurity, and a rapid torrent of impetuous Eloquence, he hurried away all before him. American Independence was then and there born. The seeds of Patriots and Heroes to defend the Non sine Diis Animosus Infans, to defend the Vigorous Youth, were then and there sown. Every Man of an immense crowded Audience appeared to me to go away, as I did, ready to take Arms against Writs of Assistance. Then and there was the first scene of the first Act of opposition to the Arbitrary claims of Great Britain. *Then and there the Child Independence was born.* In fifteen years, i.e. in 1776, he grew up to Manhood and declared himself free.

This work of historical fiction describes my rendition of some key people in pre-Revolutionary Boston, people like Samuel Adams, John Hancock, and Crispus Attucks, whom you have probably heard of, as well as James Otis, Mercy Otis Warren, and Ebenezer Mackintosh, who may not be known to you.

My initial motivation was to shine some light on a distant ancestor, James Otis the Patriot, who sparked resistance to British rule in Boston. As you read above, John Adams credited Otis' brilliant argument against the Writs of Assistance in 1761 as the moment "the Child Independence was born."

The more I read, wrote, and thought about the people who led our nation to revolution, and then to the establishment of the world's oldest and greatest democracy, the more I thought their words and deeds could help us remember what this country should be all about.

The men and women who led us to resistance and then revolution were not paragons, and they, like everyone, had flaws. They were driven and guided by a hodgepodge of feelings and desires. But underlying their actions and reactions to British rule were beliefs and ideals that we Americans must embrace anew.

What a time to reflect, and redirect our values! What is the new normal we can create today and what kinds of leaders will we select to guide us? Will they usher us to a place closer to the founding ideals? Or will they let us remain untrue to our highest ideals, keeping them and their financial contributors comfortable and powerful? Actions taken and words spoken between 1760 and 1775 in Boston can inform and inspire us about what to choose and how to come together for a common cause.

Of course, all of this book's dialogue is invented, for obvious reasons. However, quotations from newspapers and public utterances by famous leaders are authentic, as are excerpts from some key documents. Those words and the actions described in this book are what I hope will inspire you.

Yes, the Boston I am writing about had only 15,000 inhabitants, and the lives they led were simpler than ours, their economy more tied to the earth and sea. The powerful engine of industrialization had yet to be unleashed. But the actions of those Bostonians and their British rulers can provide us with reminders and lessons well worth noting.

I invite you to read this book, and then visit the "Lessons Learned" section at the very end to see if you agree.

I hope you enjoy this fictionalized glimpse into the lives and actions of some of the men and women who sparked a revolution that ushered in a new democracy and changed the world. If we are wise and brave enough, their ideals and qualities can guide us to a more perfect union.

Todd Otis

Part I

The Spark

❧ 1 ❧

Boston, Massachusetts—1760

The sweat was dripping down Otis' undergarments in the boiling Boston late afternoon as he hastened to the Green Dragon, a place to wet his whistle and join the throng and where he could be himself. He was aware, and a little chagrined, that an expanding dark patch stood out in the rear of his gray breeches. It caused the filthy little boys who were playing tag in the dirt road to point at him and laugh. At thirty-five, James Otis, Jr. usually tried to keep up appearances as a distinguished lawyer, but he felt no need for pretense with young children. He just waved back to them and smiled.

Entering the tavern gave its customers the sense that they were joining an old friend who might not be fastidious, but was accepting and fun. Patrons felt like they had been friends with the tavern their entire life. To be sure, the floors were gritty and the windows unwashed, but the solid wood pillars that separated the spaces in the tavern were like strong sentinels keeping watch over its patrons, their secrets, and their wild dreams. The clinking glasses and the constant buzz of conversation in the Green Dragon animated the place with the energy of a powerful, prowling bear. Gossip, rumors, and some good information always flowed with the beer.

The unscrubbed mirror behind the bar was like a messenger telling you to forget yourself, to dive into your conversation and your friendships, and to allow your cares to dissolve into the spilled-whisky-smelling air, but Otis couldn't help himself. He always looked into that mirror to admire his wide face and thin lips, which seemed to be in a perpetual near-smile. He felt his dark brown eyes exuded a benign intelligence.

A discontented group had summoned Otis there: five merchants of considerable means, the chief of whom was William Mackay, an importer of textiles who had grown to hate the British customs officials. The men bridled at having their homes and businesses invaded at will by the local British agents who were looking for smuggled goods, all in the name of the Crown.

Mackay was a very large man in height and girth. His generally friendly nature and lively blue eyes belied a toughness that customers and his competitors misjudged at their own peril.

"We are expecting a couple of other men, but let's get started," he said, introducing Otis to the other four who seemed to understand they were there to agree with Mackay, and to drink.

"We greatly appreciate your willingness to meet us," said Mackay. The other four echoed the sentiment with a common murmur and nodded heads.

"Our patience," Mackay continued, "has been overtaxed by the customs commissioners and their flagrant misuse of the so-called Writs of Assistance. They disrupt our businesses and terrorize families and children with their brutish raw display of power. They need to be stopped."

The Writs of Assistance were general search warrants issued to customs officers by the colonial superior courts, and they were hated by merchants and, indeed, all citizens.

Otis smiled and nodded. He knew what they wanted and was proud of the reputation he had already earned as one of Boston's ablest lawyers. He was always assiduous in his preparation of cases, always more articulate and insightful than opposing counsel.

"So, what is it you want? As you know, I am a loyal British subject proud to live in a colony of the greatest nation on earth—a nation of great honor and magnanimity. I love the Crown."

Otis enjoyed exaggerating his love of England, possibly because he suspected his true beliefs and well-considered ideals might one day be subversive to the authority of the very Crown he claimed to adore.

"We love the Crown as well, Otis, but these Writs are an abomination. None of the King's subjects would have to endure this in England. The Writs are like a spit in the face of all loyal British subjects." As Mackay spoke, the group heard a loud and gross expectoration into a nearby spittoon. A scraggly, dirty stranger, top hat askew, waved to them and winked.

"Good timing and nice figure of speech," Otis said in a gently mocking tone. "So let me ask again, what is it you want?"

"We want you to let us engage you and your considerable talents to challenge the Writs and demonstrate that they are an illegal infringement on the rights of all loyal British subjects,"

Mackay said a bit too loudly, causing the rest of the hall to come to a brief, awkward silence.

Otis straightened his back, bringing his body fully erect in the two-posted oak chair he occupied. He moved the chair forward, both hands placed sturdily and strongly on the round table.

"Are you not aware that I am the Advocate General of the Admiralty Court? I am employed by our royal Majesty, the King. If there is a case to be argued, I daresay I will do it on his behalf."

Silence. Of course they knew. Otis knew they knew. They knew he knew they knew. The brilliant lawyer was enjoying himself.

"Of course, your primary concern lies with the rights of British subjects and nothing as mundane as your business success," Otis added. "And you would never evade the law."

"Of course not," Mackay and his men muttered in unison. Each merchant's face played host to a smirk. It was the rampant smuggling in Boston that had precipitated use of the Writs of Assistance in the first place, and all five men seated with Otis had done more than their share of evading the duties on imported goods. The citizens of Boston understood the value of smuggling—it kept the price of foreign goods more affordable to them. And avoiding needless costs for their products was good business for those selling them. It just made sense.

The innocent conspirators fidgeted in their chairs and cleared their throats. The pause in the conversation was broken by the entrance into the Green Dragon of a young and very prosperous-looking young man. Dressed in his maroon velvet frock coat, which covered his silk embroidered waistcoat and his perfectly white shirt with its ruffled sleeves, the twenty-four-year-old John Hancock was a man with a trim frame and a chipper stride. Hancock's handsome, thin, and angular face exuded confidence and optimism.

"Come over here, young man, and have an ale!" Otis shouted to Hancock. "What are you doing here? I thought you were in England." An easy familiarity existed between the two despite their twelve-year age difference; they were both Harvard men.

"I will not be satisfied with one drink; I need three," Hancock said, looking toward the popular and attractive barmaid. "Beth, bring these nice gentlemen another round. Bless you."

As they settled into the next round of conversation, Hancock and Otis did all the talking. They never even mentioned the Writs of Assistance. Mackay's complexion gradually changed from pink to a deeper red, and his eyes became slits of anger.

"Is there something wrong, Mackay?" Hancock asked. "You look a bit out of sorts."

"No, nothing is the matter. Everything is just wonderful. But might we go back to the subject of the Writs of Assistance?"

"I think for now we have exhausted that subject," Otis said. "I appreciate your time."

Mackay jerked his chair from the table so hard the wooden screech could be heard throughout the tavern. He and the other four elbowed their way through the growing, thirsty crowd and burst through the front entrance.

Hancock looked at Otis quizzically. "Why so abrupt, James? Mackay and his associates have serious concerns they needed to convey to you. I thought Adams would be here too."

"Why are you asking me that question, John? Mackay is the one who barged out of here without so much as a 'Farewell.' He roars and charges like a bull. Someone should teach him manners."

The two remained at the table as the room grew more crowded and hearing one another became more challenging. As they enjoyed their third ale, the conversation became animated and the insights brilliant (or so they thought). They discussed the Writs of Assistance with great enthusiasm and gossiped eagerly about the commissioners of customs who were abusing their new authority.

"Robinson is a toad, I swear," Otis said, speaking of a prominent customs agent. Hancock made a croaking sound, to the amusement of the surrounding patrons. "Or maybe he is a duck; he waddles like a duck." To which Hancock clucked, again loudly enough to bring smiles to the swilling crowd who heard him.

As the two men prepared to leave, Hancock asked Otis if he had rejected Mackay's request out of hand. "So, Boston's most brilliant lawyer refuses to stand up for the rights of his neighbors and of all loyal British subjects in these several colonies? Is that what you told Mackay?"

"Not exactly," Otis said. "But I fear that is what he believes."

⹀ 2 ⹀

James Otis trudged through Boston's tapered and crooked cobbled streets after leaving the Green Dragon. He passed the teeming marketplace where farmers were hawking fresh turnips, cabbages, parsnips, and hard apple cider. At this time of day, the vegetables seemed as wilted as the vendors, and the customers and sellers began to consume applejack in increasing quantities. (Fresh, clean water was a rare commodity and never sold.)

The streets' contours were so uneven, and the ale in Otis was of sufficient quantity that walking was a challenge. He did not want to appear to be staggering as he started his ascent of Beacon Hill, a neighborhood he never could have afforded to live in had he not married the beautiful Ruth Cunningham. To be sure, he came from a distinguished family, his father having been a successful lawyer, judge, and colonel, but lawyering and public service alone could not provide the resources required to build a home on Beacon Hill. One did not want to stumble in a Beacon Hill street after drinking at the Green Dragon. Everyone knew that while the wealthy enjoyed their money, they prized their reputations even more, and more than that, they enjoyed gossip and recounting the foibles of their peers.

Otis dreaded the conversation he was going to have with Ruth. She loved the British royalty, she loved being a British subject, she loved the heritage of the English people, and she loved the dominant power of the British Empire. She followed the affairs of state in Great Britain, savoring whatever rumors and scuttlebutt there was regarding the king and his various ministers. A part of her, a part she never confessed to anyone, told her she would have loved to be the Queen of England. She believed she had the grace, wisdom, and compassion to be a great monarch. Her subjects, especially the men, would have enjoyed that she was remarkably beautiful; she had the kind of beauty that engendered in men far more than simple appreciation.

The last thing Ruth would want to discuss with her husband, or anyone else, was the abuse of power by British customs officers and the damage done by the Writs of Assistance. She most certainly would not want to side with the whining colonists. The British leaders knew what they were doing; they had to address the fact that too much smuggling was occurring throughout the provinces. England needed to have a way to enforce the rules of importation. The scheming, smuggling American merchants tried to dress their evasions in the cloak of freedom and the rights of British subjects, but Ruth understood their true motivation was greed.

Part of what had attracted Otis to Ruth was her lovely blend of strong beliefs and her gentle, understated manner. The somewhat awkward reality was that it was Ruth who had brought wealth to their union, and it was Ruth's father's merchant friends who had helped Otis start his practice. Being educated at Harvard and now swimming in the warm pond of Boston's elite society had provided Otis status of a sort, but he always felt the true elite were known by their intellect and the higher causes they followed. This sense of his own superiority kept him from fully respecting and appreciating his good wife.

Otis entered the parlor with its rich crimson motif of French wallpaper and drapes, its upholstered wing-chairs, and its pristine scrubbed pine floor. The house was always in a neat, uncluttered state. His eyes ignored the familiar surroundings and were riveted on Ruth.

"Hello, my beautiful wife," he said. Inexplicably, he was always surprised by the effect looking at her had on him. Legal cases and high ideals, British arrogance and unjust acts melted away when he was swept up by that initial gaze. She exuded grace and a soft, alluring quality of sensuality. Auburn hair, hazel eyes, an elegantly straight nose, high cheekbones, and a body exquisitely suited to the new fashions that accentuated a narrow waist—all these assets combined to create more than a vision; it was an aura of stunning, powerful femininity.

"Hello, James," she said. "You have been at the Green Dragon, I see." Ruth felt no affinity for the tavern's clientele and could see Otis had consumed a bit too much.

Otis knew it was probably a poor time to discuss law or politics, but he could not help himself. His sense of urgency overpowered the common sense he would have possessed two glasses of ale ago.

"I want to tell you about a conversation I just had with Hancock and some merchants." Ruth knew and liked young Hancock; they shared the same refined sense of fine clothing and elegant home furnishings, and he was fun to be with.

Otis continued speaking, now with the self-protective tone of a man giving a speech, not one who was interested in a real conversation and likely a disagreement. Ruth averted her eyes as he spoke, a bad sign. He told her of the request the merchants had made, the argument Hancock had put forward, the rumbling insurgency that the Writs of Assistance were causing among the citizens of Boston, and his powerful inclination to defend the highest principles of England itself. He professed his undying love for her, his understanding that they held differing views on adherence to the wishes of the Crown, and that he was giving serious consideration to accepting the case on behalf of the colonists.

"You are serving the king in the Admiralty Court," Ruth said softly. "You work for our British government. You are a loyal and able subject. Doing this would destroy your reputation as a solid public servant who can be trusted. You cannot switch allegiances like this; this is not like choosing the right frock or set of stockings. How can you even give this a moment's thought?" Then her expression and complexion changed as quickly as a sudden squall on a quiet lake. A primal sadness settled on her exquisite face.

"Doing this risks destroying the harmony of our family. What is more important to you: our love or your interpretation of the rights of English subjects?" Her tone was resigned, subdued. Their life together had started with such promise, such joy. Now, just a few years into their marriage, she seemed to see them headed into hostile, uncharted waters.

Otis was struck by her resolve and somewhat surprised by its depth.

"You know the answer to that question," he replied. "Nothing is more important to me than you and our little James. But I do not understand why the rights of Englishmen must be opposed to our love. Why?"

"You make it sound so simple, James," Ruth said. "But you know and I know that the rabble of our city are wanting more; they want violence and what they call liberty. Your advocacy of their cause will only inflame them, mark my words. You may still be a loyal British subject, but the people you drink with at the Green Dragon are not cut from the same cloth. Some of them even want to be independent of England—a ridiculous idea. That would make this colony a weak orphan in a hostile world. Certainly you understand this."

Otis attempted to collect his thoughts through the haze of familial guilt and alcohol. Then a new presence entered the room, unannounced. It was a person of great importance to Otis and the broader community of radicals, a person whom he loved and encouraged and of whom he was proud, yet also a person who, when he was in her presence with Ruth, made him feel uncomfortable, self-conscious, and tugged in two directions. It was his sister, Mercy Otis Warren.

"Am I interrupting? Of course I am. I am so sorry. I will come back later," Mercy said, looking at Ruth, whose scowl gave off more sadness than anger. Mercy had fond feelings for her sister-in-law, feelings she was not sure were reciprocated. While they shared the bond of gender and many of the common sensibilities of women, a gulf of growing magnitude had begun to separate them.

Mercy was attractive largely because of the remarkable energy she emanated. Possessed of a diminutive frame, she carried herself with erect dignity. Her eyes sparkled like sapphires, her sharp chin raised high, and her thin body moved surely and with undomesticated feline energy. She filled up any room she entered, not by overt conversational dominance but by a special sort of physical and intellectual power that her very being generated. She vibrated with vitality.

Mercy Otis Warren was an aberration among women. The anomaly in Mercy was not that she had grown up in a family that tended toward resistance to the Crown. Far more odd (as seen by many men and women of Beacon Hill) was her unquenchable appetite for learning and her incessant curiosity. She did not read books; she devoured them. She possessed the unconventional belief that being a woman was no reason to discount the validity of her ideas. Equally odd in the minds of many proper Bostonians was that both her father and brother actually encouraged those beliefs and qualities.

"No, stay Mercy, my dear," Ruth said, and not out of a false sense of politeness, but sincerely. "Tell me, has James already made his decision?"

"Decision about what?" Mercy asked innocently.

"About the Writs case," said Ruth. "I think you know what I am talking about."

"Not that I am aware of. Have you, Jemmy?" Mercy was not lying to Ruth. Her bond with her brother in support of what would become the Patriots' cause had not yet been fully forged. Otis had not even consulted his sister on the matter. Yet they both knew without speaking how the other felt.

"No, my darling, I have not yet decided. Truly, no," Otis replied.

Ruth's face softened and her lush lips curled into a small smile of satisfaction. Mercy felt awkward in the scene, sensing the likely decision her brother would make, yet watching her dear sister-in-law seem to believe Otis really was undecided. Mercy left after embracing both of them, leaving Otis and Ruth in a quiet place of deceptive harmony. They retired early to their elegant bedroom, made so by Ruth's unerring sense of design.

While his wife had the capacity to fall asleep instantly and move into a nearly impenetrable slumber, Otis was not so blessed. Thankfully, his fidgeting and muttering to himself had no impact on Ruth. He felt compelled to get out of bed and out of the house to sort things out. He wandered the quiet streets and alleys of Boston on his way to Boston Harbor. A smattering of neighbors had the same idea, and he greeted them briefly or, where possible, sought to avoid them altogether. He could not remember any of their names.

The sea air became more prominent as he progressed to the harbor where he could think most clearly. The quiet rippling expansiveness of the water opened his mind. The gentle sea and sky seemed to meld. Occasional puffs of wind cooled him off. The harbor was eerily devoid of dock workers and ship hands. The sounds of his freshly cobbled shoes created an exaggerated reverberation. The pier seemed changed, even strange, despite its familiarity. A voice then interrupted his unsettled thoughts—a voice that was at once surprising and calming.

"Good evening, Mister Otis," the stranger said, even before Otis could set eyes on him. When Otis stopped and pivoted, he saw a handsome man, sturdy in stature, whose face blended the African and Indian in a striking and distinctive way. The man appeared to be in his mid-thirties, clad in the simple garb of a dockworker, wearing no cap, with meticulously coiffed black hair, which matched his unblinking and penetrating eyes. His lips and the contours of his lower face gave the appearance of a familiar and permanent half-smile. Strangely, Otis liked the man immediately.

"What is your name, sir?" he asked.

"Michael Johnson, sir," replied the stranger.

"Any relation to Samuel Johnson?" Otis asked, smirking internally, certain the stranger had never heard of the esteemed English writer.

"No, but I did enjoy *The Life of Richard Savage* and do admire his poetry," Johnson replied.

Otis paused. The experience was becoming bizarre. Who is this man? Otis asked the man—or was it a mirage—how he possibly could know about Samuel Johnson, much less have read him.

"I am a curious man and greatly enjoy reading, sir," Johnson replied.

"You are a curious man, indeed. Do you tell the truth?" Otis blurted out.

"It depends on to whom I am speaking," Johnson replied.

"Obviously, an honest man admits that he lies," Otis said, appreciating his own muted cynicism. He gazed at Johnson with deepening interest. "Please tell me of your heritage."

"I come from royalty on my father's side," Johnson replied. "He was Prince Yonger in western Africa before he was captured and made a slave in this country. My mother was Nanny Peterattuck, a native of Natick. I consider myself a rich blend of races and cultures, but when asked my tribe, I tell people I am Wampanoag. I am many things, just as you are, sir."

"Are you a runaway slave or a free man?" Otis asked.

"Yes," Johnson replied, smiling.

They walked out to the end of the pier in the comforting darkness, as the light fog rolled in. Totally alone, they settled themselves on the slightly rotting wooden bench that faced the harbor. The conversation turned to the politics of the day, starting with their shared loathing of the customs commissioners. Johnson led the conversation with his questions, which quickly gravitated to the Writs of Assistance.

"How can you possibly defend the use of the Writs?" Johnson asked. "You, a loyal British subject? The king is treating colonists like primitive savages whose homes can be invaded willy-nilly. He is almost treating you with as little respect as you treat us, the native people! I exaggerate, but you see my point."

This man could be my friend. I trust him, thought Otis. The brilliant lawyer yearned for a friend. He could handle himself gracefully in Boston society and was a cordial and thoughtful acquaintance to many. But beneath it all was a deep void in him, the exact contours of which he could not discern. What a gift it would be to have a man who could be his friend! But entertaining this thought also gave him pause. Was the thought of this particular man being a trusted friend utterly foolish? Of course it was, and he embraced the idea.

"First of all," he replied, "do you think the king really even knows what is happening here? I have heard he is well-meaning but poorly informed. Setting that aside, let me confide in you. I have been approached by five merchants to argue the case against the Crown in the Admiralty Court, of which I am the advocate general. My wife Ruth is adamantly opposed to this idea and to her core she loves the Crown and England. I risk creating a deep and unbridgeable chasm between me and my beloved. Yet I am inclined to take the case on the part of the merchants. I welcome your advice, Mister Johnson." The "Mister" was unexpected. Confiding in a mixed race stranger was even newer and more unlikely. *What is happening to me?* Otis wondered.

"Far be it from me to advise you, Mister Otis. You are said to be the most brilliant lawyer in Boston."

"Please, Mister Johnson, help me think this through. You appear to be a wise and honest man," Otis said with an air of supplication.

Johnson looked at the harbor for what seemed like forever, and then said, "I believe nothing is more important than freedom. It is the source of a meaningful life. One cannot really claim to be alive without freedom. Any and every human being deserves to be free. And I know of what I speak, having at times been deprived of my freedom in ways you can only imagine, sir. To take another person's freedom is to commit murder of the soul. And most insidiously, true freedom can be nibbled away in ways that are not fully comprehensible to the victim. Freedom is not license to act like a wild animal. Human freedom is holy, but only holy when its full expression enhances more than oneself. It is only holy when its fruits help one's family, friends, neighbors, and fellow citizens.

"You are asking me to weigh the value and need to champion the cause of freedom against the exigencies of the holy state of your marriage. This is a judgment only you can make. That said, consider this thought: If a marriage seeks to embody the realization of Divine love, how can there be such a marriage if the partners are not free? To champion the cause of freedom, sir, is ultimately to champion the cause of all men and women reaching their highest potential to love. Suck the life blood of liberty out of their bodies and you steal their full humanity.

"I have never been married, Mr. Otis. Only rarely have I joined a woman in a way that ignites my deepest passion and sets her afire, as well. Only rarely have I felt the sweet and soothing caress of one who wants nothing of me but my loving presence. Only rarely have I had the feeling that I am not alone. Yet rare as those experiences have been for me, they are alive in my body, heart, and mind. Recalling them gives me joy and an abiding hope that I will meet the woman who will share her life with me. If you truly love Mrs. Otis and she truly loves you, then you both are beneficiaries of a treasure I have never known. If your love is as deep as I hope it is, sir, then your arguing against the Writs of Assistance should be a minor affair. A brief thunderstorm on an otherwise sunny summer day.

"I will tell you this: I hope and pray you take up the cause of freedom," Johnson concluded in a voice so quiet Otis had to strain to hear the words. He did hear every word. Every one.

"A final question, Mr. Johnson. What is your real name?" Otis wondered why he asked.

"Crispus Attucks, sir. I trust you will tell no one."

"You have my word, sir."

"How can I reach you in the future, Crispus?"

"I will reach you, James." A fog had settled over the harbor and pier, and Attucks disappeared into it.

≈ **3** ≈

Morning was Otis' best time of day, and this kind of midsummer morning sang to his soul. Usually as he walked to his tiny, messy law office, he felt far more comfort than he did in his own home, especially now. All the tension of being married to Ruth and being a young father would ordinarily evaporate as soon as he started his brisk walk to work. Not today. The anxiety he had felt the day before with Ruth, when raising the possibility of arguing the Writs case, was even more pronounced since he lacked the numbing influence of alcohol.

Offsetting that was Otis' reflection on his strange and pleasing conversation with Crispus Attucks. Why did Attucks resonate so deeply with him? But the meeting was the night before, and today he needed to face the harsh reality of a decision that would cause anguish, no matter his choice. He experienced a shortness of breath.

As Otis reached the small, gray, wooden building that housed his law office, two customs officers approached him. His apprehension grew; while he did not respect the men, they did represent the Crown. The two men, John Robinson and Harry Longworthy, were people he had known for several years. They seemed conscientious and loyal to the king, and to Otis' knowledge, they were honest, not known to have sought or accepted bribes. Of the two, only John Robinson showed a modicum of intelligence and imagination. Robinson's gait was a trifle strange, but his physique was impressive; he was tall and thick-boned, with sandy hair and deep blue eyes. He was possessed of a gracious temperament and an apparent modesty that women found vastly appealing. Longworthy was a self-important dullard whose simian appearance seemed to reflect his mental limitations. Thankfully, he let Robinson do the talking.

"Hello, Robinson. What are you two gentlemen up to today?" Otis asked with fake joviality.

"Mr. Otis," Robinson replied, "we come with a message from the governor and chief justice, on behalf of the king and his administration. They are providing you the honor and the

18

opportunity to represent the king in a case some misguided merchants have brought, a case that challenges the legitimacy of the Writs of Assistance. Your well-earned reputation as a lawyer and your loyalty to the king combine to make you the ideal candidate to dispel this ill-considered case."

"I also happen to be the advocate general of the Admiralty Court," Otis said. "Why do you feel obliged to flatter me since I am charged to represent our government in such matters? If I believed in the fairness and wisdom of the Writs, it would be my duty, my simple task to execute the will of the king and his government. But I believe the Writs are an abomination, and they insult every loyal Englishman in this, and every other colony, in this land. The Writs make a mockery of our British Constitution and the rights of Englishmen everywhere in the world. No true Englishman can justify, much less defend, this abuse of power and degradation of loyal subjects. So, no, sir, I will not take this case."

"Let me understand, Mr. Otis," said Robinson. "You, the advocate general, are refusing to support the king and the administration of justice in this matter?"

"Your ears have not deceived you, sir," Otis replied.

Longworthy looked at Robinson with a gaze of deep confusion that asked how a man in Otis' position could make such a decision. He was paid to be the chief advocate for enforcing the laws of the Crown. Yet he was now refusing to do so. How could this be? Robinson seemed nonplussed by this odd decision. He was unsure how to proceed.

"What do you suggest I tell the governor and the chief justice?" Robinson asked.

"Send them my best wishes, tell them of my decision, and suggest they cease using the Writs immediately. I would give them this advice: Stop this now and regain the goodwill of our fellow citizens," Otis said. Then he added a thunderbolt.

"I will be taking the case on behalf of the merchants."

* * *

Otis sat at his littered desk on his old mahogany chair and began to reflect on what he had just done. At first he was flushed with the excitement of the new challenge, the thrill of going into battle, but those feelings subsided quickly.

How am I going to tell this to Ruth who has held out so much hope, who has given herself so freely, and who feels so deeply that

19

I should not do this? Will this break her heart? Will it truly drive a wedge into our marriage? Can't I persuade her that I, too, love the king and view this action as an act of love, love for the highest principles of our great nation? Why can't she join me in asserting the ideals that are great about Great Britain? How can she not see this?

And what does it mean for the family? Will it create a plague of ill-will that infects all of our relations? And the tidy little sum I earned in the Admiralty Court, that will vanish. We will need to rely even more on Ruth's fortune. And some of our friends, what of them? They will be confused at best, and more likely estranged, even bitter. Am I turning Ruth into a social widow?

Is this worth it, and what will it accomplish? I know to my bones this is the right thing to do, but why cannot someone else do it?

Because I was meant for this moment; that is why. Everything I have learned from my father, from Rev. Russell in preparation for Harvard, from all my studies there and under Jeremiah Gridley in preparing for the law drives me in this direction. I am the best lawyer in Boston. Confucius has said, "To see the right and not to do it is cowardice." I cannot be a coward, but I am sacrificing so much more than my own standing and income; I am giving up a tranquil and secure home. And in some deep way betraying Ruth.

And I will not win the case; that is certain. The five judges will decide long before they hear my words or those of the new advocate general. It will be rigged, but the real jury will be outside the courtroom. How will my words, or the unfair verdict likely to be rendered, affect the citizens of Boston? I do not wish to inflame the rabble. I want this to be a dialogue among gentlemen that will lead the king's ministers to treat us with the respect they would show any Englishman. I pray the rabble does not get stirred by this, yet I fear they will. The harassment of customs commissioners, much though they deserve it, will only worsen if the mob engages, and that, in turn, could cause London to bully us, loyal subjects who are so close to them in breeding and education.

How can I disregard Crispus? His arguments were so cogent, his sensitivity to degrees of slavery so acute. What a wise and good man! I need him in my life; I must be true to him. Crispus said there can be no love when there is no freedom. That must be what

I tell Ruth. This decision will only expand our love, if not now, in the future. She will come to understand that.

Otis breathed more easily and began to contemplate the case, almost eager to see Ruth in a few hours. Everything would be fine.

He always walked more slowly when returning home at the end of the day; today, he was even more dilatory. The pit in his stomach was like a stone, and his mind's eye kept picturing the likely look on Ruth's face when he told her the news. It would reflect disappointment, and she would say very little. She could make him feel like he was a young child and that he had failed yet again to measure up to her expectations. Everything had been so different when they had met and courted, and even in the first few years of their marriage. One aspect of Ruth that drew him to her was her willingness to try anything and to have fun. They had danced and even played quoits together, and her laughter, with its silly trill, had calmed and softened his heart. Her violin practice, ear-piercing though it was, reminded him of those days when everything seemed simpler, less fraught with anxiety. They could just be themselves then, and that was enough. His vanity had been stroked in those days when she spoke admiringly of his brilliance, his mastery of the classics, the scholarly book he authored on prosody, and even his snobbish disparagement of how most people used the English language. She would lovingly mock his earnest devotion to big ideas; they were endearing then, not threatening to her whole world, as they were now.

What happened? Why did things change? To be sure young James III had been born, and the baby became the center of her love and attention, but that could not have been enough to bring on this new, sadly cool, atmosphere. Was she jealous of his growing reputation and his expanding world of associates both in and out of the practice of law? Possibly. But there were forces and facts of the heart that he did not begin to understand. *She cares so much about things, and I do not,* he thought. He never commented on her gorgeous new scarf from China, or the new serving table in the dining room, the selection of which she had agonized over for weeks. She expressed such dismay when he did not notice things. He did not mean to hurt her, but he knew he surely did.

As Otis entered their parlor, Ruth instantly sensed his trepidation. She was not inclined to put him at ease.

"Well, I need to tell you, darling Ruth, that I have made my decision about the Writs of Assistance. I told two customs officers today that I refuse to argue the case for the Crown, and indeed, I will be arguing the other side," Otis stated, a bit too firmly. His unsteadiness was transparent to Ruth. He only spoke with bluster when he was wavering inside. She knew him.

"I know you do not agree with this," he continued, "and that fact has weighed heavily on my mind. I value what you think. But this is something I must do. I hope you understand and can even forgive me for the discomfort this will give you, including with our friends."

Uncharacteristically, Ruth stared into his eyes as he spoke. As Otis had expected, she said nothing after his announcement (it was an announcement and not an invitation to discuss). Then her brow furrowed as if a new question had arisen in her mind, but she remained silent. Was she making decisions, considering options, or seeking the right words? The longer she waited, the more unclear and uncertain of her likely response Otis became. Ruth bowed her head and stared at the floor. Seeing her husband in all of his not-knowingness, not knowing how profoundly distant she felt, not knowing her sympathy for him in all of his earnest obliviousness, and not knowing what was in store—all his not-knowingness made her sad and softened her. She looked up and saw a man, so hopeful and true, so well-meaning and dedicated to her and their new son.

Ruth looked sympathetically at Otis and spoke in a soft voice. "James, you must do what you believe is right and is most important to you. I know I cannot stop you, and I will not try. You know that this will change things between us; it already has. I think you are making a mistake of enormous proportions. You will never again be trusted by any of the king's officers. You may cast your actions in terms of the rights of man, but I see it as a level of disloyalty that is a first cousin to treason. I will be ashamed to tell my friends of your decision, but I will want to tell them very soon so they do not learn of it from other people. This will bring a kind of disgrace, and please do not take offense, but many people will see this as another example of your imbalance. You are a good man, so go forth with a good spirit. I wish I could join you and support you, James, but I cannot."

Otis extended his arms and moved toward her; she stepped back, shaking her head.

"No, please, James. And I think it best for you to occupy the guest room tonight."

"Why must it be this way, my darling?" he asked. "Can't we leave public affairs at our doorstep?"

"This is not simply 'public affairs,' James; this is who I am. I will always be a loyal subject to the king and cannot be complicit with you."

Otis realized he had just crossed the Rubicon. Ruth and he would share a household, share children, even share most of their friends, but they would never share the whole bond of a loving marriage. Would this enormous sacrifice be worth it? It was a question that might never be answered.

They heard little Jemmy cry in the nursery, and Ruth walked briskly to care for him.

This time, the sounds of his son only brought forth a dull pain, a pain that would never entirely leave Otis. The nagging guilt he felt would always haunt him and keep him from the full and rich enjoyment of his children.

⸗ 4 ⸗

February of 1761 in Boston was dreary and seemingly endless; the days felt like months. The moist breezes penetrated the marrow of one's bones and sent the heartless reminder that, without the right clothing, one could easily fall prey to hypothermia, pneumonia, and even death. Its relentlessness could kill the sickly and aged and dampen the spirits of even the most optimistic. The snow had become dirty in the waning days of winter, and the ice underneath was treacherous, even deadly to the careless or drunken walker. The sunny days did not bring joy; they were ironic breaks, and only served to make the usual grayness of the skies more oppressive to the spirits of Bostonians. This time of year even the air, full of the smoke from the thousands of wood-burning stoves, had a stifling effect on the soul.

But as Otis approached the Massachusetts Superior Court, his spirits sparkled with gleeful anticipation at the prospect of arguing the Writs of Assistance case, the most significant case of his life and possibly the life of Boston. Writs had been issued by the unloved Lieutenant Governor, Thomas Hutchinson, and now he was about to pass judgment on their legitimacy. To Otis, that obvious conflict of interest bespoke a man without principles. Hutchinson's pale face was youngish for a man of fifty, and it conveyed smug self-satisfaction. The lieutenant governor was tall and thin, yet his effeminate gait diminished the air of authority he hoped to project.

Hutchinson enjoyed impugning Otis' motives for switching sides and opposing the Crown. He would tell anyone within the range of his thin and whining voice that Otis decided to challenge the Writs because his father, James Otis Senior (the Colonel), had been passed over for the position of Chief Justice (a position for which he was abundantly qualified). It was a post to which Hutchinson himself had been appointed (and as a non-lawyer, for which he was most assuredly unqualified). This gossip was only part of a pattern of lies and odious personal attacks against Otis and propagated by the agents of the Crown. Otis pretended to take these jibes in stride.

Hutchinson was joined by four other judges hostile to the plaintiffs. The loyalty of these five men to the Crown was total. Otis and his colleague, the brilliant Oxenbridge Thatcher, would never see a verdict upholding their position, but the argument of the case itself, and the publicity surrounding it, had the prospect of killing the use of the Writs in reality, if not in law.

Opposing counsel was none other than Jeremiah Gridley, the man who had taught Otis the law sixteen years earlier. Gridley had been a member of the General Court of Massachusetts and was a Whig, called so because the jargon of the English political order had come to the colonies. Until his appointment by the Crown as Attorney General, Gridley had been more sympathetic to the colonists than the mother country. He was an exceptionally able lawyer and a fine man. He exuded great affection for his former student and pride in Otis' growing capabilities. Otis had persisted in the challenging study of the law with virtually no law books to refer to and no authoritative works on how to plead a case, or the use of evidence. He had to study the Acts of Parliament, the decisions of the King's Bench, and other dissertations on the common law. It had been an intensive two-years' experience Gridley and Otis had shared. The difficulty of the task had brought teacher and student closer.

However, a profound gulf now separated them, even with their deep mutual affection and respect. Otis was on a mission, fully committed with his heart and soul. As a student of history, he could sense that, with this case, he might be entering history itself. He knew the men who made history were instruments of profound change, not simply skilled guardians of the status quo. While he continued to profess the belief that he was demonstrating a higher kind of loyalty to England and its principles, he also sensed he could well be unleashing something monumental. He so believed in the righteousness of the cause that he refused to accept a fee for this case. On the other hand, his teacher, Gridley, was simply doing a job, serving the king, with no greater purpose than asserting the primacy of the Crown and Parliament.

The trappings of tradition sent their own message to those bold enough (or foolish enough) to resist the king. The splendor of the trial's setting conveyed to all in attendance the supposed power and legitimacy of history. The Council Chamber of the Old Town House was an intimidating room, gorgeous in its decor and decorated with full-length portraits of Charles II and James II. The wardrobes of the judges magnified the seriousness of the endeavor at hand: the scarlet robes of the five judges flowed with tradition and the intimations of power, as did their voluminous wigs.

The Chamber overflowed with British functionaries and Boston's most important civic and commercial leaders. The hard wooden benches were crammed with excited men and a tiny smattering of women. The anticipation felt by the crowd brought out the kind of intense focus that lay somewhere between a cockfight and a brilliant debate. The setting, the opposing lawyers, and the trial's stakes provided a level of high drama the city had never seen. In attendance were Mercy Otis Warren and her husband James Warren; Ebenezer Mackintosh; Samuel Adams and his younger cousin John Adams; several customs commissioners, including Robinson; William Mackay and his merchant friends; Reverend Merrywell; and Crispus Attucks (in disguise).

When the five judges entered the room to assume their elevated judicial thrones, everyone in the audience rose, creating a muffled rustling of clothing and a common clatter of shoes stepping on the pine floor. The last of the five to enter was Hutchinson, the slumping, least imposing of all the men who were to hear the case. After the pleas were presented, and the usual perfunctory comments and explanations were made, the chief justice yielded to Gridley.

As the king's attorney, Gridley rose to speak. He had the full force of the Crown and the British government behind him. He was humbled but undaunted by the significant role he needed to play. He defended the Writs of Assistance as necessary, legal, and just. He referred to two statutes enacted at the time of Charles II that empowered the exchequer to issue similar writs as well as statutes under Queen Anne that further legitimized the writs. Then Gridley addressed the most loathsome aspect of the colonial Writs, adducing provisions under William III that authorized collections of revenue in the British territories by officers who could enter public and private houses at will, just as was occurring in Boston. He also asserted that "the Parliament of Great Britain is the sovereign legislator of the British Empire." Who could possibly take issue with the legitimate power of the Parliament in these matters?

Otis' response was preceded by a solid counter-argument made by his colleague Oxenbridge Thatcher. Thatcher pointed to other contrary precedents and distinguished between the current Writs and those referred to by Gridley. Thatcher's legal acumen shined through his comments in such a way as to show that he and Gridley occupied the same high level of expertise and commitment to legal exactitude.

When Thatcher was finished, Otis rose to his feet, his shoulders squared, his jaw held high, the energy from his body almost palpable. He felt as though he had been taken over by a larger force. The chamber was perfectly silent. He spoke in slow, modulated cadence:

"I was desired by one of the Court to look into the books, and consider the question now before them concerning the Writs of Assistance. I have accordingly considered it, and now appear not only in obedience to your order, but likewise in behalf of the inhabitants of this town, who have presented another petition, and out of regard to the liberties of the subject. And I take this opportunity to declare that, whether under fee or not (for in such a cause as this I despise a fee), I will to my dying day oppose with all the powers and faculties God has given me, all such instruments of slavery on the one hand, and villainy on the other, as the Writs of Assistance is.

"It appears to me the worst instrument of arbitrary power, the most destructive of English liberty and the fundamental principles of law, that ever was found in an English law book."

At this point, Otis' sister turned to her husband and whispered, "How do you think he really feels about this matter?" As he chuckled, she clutched Warren's hand, sensing now that the coming months and years could be a wild ride, fraught with danger, opportunity, and the exhilaration that comes with a fight that could have enormous consequences.

Otis continued, summarizing the most egregious aspects of the Writs. His remarks, which ultimately continued for four hours, made points that transcended petty legalisms and stirred the audience. Young John Adams later observed that a hero was emerging in the courtroom.

"In the first place the writ is universal being directed to 'all and singular Justices, Sheriffs, Constables, and all other officers and subjects;' so that, in short, it is directed to every subject in the

King's dominions. Everyone with this writ may be a tyrant in a legal manner, also may control, imprison or murder anyone within the realm.

"In the next place, it is perpetual, there is no return. A man is accountable to no person for his doings. Every man may reign secure in his petty tyranny, and spread terror and desolation around him, until the trump of the arch-angel shall excite different emotions in his soul.

"In the third place, a person with this writ, in the daytime, may enter all houses, shops, etc. at will, and command all to assist him.

"Fourthly, by this writ, not only deputies etc. but even their menial servants, are allowed to lord it over us. What is this but to have the curse of Canaan with a witness on us; to be the servants of servants, the most despicable of God's creation? Now one of the most essential branches of English liberty is the freedom of one's house. A man's house is his castle; and whilst he is quiet, he is well guarded as a prince in his castle. This writ, if it should be declared legal, would totally annihilate this privilege."

Those in the courtroom seemed enraptured for the duration, adding to Otis' confidence and resolve.

As the formalities concluded, young John Adams turned to his older cousin Samuel and asked, "Does he know what he has unleashed?" Samuel Adams replied, "Possibly."

When the proceedings were finished and the courtroom was emptying out, a strange quiet and calm marked the crowd. The array of Boston citizens and British officials walked out with little chatter, as if both sides were needing time to absorb what had just occurred. If the colonists had come to see the Writs of Assistance demolished, they could not have been disappointed; success at that task was total, however the case would be decided. (The five judges would lay the case over for future consideration.) If the loyalists had come to see their side successfully justified, only the most dimwitted of them could conclude that their side had prevailed.

Otis believed that not only had he carried the day as a lawyer, but he had also proven himself as a defender of the rights of British subjects everywhere.

A surprising number of citizens had waited outside the town hall even in the cold and dreary February early evening. They quickly became energized as they heard from their friends who had attended the trial what had transpired. More Bostonians arrived; their sound grew louder, and a new energy bordering on joy was coming forth. When Otis emerged, the roar of adulation shocked him. He had begun to feel exhausted from the legal battle, but the crowd delivered a jolt of energy to him. When he realized they were roaring for him, he blushed and felt light-headed, more so because he had not eaten since breakfast. He greeted those he knew as he walked slowly, a smile cemented on his face. Samuel Adams joined him, and they headed toward the Green Dragon to discuss the day and relax.

Adams and Otis had much in common. They had both graduated at an early age from Harvard, and they came from established Massachusetts families. They strongly opposed the Writs of Assistance and were personally offended by the arrogance of the local representatives of the Crown, especially the customs officials. And both believed that at times the other man demonstrated questionable behavior. They felt a real affinity to one another, but at this point, that did not translate into a deep personal friendship.

Adams was an interesting blend of failure and genius. Adams' business failures were well-known, yet his intellect was well-respected. He had failed as a malter but was unsurpassed when it came to organizing resistance. He was more than a worthy ally; he was a force of Nature. (If only the poor fellow could lighten up and cheer up.)

Samuel Adams carried himself with an air of authority despite his prosaic role of tax-collector, a position awarded him by the governing Town Meeting and which paid a paltry sum for a man of his breeding and education. His job was to collect taxes from citizens all over, including printing shops, staves, and rope-walks. He was not zealous in his mission. The exchange of money that his work entailed on a daily basis had a certain poignancy for the thirty-nine-year-old Harvard graduate. Because currency took many forms, it was valuable to the city authorities that Adams could evaluate each and understand a rough equivalency, whatever form the "money" took. Yet the fine arts of commerce had eluded Adams, for lack of interest. He had failed as a maltster and squandered the thousand pounds his father had lent him to start a career in business, giving half of it to a friend who never repaid him.

Adams had a broad, stern handsome face with a straight nose, penetrating deep blue eyes, and a chin that protruded just enough to say, "Please do not cross me." Adams was not "high hat" and was often seen in a gray wig, shabby clothes, and a stained red cloak, accompanied by his Newfoundland dog. Nearly all Bostonians knew Adams was on their side, and not on the side of the elite from which Hutchinson came. It was said that Adams even supported independence from Britain, a rumor that persisted throughout the city.

When Adams and Otis entered the tavern, it was pulsating, and customers were pressed together in a swarm of celebration. When the two were spotted at the door, the crowd burst into a raucous cheer, and those who had been seated stood up, applauding and whistling wildly. They chanted, "O T I S, OTIS," and shouted, "HUZZAH!", again causing Otis to blush. He raised his arms and made a calming gesture, his face still unable to stop grinning. There were no empty tables, but two young blacksmiths rose and ceremoniously gave Adams and Otis their table. Even in this jubilation, Otis wondered what this all meant. He was not given to the rowdy expression of emotion, and he dimly sensed that what he was experiencing was the letting loose of a creature that might not be easily tamed.

Beth Frothingham brought them the best ale the tavern sold and insisted they not pay. This embarrassed them both; neither liked public displays of privilege. But if the special treatment were uncomfortable for Otis, beholding Beth was not. An extra button of her blouse below her opened green smock was undone, and the proportions of her body were exquisite, her energy natural and frolicsome. A smile linked her lovely, dimpled cheeks. Her long black hair moved freely with her many gestures. In Otis' eyes, she had never looked more comely than at this moment. He couldn't help but follow her movements as she served the other customers. She was fully aware of this attention.

After Adams and Otis had been seated, the noise subsided and they could actually hear one another. Adams was in a good mood—not a common occurrence.

"Well, are you silver-tongued Cicero or mighty Caesar? How do you feel, you conquering hero?"

"Most definitely not Caesar! I am hungry and thirsty and tired and feel extremely satisfied. Today was all I had hoped for and more," Otis replied, as he glanced at Beth leaning over another table and delivering mugs.

"The British may be stupid," Adams said with total confidence, "but after today, I think even they will not attempt to enforce the Writs of Assistance. The Writs are as dead as the mummies in Egyptian tombs. Congratulations, James."

William Mackay, the large merchant who had approached Otis months before to take the case, appeared next to them. His face was impassive, not jubilant, and he exuded a solemn sincerity when he said to Otis, "A simple 'thank you,' sir. You have made us all proud to be citizens of this town. You have served the people and the merchants of Boston well." Mackay probably could still recall how slighted and irritated he felt when first he and his colleagues approached the brilliant lawyer.

"You are very welcome, Mr. Mackay, and let me apologize for my behavior when you first approached me. I was small-minded and coy, and I am sorry," Otis said. Mackay smiled and then returned to his crowded table with a spring in his step.

Otis summoned Beth to the table for another ale, and he and Adams continued to drink with gusto. The conversation that followed was of two men who were in vastly different states of mind. Otis was in an emotional swirl—excited and proud of his performance and the reactions it had triggered from friends and foes alike; deeply sorry that Ruth strongly opposed his efforts and would not attend the trial; reassured and relaxed by the ending of the day, a momentous day which now required nothing of him; increasingly aroused by the sight of Beth; ashamed of that attraction but even more stimulated by it; suddenly famished and, with the empty stomach, quickly reaching a rapid state of drunkenness of the most agreeable kind. The Green Dragon was becoming very warm and smoky, and it didn't bother him a bit. The ale and the achievement of the day gave him a peace of mind the likes of which he had never experienced.

Adams, on the other hand, felt compelled to discuss with cool rationality the meaning of the day's events and spoke in a way that seemed more like a well-constructed lecture than a natural conversation. Otis was pleased by the enthusiastic support he had elicited from his fellow Bostonians, but Adams expressed concern about those emotions.

"The people have become hot from this case, and that can be dangerous," he said.

"They were already hot," Otis replied. "The trial today just gave them hope."

"I believe in every grand principle you affirmed today, James," Adams said. "The rights of man and our rights as British subjects are supremely important. You did well not to villainize the officers of the Crown, but the people in the courtroom and in the streets may not be so dispassionate. You are reasoned and hopeful; the mind of the mob can be just the opposite. Today, you became a public leader, not just a lawyer, and your challenge will now be to tamp down the inflamed sentiments of the people of Boston. It is glorious that you addressed the grievances that the Writs created, but the resolution of those grievances must continue to be done in a peaceful way that respects our British customs. It's wonderful that patriots like you and me want to address their concerns, but as we do so, we cannot inflame the populace, or our actions will be self-defeating."

Otis could absorb only a portion of Adams' comments. He was ravenous, and the sight of Beth was delightfully distracting. He feigned interest in Adams' words and said he agreed with him, but thought this was not the time to pontificate or plan. Adams, as the tax-collector in daily contact with a wide array of Bostonians, was far more attuned to, and worried about, public opinion and the concerns of the mob. Otis was just relieved and basking in self-satisfaction. He felt no need for hand-wringing.

Adams added a final warning. "You should know, James, that what you have done will be seen as a humiliation to Hutchinson and the other officials. You might well become more of a target of their attacks and jibes and even character assassination. It could become quite unpleasant for you, my friend."

"Oh, Samuel, you exaggerate. We are all loyal British subjects," Otis replied, smiling with wise benevolence at his worried friend.

Adams' face compassionately expressed that Otis had no idea what was coming his way.

5

The evening of his greatest triumph, Otis sat alone in his parlor, sipping cognac and reflecting on the day. The cold draft of the bitter February wind penetrated the house, causing him to place Ruth's beautifully embroidered blanket over his lap. Young Jemmy, who had been colicky and inconsolable all day, was finally asleep. How sweet it would have been to share such a day with Ruth, but in this case, he was glad Ruth was also deep asleep, knowing she opposed what he had done. His brain was still buzzing too much to allow him to settle into his rereading of *Henry V*, and too agitated to go to bed.

He heard a faint knock on the window that faced the backyard, possibly a pinecone the wind had blown up as the night breeze stiffened. Then he heard it again, but in a double cadence. Otis arose and approached the window, the snowflakes now darting in the cold air outside, playing around the dark, smiling face of Crispus Attucks. He hurried to the back door and let Attucks in.

"Crispus, you must be freezing. I am so glad to see you! You have picked a momentous day to reappear. It seems like forever since we last met."

"James, I am so glad to be with you, and I feel honored. I observed you all day in the Town Hall, and your performance was astounding!"

"What do you mean?" Otis asked, puzzled. "How could you have seen me? I did not see you in the courtroom."

"I was there, but thankfully undetected by those who don't like 'negers.'"

Otis smiled and looked at the floor. "Would you like some Cognac, Crispus?"

"No thank you, James, but I do want to talk to you. Is this a good time, and would Mrs. Otis be offended to have me here? I know she views the world very differently from you."

"A thunderbolt could rock this whole house and she would not awaken. We are safe," the host replied.

"It could be argued that a thunderbolt already has hit this house, and its name is James Otis," Attucks said. "I am here to express a concern and to ask a question. I appreciate the courage you have shown and the odyssey you have entered upon. If it is not too presumptuous on my part, I would like to tell you my thoughts and give you advice on how to proceed from here. You have, today, entered a new world, and it is full of promise and potential peril. But let me first ask my question: Will you be discussing slavery in the coming months and years?"

Otis looked silently at him, still not certain if Attucks was a freed man or a runaway. If it were the latter, his owner was not working very hard to retrieve what he considered to be his property. Then Otis caught himself, embarrassed at even wondering about that, and answered, "I hate slavery. It is an abomination. And slavery as it is practiced in this country is even more barbaric than what was done in ancient times. Back then, there was some dignity in it, at least a small sliver of dignity. Far too many of today's slaveholders and their accomplices treat human beings as chattel. In the southern colonies, they breed them like horses and pigs. Never in history have human beings been so treated like farm animals, like livestock, and with the sickening protection of the law."

"I appreciate what you are saying, James. Will you speak out on this? Will you tell Boston this? You have catapulted into prominence today; people will listen to you now more than ever."

"Did you not hear me state my views on slavery in the courtroom this morning, Crispus?" Otis asked.

"Yes, and I appreciate it. But will you keep speaking out on this?" Attucks asked.

"I need time to think about this. I am still trying to understand what has happened today. How can I be most effective? Slavery is not really a Massachusetts problem."

"A Massachusetts problem?" Attucks hissed. " I can't believe my ears. 'This is not a Massachusetts problem.' Is that what and how you really think? There is an abomination loose on the land, but you don't think it is a 'Massachusetts problem'? There are five hundred slaves in this colony!"

"No, no, that's not—"

Attucks interrupted. "I misjudged you, James. The man I saw in the courtroom today would never say slavery is not a 'Massachusetts problem.' The man I saw today spoke for all men, and may I add all women. I saw a brave and eloquent warrior for what is right, a man who believed in the rights and dignity of all people. I was moved by that man. Is that the same man who stands here? It appears not."

"You are right, Crispus," Otis quickly replied. "Let me consider the best course of action. All my friends tell me I am impetuous, so I need time to consider what would be most effective. I apologize. Slavery diminishes us all. Forgive me."

"Slavery is a sin, James."

"Indeed it is, Crispus." A long and heavy silence followed. Finally, Otis asked, "And what advice do you have for me? You said you had some thoughts on how I should best proceed from here. There is nothing you would say, Crispus, that I would not want to hear and try to understand. Please feel free to tell me what is on your mind."

"When I said you have entered a new world, I meant it. After today, you are in danger. In both the African and Wampanoag cultures from which I come, and indeed in nearly every culture, when a person humiliates another person, the one who did the humiliating can find himself in great danger. Today, you humiliated Hutchinson and the other agents of the king. They were not equal to you. The weakness of their position, even their contempt for the colonists, became clear through your words. They will now attempt to destroy your reputation. They know that killing you would strengthen your message. Instead, they will choose a more insidious way to get you. And they will be relentless."

"Have you been talking to Adams? You're telling me the same thing he told me."

"No, but we are both correct," Attucks replied.

"Well, assuming you are right, what am I supposed to do about it?" asked Otis. "I can't control what they say!"

"I think the best thing you can do is be prepared. They will take more actions that will call out for resistance, and right now, you are the best voice for freedom and dignity. We cannot afford to have you be discouraged, dispirited. Just knowing that the lies and abuse will be coming can enable you to be strong," he said.

" And now I really must leave you and your lovely home. Above all, thank you James," Attucks added.

Otis nodded and smiled as his guest left through the kitchen door, into the dark, cold night.

Suddenly, Otis felt his home was not really his anymore and his beliefs were pulling him in a direction he could not fully predict or control. The first encounter with Attucks had given him a sense of calm and clear understanding. This time, it seemed Otis was nearing a precipice, one he could not avoid. He trusted the message of his new friend and the cause he cared so deeply about, and yet he felt a chilly kind of grief for the passing of his old, more centered and secure life.

Otis heard a sharp, piercing scream from upstairs, from Ruth. He bolted out of his chair and ran upstairs. He ran into what was now only Ruth's bedroom and saw a terrified woman on her back, both arms extended with a peculiar expression of terror on her face. She was writhing as if trying to free herself.

Otis leaned over and shook Ruth, trying not to hurt her. He had not touched her body in five months and even in this anguished scene, it felt good to feel her smooth skin. It was difficult to awaken her; did his shaking her appear as an attack in her nightmare? Her body was drenched in perspiration and she kept muttering "No. No" in muffled terror. He shook her harder and she opened her eyes wide and wildly. Then confusion took over her face, baffled by the sight of her husband, only gradually remembering where she was. (Amazingly, the baby had not woken.) Otis reached down to stroke her cheek, but she recoiled.

"Please don't touch me, James," she said. Otis lowered his head and looked at the side of the four-poster, sighing deeply.

"Can I do anything? Do you want to tell me what you were dreaming? Is there anything at all I can do?" he asked, plaintively.

"No, please, just let me be," she replied. "I am fine." Just when Otis thought the chasm between the two of them could be bridged, when he thought his reassurance and comforting would help bring them together, the gaping wound that was their marriage had been reopened.

"What is the next step for your precious little campaign against the king and our British guardians?" Ruth asked, with an uncharacteristic cutting edge in her voice.

"Why do you care?" Otis icily replied. "You really have no interest in my life, or my friends outside our proper little Beacon Hill circle." As he grew colder toward her, he felt more like he was a stranger to himself, lonelier. This was not who he was, but now, with her, it was how he was. It was a terrible contradiction; the man he thought himself to be, a loving, hopeful man, was now cutting himself off from the woman he had loved.

"Fine. From now on, I want none of your friends in my house, James. You have consciously set yourself on a course that will upset our lives. You must know that. You do not put a supreme value on our family."

Otis and Ruth were both injured accomplices in the gradual death of their marriage. And they both knew Otis loved his cause more than his family, a fact he would never admit to himself, much less to Ruth.

They then heard Jemmy begin to cry upstairs, pricking their hearts like a needle as they were reminded of their responsibilities. Who would go to the child?

"I will take care of him," Ruth said and rose from her bed. She put on her crimson silk bathrobe and walked into the nursery. The baby's cries persisted through the entire night. Neither of them would sleep.

Shortly before dawn, Otis entered the nursery to hold his son. Ruth gratefully handed him little Jemmy and retired to her room.

Part II

"Taxation Without Representation Is Tyranny"

6

The luster that surrounded Otis after he argued the Writs of Assistance case had dimmed considerably as he undertook his duties as a legislator in the General Court in 1762. The prickles and grit of politics and law-making brought Otis down to earth, but not the entire way. He still saw larger principles and ideals even in prosaic matters. A case in point was brought forth by the fishermen of Salem and Marblehead.

To protect them from potential French marauders, those hardy souls of the sea had requested help from Governor Bernard in the form of additional crew in the colony's armed security sloop. Bernard agreed to give them that protection and unilaterally used warrants to access the provincial treasury to do so. Otis loudly and incessantly protested the governor's action as another unilateral invasion of the House of Representatives' prerogative.

The citizens of Boston, and even many of Otis' allies, just did not care. The larger ideals Otis obsessed over seemed to be as nothing for people who just wanted to get on with their lives. Moreover, Otis' party was in the minority in the General Court, so his words rang with even less power.

When Otis entered the Green Dragon on a cool November night in 1763, the reception by the patrons was subdued. The place seemed quieter than usual as Otis looked around to see where Samuel Adams was sitting. Then the calm was shattered by a loud voice.

"Look who is here—James Otis, the incendiary pontificator!" the tall, slender, inebriated customer shouted. "What brilliant ideas do you want to foist on us today?"

It was John Wobbly, a merchant known to cheat his customers and a close ally of Lieutenant Governor Hutchinson. As Otis approached Adams' table, Wobbly shouted out again, "Look, two losers about to drink together; what a pair!" Adams had struggled in finance and commerce, and his malting business was not thriving.

Both Otis and Adams smiled softly and looked down at the table. They would not rise to the bait. The atmosphere in the tavern had changed abruptly, and everyone wondered who would speak out for the two men. They would be surprised.

Beth Frothingham, the beautiful barmaid, walked over to Wobbly, and standing right next to him, she said, for all to hear, "You are a despicable boor, and you should apologize to these honorable men!"

Wobbly looked up at her and smirked. "Oh, I am so sorry, madam, if I have offended you. I am sure your manners are exemplary, but I am simply telling the truth." He did not apologize.

Beth gestured to two good-sized blacksmiths to have Wobbly removed from the Green Dragon, which they did quickly. The barmaid elicited loyalty from the tavern's patrons.

Otis turned to Adams, who continued to view the brilliant lawyer as an interesting blend of mentor and protégé. Adams remained in awe of Otis' intellect, his range of classical allusion, and his fervid commitment to the rights of man. But Adams was concerned about Otis' judgment and sense of proportion.

"So, what did you want to talk to me about, Samuel? Do you want to give me some advice, or take some? What are you hearing in the streets as you collect our citizens' taxes?"

Adams' face conveyed to Otis a blend of affection and respect with a hint of exasperation.

"It is very important," said Adams, "that Bostonians continue to listen to your words with genuine interest, but their endurance is limited. Your droning on about high principles can cause them to become deaf to what is truly important, and I worry about that if or when there comes a moment or incident of real consequence."

"So," Otis said, "you think my speaking out on the rights of man is just 'droning on,' and we should let the things Bernard and Hutchinson are doing slide by without protest? They do so much that is so wrong!"

"The people respect your high ideals," Adams replied, "but they also think 'Why not help the fishermen of Salem and Marblehead?' People want a sense of security and support, and that is what Bernard was giving them."

Otis did not reply. He summoned Beth to bring them some ale. Her eyes sparkled at the sight of Otis. As for Adams, she had always felt a kinship with him because of the obvious respect he showed to working people like herself. As she was cheerfully bringing them their beverages, the Green Dragon experienced another unwelcome interruption.

Two large customs officers, Robinson and Hutton, burst through the door of the tavern, followed by John Wobbly, who was walking unsteadily but with fire in his eyes.

Robinson bellowed to all the patrons, "It has come to the attention of Lieutenant Governor Hutchinson that this gentlemen," pointing to Wobbly, "has been insulted and molested. Who has done this? This behavior will not be tolerated."

No one spoke or moved. Then Beth walked forward, approaching the two menacing men, and said, "I was the one who characterized Mr. Wobbly, and if the truth is an insult, so be it." Robinson and Hutton remained mute briefly, and then they asked who had molested Wobbly.

First, the two blacksmiths stood up, but quickly half the room moved toward the two customs officers. In response to the question, a common chant came spontaneously from the room, with increasing volume.

"We did. We did. We did."

Robinson and Hutton looked briefly at one another and shrugged simultaneously. Then Robinson shouted lamely, "Never do that again!" Many of the patrons hooted and jeered. Robinson, Hutton, and Wobbly retreated into the night.

After the tavern had settled down, Otis turned to Adams and said, "Were those two clowns giving the people the 'sense of security and support' you were talking about? Or were they just doing the bidding of a corrupt politician named Hutchinson?"

"This whole episode proved both of our points, my dear friend," Adams replied. "Small offenses should be resisted but only when the people are direct witnesses to the injustice."

"I will reflect on your words, dear Samuel," said Otis, "but I will not relent."

"I am sure you will not, James; I am sure you will not," Adams replied.

Then the two shared stories of their families and gossiped briefly about their friends. Both sensed a larger storm was brewing, but for now, familiar matters were more calming.

❧ 7 ❧

In 1764, the British rulers foisted on the colonists another unpopular measure, the Sugar Act, a revenue-raising effort that distressed and disgusted merchants and other citizens throughout the colonies. It taxed imported sugar and molasses, which were used to make rum, an important export in trade with other countries. Worse, it was levied to subsidize the British soldiers' presence on the American shores.

On this late summer afternoon, the gathering at the Warrens' Plymouth home was small: Mercy and James Warren, Samuel Adams, John Hancock, and Otis. Otis envied Mercy and her husband James. Like the other men and women in their eclectic circle of friends, he could not help but notice they were deeply and unwaveringly in love. It was impossible to be in their presence for more than a moment and not sense it. There were no public displays, no doting words or even loving glances, but the respect, appreciation, fun, humor, irreverence, and jibes they exchanged all cried out, "I adore this person!" They were loving, lenient parents with five boys, including the infant Henry. ("All boys!" Mercy would say with loving exasperation. "Oh, merciful God, what have I done to deserve this?")

The Warrens' home was a two-and-a-half-story building with wainscoted walls and nine large windows. Their stately front door welcomed guests into a large sitting room with an imposing fireplace. From the front door, a wainscoted staircase led to the bedrooms, and in the back of the house was the kitchen. Their home was often in the state of happy chaos that only five boys can cause, and it seemed sometimes to border on disrepair. Mercy and James were both busy doing more important things, in their minds, than home repairs. Their focus was on their boys, their books, and especially the political life of Boston. They often hosted small groups who discussed resisting outrageous British acts when they occurred. Both of them descended from *Mayflower* forebears, but they paid scant attention to genealogy and harbored disdain for privilege, even though they were both beneficiaries of it. They

43

came from the proper, traditional, established order. And both were on the threshold of turning that order on its head.

When the topics of conversation were heated, the two of them created an atmosphere of trust and goodwill that not only permitted, but enabled, spirited disagreement. They loved to convene political meetings, and in 1764, Boston was alive with resistance, rumor, and resentment.

Mercy and James enjoyed watching Samuel Adams occasionally yield to irritation in the presence of Hancock, the happy peacock, who had recently returned from England. They found it amusing, in a gently perverse way, to see the two together. Hancock was oblivious to the effect he had on Adams, the serious political Puritan. At the core of the humor was Hancock's apparent lack of awareness and Adams' inability to conceal his own irritation. Hancock was a "macaroni," a true dandy who spent more money on his wardrobe in a week than Adams spent to maintain his household expenses in a month. Hancock, if unchecked, could go on for hours, expounding about wine, European fashion, home furnishings, and simple gossip. Adams sometimes thought Hancock a blow-hard; far more interested in ideas and ideals, he disdained Hancock's superficiality. Otis' temperament was closer to Hancock's—cheerful and hopeful, but his interests and sense of mission were closer to those of Adams.

The five of them were seated in the Warren parlor surrounding an elegant, if misplaced, marble-topped end table that sat in the middle of the circle of chairs and was used to hold the tea tray with its plate of freshly baked muffins.

"Tell us more, John, about the new fashions in England and the Continent," James Warren asked Hancock, watching for Adams' reaction. The question achieved its intent. Adams literally started to squirm in his chair and sigh loudly. Hancock was prepared to launch. "Well, in France, the lower classes have not changed their garb for centuries, but more recently, they have tried to emulate their superiors, just using cheaper materials. In Paris, it can be difficult to tell the rich from the poor. But in the countryside, the children still often lack shoes and must improvise. As for the more well-to-do, the fashion in headdresses has gone crazy; there are so many styles that Paris now has 1,200 hair-dressers, and...."

"May we continue this part of our conversation later?" Adams asked, without apology for his interruption.

"Oh, Samuel, don't be such a stick-in-the-mud," said Mercy. "This is interesting." She was as bored by the subject as her husband, but she enjoyed watching Adams react to Hancock. Otis saved them from further boring blather when he nearly shouted, "No, it is not interesting! The only person I know who would care about this is my wife, and she is not here. Let's talk about something truly interesting."

Hancock smiled benignly at Otis, his dear friend.

"James," he said, "you are only interested in your grand mission. You need to broaden your horizons. The meaning of life is as much in petticoats as principles. You must come to understand that. Life is here and now, not only in some world of grand ideals."

"Fine," said Otis. "Let's discuss something we can all agree on: the remarkable stupidity of the English rulers. The English people themselves are fine people with the same hopes and dreams we ourselves have. It is only the political class in London that is feeble-minded."

"I wouldn't want to be the leaders of England and try to govern or control us," said James Warren. "Something beats in the hearts of Bostonians that is of a different nature from anything seen in the British Isles or on the Continent. What needs to be governed here goes well beyond the skills of almost any leader. There is a new power here, a fierce commitment to freedom that the Old World will never fully grasp. We may not create elegantly argued theories, and no, we may never grow a William Shakespeare on our shores, but the spirit alive in our land transcends the arts and conventional politics. We will not be denied. At its core is the belief that all men and women are created equal, and freedom is our divine right. I defy you to find that sentiment in practice anywhere else in the so-called civilized world."

"I am not sure I agree," said Adams, turning to James Warren. "England's military power is unsurpassed, and their leaders are not fools, not all of them. Their power to suppress the noble ideals you speak of, James, is extraordinary. And as for our fellow citizens here, I talk to Bostonians every day, and I don't think they thirst for freedom to the degree you suggest. I do not think your fellow countrymen share your passion, James."

Adams spoke with authority; he knew the people of Boston. His words dampened everyone's spirits. Otis reached for a muffin and said, "The people of Boston may not yet thirst for freedom, but they are entitled to it, and when British tyranny goes too far, and their officers become too arrogant, people on this side of the Atlantic will not countenance it. We need to convey to London what is, and is not, acceptable. I remain confident that they can reform their ways and treat us with the respect we merit. We are all Englishmen!"

"And women, " Mercy added with a smile. "Dear brother, the fact is we are not treated like English subjects, and we do not have their rights, and we have no representation in Parliament. They just want to use our resources; to restrict our trade and use us. We are no better in their eyes than the other colonies. They are money-hungry leeches and want to bleed us, not respect us. They treat us like renegades."

"Well," James Warren replied, "we are renegades, and you, dear John Hancock, are one of the worst. You are a flagrant smuggler, so you are renegade number one. It is because of people like you that the British government feels driven to take measures like the Sugar Act. You and scores of merchants mock their laws and take what the British think is rightfully theirs, as our masters." Warren knew the word "masters" would inflame his brother-in-law, and, indeed, everyone in the room.

Before Otis could respond, the two oldest Warren boys, James seven and Winslow five, ran through the far end of the parlor, screaming and laughing at such a high-pitched timbre they sounded like wounded wild turkeys. Young Winslow was carrying their pet squirrel on his little shoulder. The commotion aroused the ire of their usually calm father, causing him to shout, "Stop it, boys. Now! You must never run and scream indoors; you know that!" The intensity of his reaction surprised even him. The boys quickly complied, ran outside, and continued to screech and run with the energy only healthy, well-fed children can muster. Their parents looked at one another with loving, familiar exasperation.

"We need to act in such a way that your boys never experience the indignities we must endure," Otis said. "They are fine lads and deserve the best in the coming years."

The joyful shouts from outside suddenly turned into the wail of an injured child. Winslow, the stockier of the two, ran to the house and shouted from the opened dining room door, "James is hurt! His head is bleeding. Hurry!"

Mercy bolted from her chair to her son. She found him lying still under the huge oak tree, his forehead gashed by the granite rock next to him. After he regained his wits, young James assured his mother he would be fine, and Mercy ministered to his wound with a level of efficiency that bespoke the considerable practice she had been given by the boys throughout their often careless, and always exuberant, lives. Mercy brought calm to the house as only she could.

Her husband was still very much engaged in the discussion.

"Samuel," said Warren, "when you said you believed the people of Boston still lack a thirst for freedom, do you really believe that? You talk to far more people than I, but the people I know continue to be distressed, and some are angry, indeed very angry. They feel the British boot on their necks. Something is happening out there." He stretched his arms from left to right in the direction of the city. "Something very significant."

"Yes, but I do not want to inflame the situation, and I don't want to inflame you," Adams said, turning toward Otis. "You do not fully grasp how your role has changed, James Otis. You are now a public man. You still entertain the illusion that the British will treat you fairly. The agents of the king want to bring you down. They violate our citizens, and because of your naive belief in their good nature, you are shocked, even volcanic in your anger, when they show their true stripes. Effective resistance requires patience and judgment. We need to manage events and not be buffeted by them. There is no finer lawyer or orator in our town than you, but you must learn to restrain yourself. A larger historical reality is emerging, and we need to manage it, not be buffeted by it."

Otis, not knowing how to respond, remained silent.

The skies were becoming inky dark, and the rain's intensity had become so strong that it made conversation difficult. Still, everyone was fully engaged because they knew their ideas when given voice would ripple across the city and then across the Atlantic. Mercy and James were able to pay close attention because their boys were asleep; Hancock was unusually quiet and attentive, and Adams sat with the slightly skeptical expression of a teacher ready to critique his student.

Otis was animated and excited to read his new creation. The arrogant and arbitrary acts of the king's officials who governed

Massachusetts conflicted at the deepest level with the colonists' rights. The injustice of it all churned in his stomach, and the daily indignities drove him to state his points clearly. These could well become words for the world to read and hear. And so Otis read slowly and clearly a document entitled:

"The Rights of the British Colonies Asserted and Proved," which included these phrases:

> Let no Man think that I am about to commence to advocate for despotism, because I affirm that government is founded on the necessity of our natures; and that an original supreme Sovereign absolute, and uncontrollable, earthly power must exist in, and preside over, every society; from whose final decisions there can be no appeal but directly to Heaven. It is therefore originally and ultimately in the people. I say supreme absolute power is originally and ultimately in the people; and they never did in fact freely, nor can they rightfully make an absolute, unlimited renunciation of this divine right....
>
> Tyranny of all kinds is to be abhor'd, whether it be in the hands of one, or of the few, or of the many....
>
> The very act of taxing, exercised over those who are not represented, appears to me to be depriving them of their most essential rights, as freemen; and if continued, seems to be in effect disenfranchisement of every civil right....
>
> Slavery is so vile and miserable an estate of man, and so directly opposite to the generous temper and courage of our nation, that 'tis hard to be conceived that an Englishman, much less a gentleman, should plead for it....
>
> But let the origin of government be placed where it may, the end of it is manifestly the good of the whole....
>
> It is the greatest "idolatry, begotten by flattery, on the body of pride" that could induce one to think that a single mortal should be able to hold so great a power, if ever so well inclined....
>
> The end of government being the good of mankind.... It is above all things to provide for the security, the quiet and happy enjoyment of life, liberty and property....
>
> But if every prince since Nimrod has been a tyrant, it would not prove a right to tyrannize. There can be no prescription old enough to supersede the law of nature, and

the grant of God almighty; who has given to all men a natural right to be free, and have it ordinarily in their power to make themselves so, if they please....

The same law of nature and reason is equally obligatory on democracy, an aristocracy and a monarchy: Whenever their administrators, in any of those forms, deviate from truth, justice and equity, they verge toward tyranny, and are to be opposed, and if they prove incorrigible, they will be deposed by the people, if the people are not rendered too abject....

The first principle and the great end of government being to provide for the best good of all the people, this can be done only by a supreme legislative and executive ultimately in the people, or whole community, where God has placed it; but the inconveniences, not to say impossibility attending the consultations and operations of a large body of people have made it necessary to transfer the power of the whole to a few: This necessity gave rise to deputation, proxy, or a right of representation.

After Otis finished reading the document in its entirety, he sat silent, expectantly. The group again encircled the small, misplaced end table, which this time held two bottles of port. They were eager to respond. Mercy was first.

"That says a lot, and some of it is hard to follow. It seems like you ignore the king and keep the rights of men only accountable and derived from God Almighty. It is as if you ignore the reality of the monarchy. Poor George might feel a bit left out, don't you think?" Mercy's eyes twinkled.

"I am not writing this for George; I am writing it for all mankind," Otis replied, smiling at his own grandiosity.

"I like your statement about slavery," said Adams. "People don't talk about that enough. If this message is for all mankind, our friends in Virginia and the Carolinas won't like that part at all. Yet it goes to the heart of what we all want: freedom and respect. Keep it in, maybe even add to it, James."

Mercy responded to Adams' comments about slavery. "There are five hundred slaves in this colony. We should refrain from self-righteousness, Samuel."

"Your statement concerning the end of government," said James Warren, "is fine, but what is new in that? What does that add? Who doesn't believe that?"

"The British don't seem to believe it is true," Otis replied, "if you look at their actions. They want to extract from us and our continent for their benefit, not ours. The purpose of their governing is not for us but for them. Our fellow Bostonians will understand this."

"I like the phrase, 'life, liberty, and property,' James," said Hancock. "It adds a bit of nobility to us merchants and men of business when you put property up there with life and liberty. But read the part about truth, justice, and equity again, please."

Otis complied. "When an administration deviates from truth, justice and equity they verge toward tyranny, and are to be opposed, and if they prove incorrigible, they will be deposed if the People are not rendered too abject."

As those words settled into the full consciousness of the group, the room returned to silence, this time a silence that bespoke solemnity and deep understanding. And then there was a thunderclap and bolt of lightning of proportions never experienced by any of them. The house shook and Mercy, who had been gazing outside during the recitation, was briefly blinded.

"I like it," said Hancock, "but I fear it is highly inflammatory, James. Our king and prime minister are sure to see the word 'deposed' and be, shall I say, nervous or distressed."

James Warren disagreed. "John, do you honestly believe the king or the prime minister or anyone in the British government fears us, or fears being deposed? They are the mightiest nation on earth, and we on this side of the ocean are most definitely not."

"I like the 'if the People are not rendered too abject' part," said Mercy. "That is a direct challenge to us and our fellow citizens of Boston and the other North American colonies. I wonder if the people of Boston are 'too abject' to oppose tyranny."

"We shall see, dear Mercy; we shall see," Adams replied. He then turned to Otis and said, "You understand, James, that as our fellow Bostonians read this and concur with the very excellent words you have put forward, any future acts coming from London that continue to infringe on our rights will be viewed with even less acquiescence. Your words could well lead to more passion, including mob actions in the streets."

"Mindless passion is not my intent. Clarifying the rights of man is my simple and honorable motivation," Otis replied, with the slightest hint of self-righteousness.

"Very noble, James, very noble," Adams said with a skeptical yet gentle tone.

The discussion, questions, and opinions continued to flow well into the night, as freely as the port. Otis then walked into the wet night, his legs wobbling from the drink. He was pleased with himself once again, pleased with his command of the language, almost preening in his righteousness.

He departed, humming parts of Handel's *Water Music* to himself.

≈ 8 ≈

The words crafted by Otis and his small team quickly spread to the citizens of Boston and percolated throughout Massachusetts and colonies to the south. The words rang true to tradesmen like Ebenezer Mackintosh, to merchants like William Mackey, and to all of their many friends and associates. Otis was learning the true power of rhetoric.

That power was a double-edged sword, and the rulers of the most powerful nation on earth were not amused. Their local minion, Hutchinson, called Otis the local "incendiary" and maligned him throughout the corridors of power in his reports to London, just as Adams had predicted. Loyalists in Boston, including people Otis had thought to be his friends, were turning cold toward him. While that hurt him, it never shook his faith in the justness of his cause. He cared far more about how the citizens of Boston felt than how Hutchinson or his kind did. But the cocoon of righteousness that Otis lived in had a thin film, as he would later learn.

The Sugar Act of 1764 galvanized the colonists to resist with concerted gusto. It led them to boycott British luxury goods and start producing their own fabric-based products. Fifty letters of protest were sent to Parliament. In 1765, the Sugar Act was effectively repealed as a result of the widespread protest. It seems that the Patriots' voices mattered. Otis' words fueled that fire, at least in his mind.

The American sense of their own power proved to be short-lived. In 1765, Parliament passed the Stamp Act. In its zeal to extract taxes from the colonists, Parliament felt it wise to tax a wide range of paper products, requiring an authorizing stamp on them. The products included all ship documents, legal papers, newspapers, and playing cards. Even the customs officials, who loved their card games, bridled at the new tax.

The response to this Act in America quickly moved from incredulity to universal outrage.

A handful of prominent Boston leaders came together that summer to form "The Loyal Nine" in opposition to this recent

British intrusion. They met at the offices of the *Boston Gazette*, the leading voice of resistance, and even opposition, to the Crown. Their host, Benjamin Edes, published the paper weekly; most resisters couldn't wait to read it, and everyone in Prime Minister Greville's office hated it, as did their agents in America.

The small structure that housed the *Gazette* was permeated by the smell of newsprint, a striking contrast to the spring lilacs outside. The editorial office, which also served as the administrative hub, was a sea of old copies of the *Gazette* and other apparently random papers, suggesting falsely an element of disorder in the minds of the proprietors. In reality, the minds of Edes and his colleague John Gill could not have been sharper. Some even called them brilliant.

Edes had the air of a hungry eagle, alert, constantly in motion, and surveying the landscape—in this case both the town of Boston and those whose company he was keeping at the time. His charm derived from remembering everything he had been told about anyone he had met or even heard about, making everyone he met feel known, seen, and even appreciated (at least those not associated with British power). Edes' energy and intelligence reminded Otis of those of his sister, Mercy.

The small group that had come together that June morning included Edes, Samuel Adams, John Hancock, Ebenezer Mackintosh, and Otis. Samuel Adams, a close friend of Edes, led the discussion.

"Thank you, Benjamin, for hosting us today. Gentlemen, we cannot let this action pass uncontested. And remonstration with words alone does not suffice. No offense, Benjamin."

Edes smiled and murmured, "None taken, my friend. You are absolutely correct."

Adams continued. "We have asked Ebenezer to join us to discuss and plan a public protest. As you know, he has a reputation as a man of strong and prudent action, and many in our city hold him in high esteem. He is capable of enlisting hundreds of our fellow citizens in visible and appropriate public demonstrations."

Mackintosh, the red-haired shoemaker, listened with keen attention, aware that Adams was suggesting he be used as the muscle in an action conceived of by the Loyal Nine. He shared their views of the British, a fact these Boston leaders were fully aware of. His popularity was such that the leaders in London did not like him but hesitated to cross him.

Mackintosh was slight in frame but powerful in action and impact, able to lead thousands of his neighbors from the South End. He was a man who could rule in a "court" of bonfires and send messages in the form of headless effigies of well-known British overlords. He came from humble roots, and men like Hutchinson called him "rabble." Mackintosh was indispensable to the cause.

"What do you think, Ebenezer?" Otis asked. He had only met Mackintosh twice before, and although he held him in high esteem for his ability to raise and control a crowd, Mackintosh's crude manners and sketchy education made it difficult to view him as a true comrade. Still, they were on the same side.

"I think this group is wise in wanting a public demonstration. Am I correct that you believe it should be dramatic but without bloodshed?" Mackintosh asked.

"Indeed," said Hancock and Adams in unison. Edes was not so sure about the bloodshed part; a small amount of blood would increase his readership. He remained silent, in apparent agreement.

"Should the focus be Hutchinson or his brother-in-law, the new stampman, Oliver?" the shoemaker asked, hoping the group would prefer the lieutenant governor. He regretted asking that question when he heard the group's opinion, voiced by Adams.

"Let us start with Oliver," Adams replied.

"When should this occur?" Mackintosh asked.

"I say we wait two months to see if London changes its mind," Otis said.

This elicited a spirited debate, but the group finally acceded to Otis' view. The decision seemed to disappoint Mackintosh; he was beginning to feel like a powerful hound on a tight leash. As the group disbanded, they shook hands, as if in conspiracy. Mackintosh commented later that he had noticed the only other hands with callouses besides his own belonged to Samuel Adams. Adams was a man he could trust.

Mackintosh's final question to these Boston leaders was: "May I carry out this plan, without your further consultation? That way you can more persuasively profess your ignorance of the details. Do you trust me?"

A brief silence was broken by Adams speaking more loudly than usual. "Yes, Ebenezer, we trust you to do this appropriately." Otis felt apprehension at that decision, but he did not speak.

* * *

The early morning of August 14, 1765 was unusually hot and humid. Sweat was already forming on the men preparing to send a message to the British. A large mob convened on the South End of Boston at an elm tree that would later be called the Liberty Tree. They placed an effigy of Stampman Oliver on it. Governor Bernard ordered that the effigy be removed, but his deputies refused. The intimation of potential future violence was not lost on anyone.

That evening, after working hours, an even larger crowd of men paraded the effigy through the streets of Boston. This group attracted a rougher crowd, including waterfront workers and laborers who had begun to drink heavily. They eagerly destroyed a small building that was reputed to be Oliver's future office. But they were not finished.

The angry mob rushed toward Oliver's beautiful estate, and as they approached, they chopped off the head of Oliver's effigy. They then burned the straw man, raising a roar of approval from the assembled crowd. The fire in the night gave off sparks that seemed to crackle with the sharpness of distant gunshots. Then the men began to pelt the mansion with rocks. Calling for a hangman's rope, they broke down the mansion's doors. Upon realizing Oliver had fled, they commenced destroying his furniture, artwork, and everything else they could find.

Hutchinson tried reasoning with them, but he was ignored. Governor Bernard ordered the colonel of the militia to enlist his men, but many of those men were in the seething mob.

* * *

No blood was shed that night. The following day, Oliver asked the Treasury to relieve him of his duties. Soon the stampmen in all the other American colonies, save Georgia, followed suit.

One week later, Mackintosh was summoned to the Green Dragon, still enjoying the after-tremor of righteous energy spent on the fourteenth. William Mackay told Otis later that the shoemaker joined Mackay's table with four other merchants who seemed distressed, even in the convivial ambiance of the tavern. They greeted him warmly, but with furrowed brows.

55

"Hutchinson has put us in an awkward position, Ebenezer," said Mackay. "We have been named in some depositions as smugglers, and we are concerned both for our reputations and for the possibility of reprisal by the authorities. You know us well enough, Ebenezer, to know we are honorable men. Yet once these lies and allegations are made public, there is no putting the genie back in the bottle. Perhaps you can help us."

"I would be happy to," the shoemaker replied. "Simply tell me where these papers might be found and my friends would be more than willing to render justice. It must appear to be a further action against the damned Stamp Act, so we must act very soon."

The merchants' countenances changed quickly with these words. A lightness came to the table like the froth of the new round of beers Beth had just delivered. Mackay provided Mackintosh with the necessary details. Mackintosh did not even blink when he learned one of the target destinations was the home of Lieutenant Governor Hutchinson. Later, before Mackay could suggest it, Mackintosh told the small group, "You have no knowledge of this, no connection with what will happen." They gave a relieved nod in unison. Mackintosh left the Green Dragon with a spring in his step, his mind racing, full of names of men he would enlist and actions that would be taken, and when.

Beth Frothingham told Otis that the next night Mackintosh brought together thirty of his "associates" and went to the back room of the Green Dragon to discuss the upcoming "project." They came from all over Boston—smiths, coopers, workers from the wharf, vendors, craftsmen, and assorted hangers-on. The room bubbled with pure male energy. There were the usual mocking and belittling jokes directed at one another, the crude language and exaggerated claims that come with such a crew.

The esprit de corps grew as the rounds of beer and the hours passed by; the jokes seemed ever-funnier and elicited responses that seemed hilarious to the men. Occasionally, a small group within the throng would break into song, usually with off-color lyrics aimed at customs officers or the local high officials representing the crown. The manhood of those officials was frequently mocked with bad puns and thinly veiled metaphors. When the time seemed perfect, when none of the men had started to depart, Mackintosh stood on a chair to address his "associates."

"Gentlemen, it is a pleasure to address you this evening," he started, talking through the hoots, jeers, and whistles that welcomed him. The smoke was thick in the room, which helped reduce the pungent smell of the small pool of vomit that had just been delivered by one of the revelers.

"Our friends from the merchant community have asked me to request you help them straighten out a little matter, a problem our dear lieutenant governor has created."

At the mention of Hutchinson, the men groaned and booed like a wounded elephant.

"Please let me finish," Mackintosh implored. "Here is the plan."

Mackintosh laid out the plan, which was simple and clear, mercifully so, given the deep level of drunkenness in the room. He then asked for volunteers, instructing those assembled to rise if they were going to join the mission. While a few needed help to get on their feet and stand on their own volition, not one soul remained seated. Mackintosh then directed the men to reconvene at the Green Dragon in the early evening of August 26.

The actions of the evening of Monday, August 26 had an even harsher tone than those of August 14. There was no restraint. Hutchinson would later write that it was a "scene of riot, drunkenness, profaneness, and robbery." Indeed it was. The homes of four officials associated with the vice-admiralty court or customs establishments were ransacked. The elegant house of Thomas Hutchinson, with its façade's Ionic pilasters and cupola-crowned roof, was destroyed. The walls were smashed, the curtains torn down. Even the cupola was dismantled. His silver was stolen, as was considerable cash. More hurtful still to Hutchinson was the destruction of papers and manuscripts he had used to document the history of Massachusetts. The rebels continued their destruction and havoc until sunrise.

Otis was furious when he heard what the mob had done. This was no high-minded protest to the Stamp Act—it was flagrant lawlessness. The next day, Otis asked Mercy if she and her husband, Samuel Adams, Hancock, and he could meet at her house. Adams wanted Beth Frothingham to join them because she heard so many voices at the Green Dragon and could provide a deeper understanding of the recent mayhem's impact on their fellow citizens. And as the tax collector in Boston, Adams' ear was close to the ground as well. Mercy cheerfully agreed to host them, and they reconvened that Friday with Beth, who gave the gentle lie to her employer that her mother needed her, to excuse her absence from the Green Dragon.

Mercy greeted Beth at the door with her natural grace. Whatever self-consciousness the barmaid may have felt was quickly dispelled. Within a minute, Beth felt she had known Mercy her whole life. They joined Adams and Hancock, who were already sipping the port the Warrens had put out; both men knew Beth, of course, from the Green Dragon, so no introductions were necessary. Hancock welcomed her arrival because he found her comely and fun; Adams welcomed her because she was "of the people" and had no airs of pretension or self-importance. An easy familiarity pervaded the room; it was the natural state of the Warren home, and even more pronounced with Beth there.

Otis had arrived serious, eager to speak his piece about recent events. He took his place on the loveseat next to Mercy, quietly fuming.

"How in the world can someone like Mackintosh do that to us?" he asked. "Who put him up to it? All we want is to be treated as if we had the rights of Englishmen, but now we are barbarians. What an idiot. Now, when we try to appeal to their better natures and good judgment, they will look at August 26 and ask why they should take us seriously. My God, what a setback. Samuel, have you been in contact with this man?"

"Yes, but not recently," Adams replied.

James Warren tried to lighten the room. "Are you feeling sorry for Hutchinson, my fellow James?" Otis was not amused.

"Don't 'fellow James' me, James," he replied, which in itself sounded faintly comical. "This is serious!"

Mercy interceded by putting her arm around her brother and regarding him with a look of affection a parent might feel toward a wild child.

"Dear brother," she said, "let us step back and look at what has happened, and as Ruth, your lovely wife, might say, 'breathe.'"

Otis hated to be patronized, even by his sister, much as he respected her. It seemed that more and more of his friends had begun to treat him that way. Strange.

"Stop, Mercy. I know what you are doing. I have spent years of my life fighting for us to gain the respect and rights of Englishmen, but a buffoon like Mackintosh can blow that up in one night of drunken excess. It is so wrong!"

Suddenly, Beth broke in.

"Ebenezer Mackintosh is a good man. He is not an idiot; he is not a buffoon. He is a man of honor. If the events of August 26 went too far, it is because Hutchinson is rightly hated. Ebenezer cannot control the mob every time. I hope your comments do not reflect your true feelings, Mr. Otis."

"For heaven's sake, call him Jemmy," Mercy interjected.

Beth's ardor and defense of Mackintosh touched Otis, taking him aback, but filling him with respect for her. She had no fear challenging the most prominent lawyer in Boston, which made her more interesting, even alluring.

"Yes, call me Jemmy, Beth," Otis said.

"If," Beth continued, "we in this town are going to resist the gross misuse of power by the king's agents, we must stand together. We cannot turn against one another." The barmaid was reminding some of Boston's leading thinkers of what was important. It was refreshing to hear her speak. Mercy appreciated her the most.

"Beth, you and Samuel are closest to the people. What do you both think we need to do next to repair the damage done to our relations with the Crown?" Mercy asked.

"Beth is absolutely right," said Adams. "No public reprimand of Mackintosh. No self-righteous pronouncements against the mob, James. Are you listening to me, James?"

Once again, Otis felt patronized.

"There need be no apologies to the Crown," said Adams, "but there must be peace and calm. I will talk to Mackintosh and to each of the Loyal Nine. I will tell Mackintosh we need his help to maintain order. I am most concerned about November 5, Pope's Day."

Pope's Day gave revelers from the North End and South End an excuse for controlled rioting and drunkenness in remembrance of the 1605 abortive plot on November 5 by Catholics to blow up the House of Lords and kill King James I. It was celebrated more for the ribaldry than anti-Catholicism.

"There must be order on Pope's Day, and Mackintosh is the one who can maintain it. His people would follow him if he marched off a cliff. He and he alone can make sure Pope's Day does not turn into even greater mayhem than usual. That is the next test."

Beth was nodding her head. "I have little to add to what Mr. Adams has said. The people are very distressed, but they do not want chaos and the savagery that can come from it. They continue to want respect, and to be left alone."

Otis was no longer thinking about Mackintosh, Hutchinson, or the British authorities. He was focused on Beth and taken over by feelings of the kind he had not had since the time he had first met Ruth. The feeling was disconcerting and exciting. He thought Beth was viewing him in a different way too, less deferential and more like an equal. Mercy also seemed fond of her, and his sister had always been a good judge of people. Otis wondered how he could justify spending more time with Beth, and possibly private time with her, for the purpose, of course, of better understanding the mood of the people of Boston.

He could justify and articulate almost anything; he was, after all, a lawyer.

≈ **9** ≈

Otis talked frequently with Samuel Adams after that meeting, discussing strategy—Adams' strong suit.

Adams was struggling with the delicate question of how to approach Mackintosh, and how to motivate him to control the mobs more effectively, without seeming to chastise him. Adams had convinced Otis that the shoemaker was a priceless asset to the cause. For advocates of resistance, Mackintosh exuded a restless but controlled dissatisfaction that inspired loyalty. His very lack of ambition gave him the moral force to lead. Because he was truly humble, he had enormous influence. And when it was necessary to resist arbitrary acts, Mackintosh generated hundreds, even thousands of citizens to protest. To the British authorities (save Hutchinson), he was also seen as a potentially invaluable force, the only moderating influence they knew of who single-handedly could avert rebellious pandemonium.

Adams invited Mackintosh and Otis to join him for a leisurely stroll through the streets of Boston in early September, ostensibly to chat and catch up on the city's affairs. He had met with the Loyal Nine to be clear on what to tell Mackintosh, and none of those leaders disagreed. While they knew Adams to be an unsuccessful businessman, they also knew him to be a brilliant and relentless political strategist. Adams knew how to connect with the shoemaker: the two men even dressed in similar simple attire, in plain trousers and flat-brimmed hats.

That radiant Saturday morning, the streets of Boston's South End were teeming with people of all ages and an occasional stray cow; far more families were wandering throughout the city than usual, with nothing more important to do than greeting their neighbors and breathing the clean air that the breeze from the Atlantic brought in. A number of the children played with their pet squirrels as their families strolled.

Adams encouraged Otis to say as little as possible, a considerable challenge. Otis seemed to savor speaking, being almost addicted to the sound of his own voice. He often needed to be told quite bluntly that others around him should have the opportunity to express their views too. In this rare case, he complied with the request to remain silent.

Two strong hands met in greeting as Adams said, "It is so good to see you, Ebenezer." Mackintosh conveyed equal warmth and comity, without words. He gave Otis a polite but cooler greeting.

"I need to hear your thoughts about the coming Pope's Day events and get your reflection on what occurred last week. The Loyal Nine are very concerned that things not get out of hand on November 5. They need reassurance." Adams' patient words did not reveal an important motivator for Mackintosh to comply with his wishes: Adams could seek the back taxes Mackintosh owed.

"I appreciate your concern and value your respect, Samuel. I plead guilty to letting things get out of hand last week, and I apologize. I truly despise that weasel of a lieutenant governor. It is personal, but it is also public. I am sure you are aware of his filthy little campaign to besmirch your reputation, James. You are our leading voice of resistance, and the little dandy prat maligns you constantly," Mackintosh replied. Otis nodded in sad acknowledgment.

Adams then took hold of the conversation. "You are a fair and fervent friend of our cause, Ebenezer, and the city is blessed to have you. But we cannot allow another August 26 unless it is duly provoked by the arrogant asses across the Atlantic." Adams seemed pleased with his accidental alliteration, but Mackintosh did not notice it.

"Samuel," Mackintosh replied, smiling, "I vow to you that Pope's Day will not deviate from the controlled mayhem it always is. At least I can speak for the South End, and since we are more numerous, braver, more intelligent, and generally better human beings than those on the North End, you can sleep easy."

Adams did not ignore the leaders of the North End. On the night before Pope's Day, Adams staged a "Union Feast" for the tough men of both groups to mingle with one another as well as merchants and politicians. That they did so reflected their great respect for Samuel Adams.

The account given concerning the events of Pope's Day in the November 7 edition of the *Massachusetts Gazette* demonstrated the extent of Mackintosh's success:

> Tuesday last being the Anniversary of the Commemoration of the happy Deliverance of the English Nation from the

Popish Plot, commonly called the Powder Plot, the Guns at Castle William were fired at one o'clock; as also on Board the Men of War in the Harbor. It has long been the Custom in this Town on the Fifth of November for Numbers of Persons to exhibit on Stages some Pageantry, denoting their abhorrence of Popery and the horrid Plot which was to have been executed on that Day in 1605; these Shews of late Years has been continued in the late Evening, and we have often seen the bad Effects attending them at such time; the Servants and Negroes would disguise themselves, and being armed with clubs would engage each other with great Violence, whereby many came off badly wounded; in short they carried it to such Lengths that two Parties were created in the Town, under the Appellation of North-End and South-End: But the Disorders that had been committed from Time to Time induced several Gentlemen to try a Reconciliation between the two Parties; accordingly the Chiefs met at the First of this Instant, and conducted that Affair in a very orderly Manner; in the Evening the Commander of the South entered into a Treaty with the Commander of the North, and after making several Overtures they reciprocally engaged on a UNION and the former distinctions to subside; at the same Time the Chiefs with their Assistants engaged upon their Honor no Mischiefs should arise by their Means, and that they would prevent Disorders on the 4th.

When the Day arrived the Morning was all Quietness, about Noon the Pageantry representing the Pope, the Devil and several other Effigies signifying Tyranny, Oppression, Slavery were brought on Stages from the North and South and met in King Street, where the Union was established in a very ceremonial Manner, and having given three Huzzas, they interchanged the ground, the South marched to the North and the North to the South, parading thro' the Streets until they met near the Court House: the whole then proceeded to the Tree of Liberty, under the Shadow of which they refreshed themselves for a while, and then retreated to the Northward, agreeable to their Plan;—they reached Copp's Hill before 6 o'clock where they halted and having enkindled a Fire, the whole Pageantry was committed to the flames and consumed: This being finished every person was requested to retire to their respective Homes— It must be noticed to the Honor of all those concerned in this business that everything was conducted in a most regular manner, and such Order observed as could hardly be expected among a concourse of several thousand people— all seemed to be joined, agreeable to their principle Motto Lovely Unity—The leaders, Mr. McIntosh from the South and Mr. Swift from the North, appeared in Military Habits, with small canes resting on their left arms, having music in Front and Flank; their assistants appeared also distinguished with small reeds, then the respective Corps followed, among whom were a great Number of Persons in Rank: These with the Spectators, filled the Streets; not a Club was seen among the whole, nor was any Negro allowed to approach near the Stages;—after the Conflagration the Populace retired, and the Town remained the whole Night in better Order than it had ever been on this Occasion.

Adams paid an unexpected visit to Otis the next morning, in a state of high spirits, eager to talk.

Otis observed Ruth as she answered the door in response to Adams' eager knocking. Her face betrayed irritation at the sight of a man she took to be a disloyal rabble-rouser. Adams barely even looked at her as he asked, "Where is James?" Then he remembered that certain social niceties should precede addressing the serious business at hand, so he lamely added, "How are you today, Ruth? I hope you are well, and how is young James?" She did not even deign to respond. She turned to Otis, seated in their parlor, and announced, "Samuel Adams is here for you, James."

When Otis rose and greeted Adams, the awkwardness with Ruth only intensified since clearly she was not welcome to be part of their conversation. Otis invited Adams into his small study with its brimming bookshelves that seemed to groan with the weight of history and big ideas. The books pushed against the walls and were so voluminous they overshadowed the furniture, including the simple mahogany desk and office chair. There was but one additional cushion-less chair for the host's infrequent visitors.

"James," said Adams, seating himself, "what happened—or should I say didn't happen—last night was extraordinary. We had asked Mackintosh to control what could have been uncontrollable and he succeeded." Adams rubbed his hands together with glee. "Do you understand what this means, my friend?"

Otis shook his head, puzzled by Adams' excessive excitement. "I am not quite sure I understand your great enthusiasm, Samuel. Forgive me, but please explain."

Adams arose from the uncomfortable chair and began to pace around the small office like a lion in a cage. A smile crept across his face as he explained to the brilliant lawyer the preceding night's significance. It was a patient, patronizing smile because once again he thought Otis had failed to see the forest for the trees. The "forest" was the fact that Boston's citizens were coming together; those who had been antagonists were uniting. For Adams, that was a crucial precondition to more sustained resistance to the British in the future. The "trees," as Otis saw it, was that Mackintosh merely succeeded in controlling the mob.

"James, you are brilliant, and so are the authors of many of these books," Adams said, pointing to the bookshelves. "But what happens in the streets is of equal or greater significance for our cause. That Mackintosh has such control of the mobs is an asset of inestimable value. It demonstrates to London that we are worthy subjects, not wild savages. It shows we are worthy of respect."

Once again, Otis felt patronized, lectured, and spoken down to. While he knew he was not the shrewd strategist Adams was, he felt he had enough common sense to know the truth of Adams' words. He did not believe he needed to have such things spelled out.

"Samuel," Otis replied, "we need to remain on the high ground, and I still distrust Mackintosh to keep us there. We may not like Hutchinson, but he did not deserve what happened to him. He is a well-educated, refined man, another Harvard man, and we should not give him reasons to disrespect us."

"Hutchinson is not a good and decent man, James," said Adams. "It grieves me to tell you this, but his efforts to destroy your reputation in this town are having some effect. His customs commissioners mock you wherever they go, and Hutchinson himself disparages you wherever and whenever he is able. He is still bitter about the Writs of Assistance case; he has felt emasculated by your brilliant advocacy against his position. He believes you have undercut his authority, and indeed you have.

Hutchinson may be a Harvard man, James, but he is also a skunk."

Otis stared at his friend. He felt confused and puzzled, as if he had been told a joke and did not understand it. What exactly was the meaning of Adams' remarks? Were his words really true? *Have I been a fool, blind to obvious things around me, unable to deduce who was doing what and why? This is so strange and contrary to the way a person should act; can Hutchinson really be this ignoble?* Coming to this new information, this new insight about what had been happening around him, caused him to feel like a fool. Who else might be betraying him? He believed so deeply in the goodness and equal rights of all men and women that hearing Adams' words greatly darkened his spirits.

"How do you know this is true, Samuel? Have you actually observed this?" Otis asked, in pain.

"I have my sources all over Boston, James. I talk to many people. It is true, I am afraid."

Otis dropped his head, stood still, and groaned.

"James, we need you to continue to lead us," Adams said soothingly, "to speak for our principles and our cause. You are a good man, and the likes of Hutchinson deserve scant consideration. Recently, I heard Customs Commissioner Robinson malign you at the Green Dragon, and his words were met with disbelief and derision. Fisticuffs almost ensued. The people in this town love you and hate the customs commissioners, so their malignant words are not ringing true to our fellow Bostonians."

Otis, speaking in a low voice, asked Adams to leave. He needed time to digest this new reality, that he was the butt of vicious words. And sadly, he could find no solace in his own home; his marriage had become more desolate and lonely than ever. Yes, he had friends of a certain kind, but he needed a person who could give him perspective and fill the bleak void he felt inside. It could be Crispus Attucks, but there was no way of finding him. For all he knew, Attucks was down the coast working on the docks of New York or Charleston.

Maybe Adams had overstated Hutchinson's efforts to malign him. The coming holidays, including the Christmas party at Rev. Merrywell's, would expose him to Hutchinson in person.

10

The annual Christmas party put on by the Anglican priest, Francis Merrywell, always gave the invited guests a blend of eager anticipation and muted trepidation. Otis wondered who would be there. It seemed that Merrywell wanted to invite people from various walks of life, possibly with an intent to broaden the base of his congregation in a town that leaned more heavily to Congregational and deist views than toward those of the Anglicans.

The smell of roast pork permeated the house, causing Otis to salivate. The lush, blue Persian carpet that covered the clean pine floors made the guests cautious about tracking dirt in. Standing to the left in the ample parlor was Robinson, and next to him, to Otis' surprise, was Beth Frothingham. Inviting a barmaid from the Green Dragon was an interesting choice for such a gathering. Inviting Robinson, a customs officer, was also unexpected. Merrywell would seldom disclose who the other guests would be at his little parties; it added to the social electricity of the events, and he rather enjoyed matching people who came from different worlds.

The host would bring in chamber musicians to perform, the prospect of which provided some consolation since it meant there would be a period in the evening when Otis would not have to be charming. And he did love music. Merrywell always arranged the evening such that the beginning would be a larger mass of people invited to enjoy the wine and hors d'oeuvres; the music would then begin; and when it finished, a select few would remain for dinner.

When the musicians had packed their instruments, Otis was aghast to see who his dinner companions would be. Once again, Merrywell was devising a way to bring unlikely dinner partners together. Besides Otis and Ruth, the guests included Hutchinson, Robinson, Mackintosh, Hancock, William Mackay and his deaf and jolly wife Abigail, and Beth Frothingham. The selection of dinner guests seemed almost perverse to Otis; Merrywell knew what he and Hutchinson thought of one other.

To make things even more interesting, the guests had all already consumed a great deal of the Portuguese Madeira that Hancock had successfully smuggled into the town and given to Merrywell, an ill-gotten holiday gift. For all but one of them, the guests' inhibitions had vanished completely, like small puffs of smoke blown away in a stiff gale. Beth was the only one who could hold her liquor.

Merrywell opened the meal with a loud and slurred expression of thanks to the Lord and an enthusiastic, if incoherent, shower of wishes, more thanks, and apologies that even the Almighty would have been challenged to understand. When he paused, several of the guests uttered "Amen," but Merrywell was not finished; the Lord needed to know how grateful the pastor was for the wise and humane leadership of the prime minister, the Archbishop of Canterbury, and, of course, the king. Finally, Merrywell finished, and when his guests were confident he was done, the conversations began. The seating arrangement created distinctive dialogues.

Merrywell and Hutchinson sat at the head and foot of the table respectively. On Merrywell's right was Ruth and Hancock, and on his left, Beth and Robinson. Abigail and Otis were on Hutchinson's right, and on his left was Mackintosh. They broke into four conversations and the volume escalated, even more so because Abigail Mackay spoke loudly due to her hearing impairment.

Hutchinson, Abigail Mackay, and Otis discussed children and all the challenges they brought. Abigail sympathized loudly with Hutchinson, a widower with five children, showering him with praise for doing the difficult task of governing the colony and raising children. When she asked him which was more difficult, he quickly answered that raising children was.

Hutchinson and Otis tried to deflect their antipathy by reflecting on their experiences at Harvard. They clucked and chuckled together, then agreed the school was heading in the wrong direction, a common refrain of ignorant alumni. Otis mellowed with the Madeira; the conversation with Hutchinson caused him to doubt that such a convivial fellow could be trying to do him harm.

Otis overheard Ruth and Hancock discussing fashion and furnishings. Their conversation was marked by much laughter and friendly touching. Hancock regaled her with the fashion news of

France which, being a fiercely loyal British subject, did not impress her. He praised her home-decorating prowess and agreed that her husband had almost no appreciation of style. She asked Hancock about his importation and shipping business and whether, as people were whispering, he was a "naughty smuggler." He responded with an easy, familiar smile that filled the room, and uttered a loud rejoinder.

"How can you possibly ask such a thing, Ruth? I thought you knew me better than that."

Otis also caught parts of Merrywell's chat with Beth and Robinson, which was largely vacuous. Beth found the conversation boring, although she concealed her feelings gracefully. She sensed that Robinson was trying to create a conciliatory tone. The customs officer seemed shamelessly sycophantic with Merrywell. The men did all the talking and, except for an occasional glance from Merrywell at his attractive companion, they ignored the barmaid. That did not disturb Beth because of the low regard in which she held both men. She was listening to the other conversations as she feigned interest in the one she was apparently in. Then the conversation took an interesting turn, a turn toward Jesus. Robinson initiated a new, unexpected focus as he chatted with Merrywell.

"We are nearing the celebration of the birth of our Savior, Francis. May I ask you a question?"

"By all means," Merrywell said. Entering into conversation about the Lord was intoxicating for the pastor. He had contemplated all the serious questions of theology and grappled with all the contradictions and incongruous parts of the Bible. He had even won awards for his scholarship. He had the glow of confidence that his superior wisdom gave him, reinforced by five glasses of the Madeira. "What is your question, my good fellow?"

"Which of the many messages that our Lord has delivered do you believe is the most often ignored or forgotten in daily life?" Robinson asked. Only God knew exactly why this question had come to the customs officer.

Merrywell paused and cast his eyes downward at the half-eaten roast pork on his plate. The chit-chat at the table stopped immediately; the room became as quiet as a deserted tomb.

Then Merrywell spoke, softly and with great solemnity. "Forgiveness; forgiveness is most often ignored."

"Please say more," Robinson said eagerly, and Beth added, "Yes, please do."

"Forgiveness bespeaks a quality of love that is difficult to attain because it overcomes the natural tendency to judge. Showing the compassion needed to forgive, when one feels the other is undeserving, requires a nobility of spirit. The act of forgiveness elevates both the forgiver and the forgiven. Indeed, the humility required to ask for forgiveness is a sign of heavenly strength. And remember, 'To err is human; to forgive, divine,' as Alexander Pope has written."

Robinson rose to his feet. He was a bit wobbly with drink, but his face was fervent. Then, pointing at Otis, he slurred with enthusiasm, "Otis, I forgive your disloyalty to our king. I forgive your betrayal!"

Otis sat silent, thinking Robinson a drunken boor and his words unworthy of a response. He could not resist letting a small smile cross his face, betraying the sarcastic thoughts and poorly veiled contempt he felt toward Robinson.

The tension created by Robinson's words created a feeling of common embarrassment among the others, but only briefly. A loud banging on Merrywell's front door was an unexpected yet welcome sound that enabled the assembled to escape the Robinson confrontation. Suddenly, a swarm of disguised wassailers entered the front hall and barged into the dining area. Merrywell was a favorite target of these unwelcome low-lifes during the Christmas holidays.

Some of the costumes were the same as those seen at the Pope's Day revelry. One wassailer was dressed as Satan in solid black linen, one like a jester with his colorful triangular tassel hat, another like the king in a red velvet robe that dragged along the floor, and a fourth like an Anglican pastor in full royal garb, while two dressed like goats leaned over in pathetic attempts to bleat. They began their obscene skit, speaking loudly and making gestures not fit for polite company. Their bodies reeked, and their flatulence seemed hilarious to their addled, drunken brains.

The unwelcome visitors expected their antics to be interrupted with an offer of money, in whatever form that might take. That understanding drove the wassailers every Christmas season. Instead, they were confronted by two strong dinner guests— Mackintosh and Robinson, who approached the troupe menacingly. Robinson picked up one of the "goats" and threw him across the room. Merrywell shouted, "Stop it! No violence in this house!" He then turned to Satan and asked him what it would take to have the wassailers cease and desist.

"Since I am the Prince of Darkness," Satan replied, "I need a princely sum. Five shillings." When both Robinson and Mackintosh grabbed Satan, the price quickly dropped to one pence, which the generous Merrywell quickly found. The foul little group exited in silence.

The guests then assumed their seats in a room that had lost any semblance of conviviality. Robinson's outburst had altered everything, as if a crazed parishioner had interrupted the sermon, rendering the congregation mute. Even eye contact was awkward. As the hot apple pie was being served, Otis broke the silence by casting out another question sure to heat up the room.

"Who among us believes the Stamp Act will be repealed next year?" Otis asked.

"Must we talk politics even at Christmas, James?" Ruth replied.

"This won't take long, my dear. Please, raise your hand if you think Parliament will backtrack again." Beth, Mackintosh, Hancock, and Otis raised their hands; the others looked down at their plates. When Otis asked Hutchinson his opinion, he did not reply. The lieutenant governor was not amused by the question.

11

The following May, the Stamp Act was repealed. The message came from London on one of Hancock's ships, adding to his popularity. Otis gloated. The dinner companions from the Merrywell party—Adams, Hancock, Mackintosh, and Beth—were greatly encouraged, as was a vast majority of Bostonians. The non-importation of British goods had been a major factor in the repeal, and many citizens had sacrificed in that effort.

When the town learned of the repeal, bells tolled throughout Boston, guns roared, ships showed their colors, music sounded, and the Liberty Tree was adorned with colorful streamers. In the evening, the celebration continued with bonfires, and on Hancock's lawn, a 126-gallon container of Madeira flowed freely.

Meanwhile, the cancer of subtle humiliation continued to take over Hutchinson, Robinson, and the other servants of the king in America.

The repeal of the Stamp Act continued the pattern of British retreat: since Otis had argued the Writs of Assistance case, the authorities rarely used them again; after the British enforced the Sugar Act more aggressively, American opposition caused them to repeal it, and then came the Stamp Act repeal. It was apparent that the right kind of public resistance would cause the rulers to backtrack.

Yet Americans still believed in their British leaders' legitimacy. They resisted as loyal subjects.

But the men who ruled England were beginning to lose patience with the American subjects, and London's thirst for revenue from the colonies escalated. The next attempt to extract it was led by Chancellor of the Exchequer Charles Townshend. In 1767, the Townshend Revenue Acts imposed duties on glass, lead, paints, and paper. And tea.

The Townshend Acts created a new kind of organized resistance, this time from the Sons of Liberty, which had come into being at the time of the Stamp Act. The Sons of Liberty included men from all walks of life in Boston, and it had developed an underground network of supporters, including allies in New York.

Their successful protest of the Stamp Act gave them energy and credibility among like-minded Bostonians. A small group of them convened at the Green Dragon on a warm summer evening to plan a new approach to oppose the latest British arrogant folly.

Present were merchants John Hancock and William Mackay; publisher of the *Gazette*, Benjamin Edes; tax collector and the clear emerging leader, Samuel Adams; and Otis. Adams had invited William Molineux, an English-born hardware store owner whom Tories called the "fist leader of dirty matters," a man of uneven temperament comfortable connecting with what the British called "rabble." Hancock was flirting merrily with Beth Frothingham as she tried to attend to other customers, so she felt relieved when Adams forced Hancock to join the "more serious conversation." For Adams, it was always all business, all the time. He was the one man in touch with all the circles of patriot resistance in Boston. Hancock, Edes, and Mackay rather enjoyed the banter with Beth and other patrons, but duty called; its name was Samuel Adams.

"The King," Adams began, "cannot be fully aware of what his ministry is doing. His ministers are fools. Here we are, stuck with recklessness and avarice from his emissaries. And those minions seem more ruthless and resolute than ever. Gentlemen, we need a plan." Molineux murmured his agreement, causing his disapproving face to look even more surly.

"Samuel, I care more about my customers than the customs commissioners, or even the almighty king, for that matter," Mackay barked back. "It is not I but my customers who will pay the duties, and that is unfair to them. Let me ask you all: Whom are we serving in our various endeavors, our countrymen or the Crown?"

"I thought we could serve both," Edes said. "I thought our protest was to serve our mother country's truest ideals. But the king's arrogant agents try to run roughshod over us. It is becoming intolerable."

In an attempt to inject hope for future governance of Massachusetts, Hancock pointed out that the colony's cause did have friends in London, including such wise and brave men as William Pitt. Hancock's optimism was quickly dismissed.

Adams looked at the two men of business and reminded them of other English allies.

"Our resistance to the Stamp Act took two forms, and the one that was less showy was the agreement to restrict British imports. The mobs gave energy to the cause, but our message only got across when other Englishmen saw their businesses decline because of our attempts at non-importation of their goods. You remember what my cousin John said in the *Gazette*: 'I'd rather the Spittlefield weavers should pull down all the houses in England, and knock the brains out of all the wicked men there, than this country loose its liberty.' Harsh language I admit, even hiding behind his Humphrey Ploughjogger nom de plume. But the point is that English business leaders can continue to be our best advocates with Parliament. We need to step up the non-importation efforts in our town as they have done so well in New York."

Hancock looked concerned, as did Mackay.

"I do not like anything that restricts the flow of goods and commerce," Hancock replied. "We all hate the duties they are trying to foist on us, but our merchants here will suffer if they have fewer goods to sell."

"John, why do you care about the niceties of the British regulations?" asked Mackay with a twinkle in his eye. "You will continue your smuggling no matter what."

At Mackay's comment, Hancock's usual good nature seemed to evaporate, but it wasn't the little jibe that had transformed his visage. He scowled, a rare expression on Hancock's face; it was the expression of a man sensing a higher mission than his own wealth, a man sensing his involvement in a cause grander than opposition to unfair taxes and duties.

"I am glad you mentioned New York, William. More now than ever, we need to think of the other colonies. We cannot resist alone; our fate is tied to our friends to the south, even those in the tobacco and cotton colonies. Nonimportation only works when the colonies are united," Hancock said.

"Be careful, Mr. Hancock," Adams said with a tiny smile. "You are starting to sound more like a patriot than a rich man of affairs."

Beth approached them carrying three mugs of ale and spilling some of it on the gritty floor. She had heard most of their conversation. Her excited support of the cause had been growing for years. It was a cause she tied to Otis, her best friend among the

Green Dragon's customers. She was proving an invaluable asset, all for the larger mission, of course.

When the Green Dragon Tavern closed its doors sharply at midnight that sultry evening, Beth's thoughts were preoccupied with Otis. She often would seek solace and perspective by wandering over to Boston Harbor so she could gaze out into the harbor and beyond to the more distant, exotic ocean. While her legs and strong arms were tired, the sea air always perked her up, giving her new life. She passed sailors and stevedores, as well as other stray night walkers, and made her way to her favorite perch at the end of the long pier, a small wooden bench that could seat two. She would always sit in the middle of the bench so no stranger would ask if he could join her. Beth was so well-known that she felt safe; if an unwelcome advance were made toward her, she only need raise her voice a bit and several strong dock workers would be there.

Beth seated herself and settled down to rest and meditate on the sea and herself, alone.

"Hello, Beth. What brings you down here?" a familiar voice asked her from behind the bench. Otis came around to her right side and looked down at her with an irrepressible smile she returned.

"Oh, James, I just wanted to get some fresh air after all that time in the Green Dragon, all the smoke and close bodies. I just wanted to breathe," she said with a pleasant sigh.

"Well, I can't tell you how happy I am to see you. Such a pleasant surprise. I love coming down here by myself and, frankly, getting away from everything. Then I see you. I hope I am not being too forward, but I cannot think of anyone I would rather be surprised by."

"You are very kind, sir," she replied with a lilt in her voice and a smile that flooded Otis with feelings he had forgotten he'd ever had.

"May I join you?" he asked.

"Please; it would be my pleasure," she replied, moving to the left side.

Beth started the conversation naturally.

"I always feel there is so much I would love to talk about with you, James, but there is never the opportunity." She quickly wondered if she should not have said "love."

Otis felt giddy. Time and space felt unlimited, his daily worries so far away. He was free.

"What do you want to discuss, young lady?" he asked, quickly regretting the "young lady."

"How did you come to believe the things you believe, and where is all of this going?" she asked. Otis gazed out at the water as she spoke. Then he turned to her.

"My family, my education, my career, and my current coconspirators have taken me here," he replied. He felt it an unworthy answer; it said nothing, but it was a start.

"My father, while a man of many talents and some considerable importance, has always bridled at the authority of the Crown and particularly the king's agents here. A somewhat grudging subject, and certainly not a Loyalist, he loves politics. He has been a judge, a lawyer, and a colonel in the militia; in fact, people call him "colonel." He put a supreme emphasis on education. That I would go to Harvard was never even a question. I was well-prepared by Jonathan Russell, the minister at Barnstable, and at fifteen, he thought me ready to matriculate."

Otis felt he was already going on too long and being too boringly literal in his response, but what should he have said?

"Have I bored you yet, Beth?" he asked.

"No. I don't know any of this, and I love hearing about your past and your family."

"All right, but you must be honest and tell me when to stop or please interrupt me, agreed?"

She agreed.

"I plunged into the classics during the last two years at Harvard and only surfaced occasionally to be with other people. I mastered the violin there. When I was lonely or felt lost, I found refuge in scholarship and began my love affair with prosody."

Beth interrupted. "What is prosody? I have heard the word but do not know what it means or why you, or anyone, would study it."

"It is complicated. It is the study of the rhythm and sound in poetry, and it can include the study of patterns of stress and intonation in language generally. I studied it, and even published a book about it, because I believe there is nothing more powerful and delightful than language, if it is fully understood and appreciated. Do you want to know something?" Otis asked.

"Yes, of course," she said.

"Nobody has ever asked me about prosody in the past twenty years, yet it is central to my life, or at least my oratory, which people in Boston seem to admire. You have reminded me of a treasure. Thank you, Beth. I am in your debt."

"The credit you give me is unearned," she said. A breeze had picked up off the harbor, causing her lovely raven hair to sweep across her adorable face.

They sat quietly for a moment, listening to the lapping waves and the occasional gentle bumps of the ships against the docks adjacent to the pier. Otis, wondering what she was really thinking, rested in a state of luxurious contentment.

Beth broke the silence. "You are a genius at expressing yourself publicly, James, but what is the source of your ideas?"

"Oh, Beth, there are so many sources," Otis replied. "Some of it comes from the ancients, particularly the Romans. The contrast between the noble republic and the dissolute empire and all the lessons from that epoch have inspired us. Our teachers from that time are Plutarch, Livy, and above all Cicero. Some of it derives from English common law. Much more recently, some of our ideas come from the Enlightenment, from Voltaire, and of course, the great John Locke. And perhaps the most powerful thinkers for us to follow are actually the English radicals from earlier in this century, visionary men like John Trenchard and Thomas Gordon, who created *The Independent Whig* and *Cato's Letters*. They have led the way both in resistance to arrogant political or religious authority and in spreading the word aggressively through pamphlets, attacking the foes of liberty. But once again, I am blathering on."

Beth seemed engrossed. She had limited formal education but had been told from her earliest years that she was very bright. Her father was a blacksmith, and her mother sold green vegetables in the summer and canned and knitted in the winter. Beth loved to read, but she had not read any of the men Otis mentioned. She was intrigued by the ideas that moved people to believe and act as they did.

"I find this very interesting, James," said Beth with genuine curiosity. "Excuse me if this is too simple a question, but what is driving resistance here in Boston? What are the British getting so wrong? What are your hopes and fears?"

"The big ideas developed brilliantly by different men revolve around natural rights, the social and governmental contract, the character of liberty and the institutional dictates needed to attain and maintain it, the laws of nature and appropriate laws of nations, and throughout all of that, the use of power, whether it is power over the citizens or power with the citizens. And with power comes the tendency toward corruption. How can that power be kept in check?

"Beth, I think those of us who are challenging the Crown simply want to be treated with the same rights and privileges that Englishmen in Britain are granted. We hate arbitrary power. We believe our shared ideals unite us; they enable us all to forge common bonds for our own good and that of the community. My own view is that those rights, and that equality itself, should be open to men and women of all races. They are derived from God himself, and are not granted by men. And the happenstance of birth should not dictate how free a person is. I hate slavery. I believe women are equal to men in mental capacity and generally superior in character. Those who disagree with me have begun to say I am not of sound mind. That is their right, however ill-founded their belief."

Beth did not respond but continued to sit quietly. Even with all the talk of abstract ideas and ideals, the night remained enchanted to Otis. He took Beth's hand and held it. Her hand fit so well in his and felt so natural. Beth's face became flushed; she sighed, but she did not resist. They stared ahead into the harbor.

* * *

At that very moment, beyond the harbor and twenty miles east in the tumultuous Atlantic Ocean, Crispus Attucks, along with a small crew, was in close pursuit of a prized target, a sperm whale. The waves were high, dangerously so, but the target was well worth the risk. The sperm whale provided the cleanest-burning oil, the best lubricant, and the spermaceti provided material for candles that attracted eager buyers in England. Attucks was a skilled whaler, sought out by the men who made their living in this dangerous but lucrative field. He could do it all—he was outstanding at harpooning and penetrating the tough skin of the whale to ensure a solid attachment; he was patient and uncomplaining as the creature swam until it was exhausted; and he was unmatched in his ability to throw the lance that enabled the team to bring the massive animal to shore.

The light cedar, doubled-ended whaleboat was now in striking distance. Attucks had never faced a challenge this daunting; keeping his balance and calibrating the throw in a situation which had such odd and quickly changing angles was uncharted territory. The other men were silent and full of expectation; each was glad that he himself had not been called upon to cast the harpoon in these circumstances. Their confidence in Attucks exceeded his own. When his throw hit the whale at the precisely correct place, the men cheered, though the cheers were almost impossible to hear in the roaring of the sea. Attucks still did not smile. They would be in for a harrowing ride, but he knew this mission would be successful. Success of this kind was his constant companion, not just in whaling but all of his endeavors. What Attucks was not yet aware of was that he himself had become a target.

John Robinson had sent out the word to his fellow customs commissioners from Boston to Charleston that Attucks was to be "hunted" (his word) and brought to justice; that is, returned to his Framingham master, Deacon William Brown. The customs commissioners were to remain vigilant and follow up on any information they may have obtained that could help accomplish this goal. Robinson believed that those in the Southern ports would be particularly enthusiastic about such a reward for a runaway slave. How wrong he was.

Crispus Attucks had become legendary up and down the American Atlantic coast. Yes, he was greatly admired for his skills by those in the booming whaling industry, but he was even more respected for his character. Stories abounded of his good and selfless deeds (some of them no doubt apocryphal), so when the sailors or stevedores told of the bounty on him, they smirked. Who would be foolish enough to cash in on this good man? Some of them even said that, were they to learn who such a bounty hunter might be, that man would not be long for this world. And they meant it.

* * *

The following summer, a momentous event would occur in Boston Harbor that further broadened the gulf between Boston and the most powerful nation on earth.

Part III

A Growing Flame

≈ 12 ≈

June 9, 1768 was a clear day with calm waters that enabled swift passage into Boston's port. One ship that had arrived belonged to Hancock—the *Liberty*. The fine sloop had a full cargo of Madeira wine. Captain John Marshall had done another masterful job delivering her in the late afternoon, and she was ready to be unloaded.

Finally, the tide-waiter, Dennis Smith, came on board as a representative of the customs commissioners, to ensure an accurate accounting of the cargo's size and nature. It was usual for him to meet with the *Liberty*'s sloop-master, Archibald Brown, over punch, before official business was done. It was an opportunity for Brown to provide a small bribe and Smith to agree on how much to underestimate the amount of cargo on board. They met in a cozy, small room next to the captain's quarters.

Brown, an affable, husky man, recounted days later how he began the chat as he sipped the tasty beverage that had been enhanced by some of the cargo.

"What do you think, my friend?" Brown asked with a confident smile. "Does two guineas sound like a fair amount for us to show our appreciation of your conscientious work enforcing the law?"

"No. There will be no greasing of my palm," Smith replied. His face remained stern as he took his sip.

"That is strange. What is the matter?" Brown asked. "Not enough?"

"It is called integrity," Smith replied. Brown did not know how to continue.

"Very well. What about the assessment of the quantity of cargo? Shall we say fifty cases, and you keep five to give to your friends in the Custom House?" Brown asked.

"The amount is far greater than that, Mr. Brown, and you know it. Once again, the answer is 'no.'"

There was a strained silence. Clearly something had changed, and the agreements that kept commerce lubricated were no longer in effect.

"I need to consult with Captain Marshall for a moment. I will be right back if you will excuse me briefly," the sloop-master said. Brown left and returned quickly, being a man of his word. He engaged the tide-waiter for another hour when they were abruptly interrupted by John Marshall and three of his strong crew. Marshall himself was a powerful-looking and strikingly handsome man with brilliant blue eyes and a straight nose that could smell nonsense. The captain asked Smith if what Brown had told him was true.

"It is, sir. It would be well to start the process of unloading, Captain," Smith said in a voice that suggested a command, a tone that did not endear him to the other men.

Quickly, the three mates grabbed Smith, lifted him from his chair, and carried him out of the cabin, his feet never touching the ground.

"Put him in the brig and keep the door locked," the Captain barked.

Smith was dumbfounded. He emitted a kind of choked sound, but he could find no words. The men did as they were told, not being gentle as they tossed him into the tiny prison.

That evening, the unloading of the cargo proceeded as usual, and the necessary papers were filed with the appropriate misinformation.

The following day's weather was sunny and pleasant, but a storm of British hostility had erupted, causing havoc on the wharf; the British authorities were outraged. The king's agents were led by the Comptroller Hollowell and Collector Harrison, and their fury was fierce. Harrison believed the *Liberty* should remain where it was with a King's Mark placed on the mast to indicate the vessel required special attention. Hollowell argued for confiscating it and moving the *Liberty* close to the British warship, the *Romney*. Hollowell prevailed and the ship was moved. They were stealing one of Hancock's prize assets from him, even though he had been far from the scene of the misadventure. And there would be no legal recourse for him. The British would later turn the *Liberty* into one of their own warships, adding fuel to the patriots' fire. The collective wisdom of the local British authorities approximated the intelligence of the wooden mast to which Harrison had suggested affixing the King's Mark.

Word quickly spread to the residents of Boston, and an angry mob was formed. A smuggler named Malcolm led the mass of men. They beat two customs officers senseless and carried their rampage to several other officials' homes, breaking windows and destroying other property. Some of the British officials scurried to seek refuge in the warship *Romney*. One Boston citizen shouted, "Look! The rats are running into the ship, not out of it!"

The confiscation of the *Liberty* catapulted John Hancock into a new place in the hearts of Bostonians: he was an aggrieved hero they could love and with whom they could make common cause. He did not give up ownership of his ship without a fight, however; he persuaded the Sons of Liberty to convene a meeting at Faneuil Hall to discuss what could be done.

On June 14, the Sons of Liberty and thousands more convened at Faneuil Hall, a stately red brick building with an eighty-pound bell and grasshopper wind vane, a place that had been built twenty-five years earlier and already endured a serious fire that had required major reconstruction. Destruction and reconstruction of rights were on the minds of the thousands of citizens who came together, so many that the meeting was moved to the Old South Church, which had a capacity of 6,000. It, too, was a strong and elegant red brick building that could host town meetings and serve as a church as well, one attended by Samuel Adams.

Otis was chosen to moderate the meeting. Ebenezer Mackintosh would serve as a kind of sergeant-at-arms.

Otis was happy to preside. He was still basking in the glow of his late night meeting with Beth, his mind racing back and forth between holding her hand as they sat at the end of the pier and anticipating the prospect of seeing her again. He had agreed to tutor her in the classics, and she would tell him what the citizens were thinking as she eavesdropped at the Green Dragon. Just as friends, of course.

The crowd in the pews was far from mellow. Otis was unsettled by the audience's size and mood as he stood on the stage. Before the swarm of hot Bostonians in front of him, he laid out the ground rules for speakers; each was allowed no more than three minutes. He reminded them of the meeting's purpose, namely how best to respond to the most recent British outrage. The focus of action would be Governor Bernard.

"Does everybody understand how we are going to proceed?" Otis asked. The mass grumbled in the affirmative.

"I will call on you as I see you, and I will call you by a number, such as Citizen One, who will be the first speaker. I will not countenance long speeches, and Mackintosh here will escort you out of the hall if you transgress; is that clear?" Otis asked loudly. It felt a bit awkward to try to seem so forceful, but once again the crowd grunted a collective yes.

Citizen One was a short man, a well-known barber who knew all of the town's secrets. When he was cutting hair, he was an admirable conversationalist, good at listening and clear in expressing his views. The mass listened with interest, in part to see how the views he was expressing now conformed to what he told them as they were getting shorn.

"We cannot permit these outrages to continue. I have always thought myself a loyal and proud British subject, but it is apparent we are being governed by lawless thieves. What will they steal next and from whom? The governor must stop this. Is Bernard with us or against us? And John Hancock deserves justice; they must return his ship."

At this, the mass roared its agreement.

Citizen Two, a tall thin stevedore, was less inhibited than Citizen One, and even this crowd was made uncomfortable by his words.

"We need to give a lesson to those little weasel customs officers to show them who's who. And we need to remind Hutchinson and Bernard what we can do. Who do they think they are, and what do they think we are? I say we have been too peaceful too long. They only understand one thing, and we should give it to them," he said. Those close to him could detect alcohol on the speaker's breath, and eventually, it was necessary for Mackintosh to escort him out of the hall. Citizen Two's comments elicited an embarrassed silence from the mass.

The forty-three other citizens who spoke echoed Citizen One's sentiments, and some put forward specific courses of action. While many complained about British impressment into the Royal Navy, most kept their comments focused on how to respond to the seizure of the *Liberty*.

As the parade of angry speakers petered out, Otis successfully preserved an atmosphere of calm and then summarized what had been said.

"I have a suggestion for what we do next. May I tell you what it is, and hear your thoughts?" Otis asked. Everyone agreed.

"I say we send a delegation to our dear governor," said Otis, "pleading with him to have Hancock's sloop returned, appealing to his higher sentiments and good sense. We need make no threats. Act toward him as if he were a wise and good leader."

These were surprising words from a man Bernard had thwarted almost since he had come to Massachusetts from New Jersey. Bernard had vetoed Otis' election as Speaker of the House and had maligned him to the powers in London at every possible turn. When Otis uttered the words "wise and good leader," jeers and catcalls followed. But when Mackintosh lifted his hand, the hall became as silent as a tomb. "Hear James out," the shoemaker said.

Otis made a few additional comments, including reminding the mass that they were all loyal British subjects so they needed to continue their quest for better relations with the British. Otis' words had the desired impact on those in the crowded pews. He then stated the obvious: he should not be one of the delegation members, and it was agreed that Hancock and Samuel Adams should also remain in Boston. Twenty-one men volunteered to pay Governor Bernard a visit at his country home in nearby Jamaica Plains.

* * *

Several days after the meeting at the Old South Church, eleven chaises set out to Governor Bernard's estate, a four-mile trip that took the horses little time to traverse, pulling light carriages with two passengers apiece. The pleasant summer weather continued, and the trip was made without a hitch. Some of the men came just to see how someone who was transplanted British gentry might live in the colonies; others came with a more serious sense of mission, and a few hoped for a confrontation. They all agreed they needed one spokesperson for the meeting and agreed on Citizen One, the barber who seemed to know all the men in Boston.

Bernard had agreed to the meeting, as well as the time, place, and size of the delegation. His estate was well-groomed, and the house dwarfed all but a few of the Beacon Hill mansions. The entry level and below were surrounded by artfully arranged field stone, and the top floors were painted wood, which had already attained a weathered gray color that hinted at its owner's personality. When Citizen One knocked on the front door, the response was quick. They were met by an aged Negro servant whose visage was eerily expressionless. When the man saw the delegation's size, he encouraged the visitors to circle around the house to the expansive backyard where chairs had already been placed in a perfect semi-circle, close to an ancient oak tree.

Bernard emerged from the house carrying a tray of glasses, followed by his servant. His visitors saw a man of average height, possessed of a diminutive nose and small mouth, which seemed incongruous for a man in such a powerful position. The governor walked with a peppy stride and gave the impression he was always trying to catch up with someone or something. All the men were served either clear well water, cider, or wine. The governor had the air of a happy host eager to be with his guests; he exuded the grace of a man who had entertained a great deal.

"Welcome, gentlemen, and thank you for making the trip here. I so appreciate you taking the time out of your lives to join me in this conversation," he said with studied charm and well-practiced sincerity. Bernard's accent seemed slightly off and reminded the men that he had not been born on their shores. Rumor said he had come to America because of financial hardship in Lincoln, England, where he had practiced law. His intention in crossing the Atlantic was believed to be more to extract from the people than to govern them. His avid cultivation of the wealthy Boston merchants seemed to give proof of that.

The circle of men sipped their beverages quietly, waiting for the "conversation," as Bernard put it, to proceed. After introductions had been made, Citizen One broke the ice.

"Governor we 'out of doors' Bostonians are not the powerful leaders of the city. You are 'within doors' and hold considerable sway over our lives. We are here to express our concern about the taking of John Hancock's sloop because it sets a terrible precedent. Some call it theft. And we are also here to let you know of our deep dismay that the imposition of taxes by Mr. Townshend has caused." Citizen One felt his words were too polite and did not reflect his fellow citizens' depth of anger, yet Otis' advice echoed in his mind. Then he was emboldened to add, "What recourse can we expect of you to set things right?"

Bernard first looked at Citizen One and then looked at the ground with a patient smile. He gave a dramatic pause before responding.

"Please forgive me, gentlemen," he said, scanning the circle of men, "but I have trouble understanding why the king and those privileged enough to be his local arms and legs should countenance the blatant smuggling of Mr. Hancock, or the confinement of one of our tide-waiters in the brig of his ship, or the wanton violence of the mob that followed. There need to be standards in this colony, and part of my job is to maintain proper order here. I hope you all understand."

"So," one of the men barked, "that means you can steal a merchant's ship and impose taxes on us without us having so much as a voice?" The statement generated a low growl of agreement from the assembled visitors.

"Good men can have honest differences about the duties and taxes that need to be levied to support the proper governance of our fine town," Bernard replied, "but none of us can condone lawlessness or violence. I hope you can understand that."

"We 'understand' perfectly well what you are doing to us," another man responded. "We hope you 'understand' that we cannot countenance tyranny, no matter how well dressed it may be." Those words hit with particular force given how the guests' simple wardrobes contrasted with the opulence of Bernard's attire.

Citizen One tried to regain his role as principal spokesperson, and to avert an impasse. "What can we expect, sir, in the way of bringing justice to Mr. Hancock and reducing the financial burdens your administration has placed on the peace-loving citizens of Boston?"

Bernard maintained his composure. "I very much appreciate your efforts to discuss this, and I am moved by your sincerity. You are clearly a cut above the rabble who only show their dissatisfaction with violence and destruction of property. And you are not like that madman Otis. You are thoughtful and good men, and I will seek to make your case to my superiors in London. You have my word on that."

His words provided some reassurance to many of the men. What they did not know was that even before this meeting, Governor Bernard had requested thousands of British troops to come to Boston as a show of force. He believed that armed and well-trained soldiers might reduce the colonists' desire to resist in any public way, and that it would restore the kind of order Bernard believed London wanted.

Bernard's guests would soon see how much they could trust his word.

⚞ 13 ⚟

Until the fall of 1768, the town of Boston had been a familiar place in the sense that families knew one another and the web of relationships created trust and goodwill among the people, notwithstanding the occasional protests. The sense of place was strong. The homes, shops, places of worship, docks, and dusty streets brought Bostonians together. A vibrant and hopeful spirit existed there. The quality of life exceeded that of London in many ways, a fact that gave Bostonians a certain self-satisfaction. It was said Boston had a higher rate of literacy than London. The town's air was much cleaner than London's, and there were far fewer poor or sick people. Bostonians knew who they were, knew their town, and sensed that they were building a great future.

That sense of reassuring place and known relationships was shattered that fall when thousands of British soldiers began to pour into Boston as a show of English power, in part due to Governor Bernard's messages to London. By the end of this unwelcome influx, the town's population had grown from 15,000 to 19,000. The dangerous folly of sending such a hostile delegation was described in different ways by two brilliant men of the time: Benjamin Franklin and John Adams.

Franklin said of soldiers who might come:

> They would not find a rebellion, they might make one.

Adams stated with obvious fervor:

> Every person who shall solicit or promote the importation of troops at this time is an enemy to the town and province, and a disturber of the peace and good order of both.

Both men spoke the truth, a truth that became manifest in countless ways. A sizable number of citizens wanted to undertake violent protest at the arrival of the troops, but Otis was one of several who convinced them not to, in part so that Boston could maintain the high ground in the eyes of the other colonies.

Instead of a public protest in the streets, a town meeting was called September 12 to discuss how to proceed.

The assembled citizens decided to ask Governor Bernard if British troops were truly coming and what his intentions were regarding convening the Assembly. What would he do to ensure appropriate measures to preserve Bostonians' rights and privileges? (Bernard's response would be characteristically misleading, implying that decisions regarding troops and convening the Assembly were out of his hands.)

A committee of the town council then reiterated the beliefs that their charter and several acts of Parliament since the Revolution of 1688 affirmed that they could not be taxed without their consent, and that:

> The raising or keeping a standing army, without consent in person, or by their own free election, would be an infringement of their natural, constitutional, and charter rights, and the employing of such army for the enforcing of laws made without the consent of the people in person, or by their representatives, would be a grievance.

The same assembly overwhelmingly passed an interesting resolution:

> Whereas by an act of Parliament, of the first King William and Queen Mary, it is declared, that the subjects, being Protestants, may have arms for their defense: it is the opinion of this town, that said declaration is founded in nature, reason, and sound policy, and is well adapted for the necessary defense of the community.

Affirming the colonists' right to bear arms was understandably alarming to the British authorities. For men like Bernard, it vindicated the secretly expressed feeling that there was a need for a show of force.

Since Governor Bernard refused to convene the General Court to address the looming discontent brought about by the advent of British soldiers, the town council decided to convene representatives from sixty-six other towns at Faneuil Hall to discuss what to do. The representatives from Boston would be Hancock; Samuel Adams; Thomas Cushing, the respected merchant, lawyer, and civic leader; and Otis. The representatives of the towns met September 22 and formulated a report that summarized their grievances and reiterated their opposition to the possible arrival of a standing army. This kind of gathering was also unsettling to the British.

The men of the Massachusetts colony who met that day at Faneuil Hall appeared to believe the British authorities would treat them with respect. The leaders of the sixty-six towns advised non-violence and peaceable conduct, partly at Otis' strong encouragement. They remained loyal British subjects, merely seeking their rights.

Otis earnestly believed there was a need to stay on the high ground with the British, a belief that would be sorely tested. The testing began with what Beth Frothingam was forced to endure at the Green Dragon.

* * *

A contingent of five English soldiers bullied their way into the tavern and forced two very old Bostonians to move so they could claim a prize table near the recently cleaned window on the north side. The loudest of the group, Jimmy Powell, a tall, powerfully built, black-haired man, called out to Beth, "Missy, over here right now!" She ignored him. "Here, now!" he bellowed again. The Green Dragon became silent. Beth finished delivering six mugs of ale on the other side of the room and walked slowly over to Powell's table. Every eye in the place was on her.

"You should learn to mind your manners, sir," she scolded.

Powell's face made a twisted cynical grin. "Oh, excuse me, your majesty," he said, smirking at the other soldiers. "Her majesty certainly has lovely little buttocks, splendid prats," he added. With those words, twenty men throughout the tavern rose to their feet, prepared to defend Beth's honor, but Beth turned to them and raised her hand. "Thank you, dear friends, but I can handle this," she assured them.

"What may I get for you?" she asked the soldiers. They answered and the barmaid departed to fetch the drinks. She returned with five large mugs, somehow managing to carry them all without a drop being spilled. She handed the other four men their beers with a pleasant smile. She then took Powell's mug and poured the contents over his head and upper body.

"Will there be anything else?" she asked sweetly.

Powell rose, a man both drenched and incensed. He towered above Beth, the veins in his head and neck bulging. As he stood up, a din of chairs moving across the Green Tavern's floor was heard, and thirty men came to their feet, moving toward the British soldiers' table from every direction, like lava from an angry volcano. Even Powell, in his rage, understood that lifting a hand against Beth would be extremely ill-advised. He glanced at the other four Redcoats as if to seek advice or support, but they looked back at him with the glazed, stupid expressions of cows grazing. Flummoxed and mute, Powell began to make his way to the front entrance, followed by his slinking comrades. The other patrons started to jeer as the five soldiers made their way out. Before they could complete their exit, Beth cried, "Pay up! You cannot leave without paying. We don't like thieves in Boston." With her words, a throng assembled in front of the Green Dragon's front door, ready, even eager, to enforce Beth's demand.

As Powell and the other four settled their account, he hissed, "You will regret this, more than you can imagine." The words elicited more jeers and sarcastic moans from the other customers. The soldiers walked out of the Green Dragon, heads down, almost comical in their deflated bravado. Yet all in attendance knew there would be repercussions. The British soldiers in Boston were not a happy lot, and when stripped of their pride, they could become dangerous.

The leader of this mass of British soldiers was Major General Thomas Gage, commander-in-chief of the British in all of North America. He and his wife enjoyed a vibrant social life in New York, but he had been forced to turn his attention to Boston. Among all the cities in the colonies, it was the hotbed of resistance.

Gage had expressed misgivings about bringing soldiers into an unwelcome community, but the powers in London had chosen this course. The tense and even violent events occurring now in Boston led to angry citizens and unhappy soldiers, so unhappy that an increasing number of Redcoats deserted. The British troops were mocked and even spit on by young rowdies who were trying to show their mettle to their cronies. Citizens of Boston could be detained by arrogant, bored British officers for simply walking down the street. The citizens showed their displeasure in varied and often imaginative ways. The result was that an increasing numbers of Redcoats tried to desert. Gage ordered future deserters to be killed, and his public whipping of his own soldiers on Boston Common disgusted Bostonians.

So, while General Gage was not pleased to hear of what had occurred at the Green Dragon, he seemed to turn his anger on his own men. He made no threats to the tavern owners, and he never even protested to the local authorities. For the time being, at least, the obstreperous citizens of Boston were not his immediate problem. But it was clear that with Gage's arrival, the heavy iron hand of British rule had also arrived.

* * *

Fifty miles south in Providence, Rhode Island, that very evening, another kind of encounter occurred at the Olney Tavern on Constitution Hill. Two husky, tanned whalers were drinking in a place that seemed more like a luxurious home than a public watering hole; it was cozy and very well-kept, with a staff that exuded a certain charming formality. That charm contrasted with the appearance of a scraggly vagabond who had taken a seat at the small table next to the whalers. He was emaciated and unshaven. His arms were like sticks, and the coal residue behind his ears suggested he was a chimney sweep. He arrived reeking of liquor and barked his order to the stately old waiter, Winston, who was as much of a fixture of the Olney as the chandelier that hung in the middle of the room.

Turning to the whalers, the unkempt visitor sought to strike up a conversation.

"Lovely place, this, don't you think?" he said.

They nodded in agreement.

"And I am told that the Liberty Tree out front is a good gathering place for the civic-minded." He sounded better spoken than his appearance would have suggested.

The whalers nodded again. They detected a Southern accent in the man. They wondered how such a scruffy person might be able to afford a tavern like the Olney.

"I know there is much discontent with our British brethren these days and concern about the rights of man, and all that. Fine to have a Liberty Tree, but I think you will agree there should be some limits on liberty. I hear tell of a crazed lawyer in Boston named Otis who actually believes that negers should be given equal rights. Very odd."

The whalers did not respond and tried to resume their conversation. They did not appreciate his use of the word "neger."

"I am going to hunt that Crispus Attucks down and earn some money if it's the last thing I do."

The two whalers had worked extensively with Crispus Attucks and felt intensely loyal to him. They decided they would need to influence this wastrel. Whenever he might decide to leave the tavern, they would accompany him outside, and if he stayed too long, they would simply escort him out for a brief conversation.

The unwelcome visitor did leave just after guzzling a mug of ale, and he commented to the two men he had tried to talk to, "Not very friendly, I would say." He was correct about that. They followed him out of the tavern and down a vacant side street, past a warehouse to an open field. The whalers then asked the man to stop, and he did, acting surprised.

"What can I do for you?" he asked.

"We need to talk to you about Crispus Attucks," the larger whaler said as he and his friend approached the man from his left and his right, drawing menacingly close. They each took hold of an arm and held the man by his wrist, stretching his arms, causing him to look like a human scarecrow. He felt the remarkable power of the whalers' hands as they continue to stretch him.

"We know many people up and down this coast. There are hundreds of us who know and respect Crispus." They tugged his arms even more forcefully.

"If we learn that you have played any role in an assault on Attucks, we will visit you again, and we will pull these puny arms out of their sockets. This is not a warning; this is a simple fact," the shorter whaler stated without a hint of emotion. "Do you understand?"

"I understand," the skinny, frightened man said, barely audibly.

The men parted ways. The larger said to the shorter whaler, "If he keeps on Crispus' trail, we should kill him. It would discourage other slimy squeeze crabs." His companion agreed.

⚡ 14 ⚡

The end of May 1769 was a radiant time in Boston; spring was in full bloom, and a splendid array of colors was back, including the dark mauve of lilacs and the darkening green of the grass on Boston Common. Even Boston Harbor seemed to sparkle more brilliantly than at any other time of the year. Azure skies and sunshine, and the lovely smells of the revived plants of spring lightened the hearts of the General Court's elected Representatives, whatever their specific political views may have been. Samuel Adams, James Otis, and many of their colleagues were eager to get back to work after Governor Bernard had shut down the legislature in 1768 because it refused to disavow Adams' Circular Letter of the preceding year.

Samuel Adams had written the Circular Letter in reaction to the Townshend Act of 1767, asserting that Parliament had no right to tax Americans since they were not represented in a legislative body. It was sent to legislative bodies throughout the colony and garnered much support. His informal assistant, William Molineux, made sure Bostonians of all ranks were aware of it as well.

As Adams and Otis approached the stately brick building to resume their duties, they were shocked to see a very unwelcome color encircling the hall of Massachusetts' government. Red. British soldiers, in their resplendent red coats and armed with the most modern rifles in the world, greeted the legislators like a red python threatening to squeeze and suffocate any attempts to express views that differed from those of Governor Bernard and Lieutenant Governor Hutchinson. The reverie of glorious Nature had given way to the gritty reality of bullying British power.

The impact of surprise only magnified the emotions. Otis was outraged and emphatic in the brief speech he gave at the very beginning of the legislative session. He said it was unworthy of any legislature to attempt to deliberate in the presence of such military force. He moved successfully to create a committee to lodge a formal protest to the governor. No business of any consequence was conducted. Several days later, the proceedings were moved to Harvard College's chapel.

The chapel hosted more than legislators. Harvard students lined the walls in little listening groups, eager to see and hear their leaders address the issues of the day. The novelty of the scene and the ideals those students had already come to prize were moving to the legislators. The students' presence made Otis feel like he was speaking to and for the Future and for the Ages, not simply to the colleagues with whom he did the often dull, but essential, work of law-making.

Otis railed against the indignity of the situation in Boston. With as much eloquence as he could summon, he told the students of their rights and duties and the need for them to pursue their principles; to fight to redress the wrongs that treacherous individuals had brought upon them; and to be prepared to be a light in the dark times that were to come. The country would one day need their support. The noblest of all duties was to serve their country and, if necessary, give their lives to do so. He cited the lessons of ancient Rome, leaving no room for interpreting which was the nobler side to support between the corrupt Empire and the noble Republic. The students listened with breathless attention, many eyes filled with tears, their emotions so aroused that they would have cheerfully gone into battle then and there. The sentiments Otis expressed may have led to a special kind of vandalism at Harvard: the portrait of Governor Bernard, which he had donated to the college, was later found with the heart carved out of it.

Otis' views had already created a deep fissure in his own family. Years later, family friend Hannah Fayerweather Winthrop would recount the story of his son, Jemmy, and his response to a comment made by a gentleman, telling the boy what a fine woman his mother was. Young Jemmy replied, "I know Mama is a fine lady, but she would be much finer if she was a Daughter of Liberty."

* * *

Several weeks later, in Mercy's home, the little team of resisters—Samuel Adams, Hancock, the Warrens, and Otis—came together again to take stock and strategize. They would also discuss the draft of a new statement Adams, William Cooper, and Otis had crafted named "An Appeal to the World, or a Vindication of the Town of Boston."

It was an overcast, humid July morning, and the only thing Mercy was offering was tepid tea. She felt compelled to start the meeting by summarizing the current troubles.

"In a short while, we will be listening to my brother and Mr. Adams discuss their eloquent indictment of Governor Bernard and General Gage and others, and that is fine. It will further inflame both sides, and as I see it, there is no harm in that. We are in the middle of a downward spiral of threats and moving inevitably toward a violent confrontation. Words matter, and the words in that document will embarrass the local British stooges and confirm Bostonians in their self-righteousness. Fine. It is fair and just that we 'vindicate' the town of Boston in the face of Bernard's exaggerations and lies. But make no mistake, it will bring us closer to bloodshed.

"The British government is currently led by men of poor judgment and represented on these shores by men of inferior moral and intellectual capacity. The political leaders of our dear colony continue to fight for their rights, and Samuel, you are organizing and guiding this resistance brilliantly. The back and forth of stupid British actions and inflamed reaction on our side is taking us down the road to war."

At this, Otis blanched. He needed to clarify his intentions. "Nobody wants war, Mercy. I do not condone violence. You know that; you know me better than anyone does, dear sister. We just want our rights. Rights for everyone. What is wrong with that?"

Mercy did not answer. Adams glanced down with an expression of gentle concern. He knew Otis' sister was a powerful force, the smartest of them all. Her literary gifts could be used to mock and deflate the local British minions and unify the town's citizens. She was a valuable asset for the cause. He knew Mercy was a realist and her words rang sadly prophetic.

The awkwardness was broken briefly when young James Warren, now age twelve, entered the room and, noticing the silent group, uttered a brief apology; he left quickly, bewildered by what was going on in his family's parlor.

As the men regained their composure, they were able to look at what was right in front of them. "An Appeal to the World or a Vindication of the Town of Boston" enumerated the many lies and misrepresentations perpetrated by Bernard in his letters describing affairs in Boston to the British rulers. The governor made it appear the wild town was filled with mayhem and incipient rebellion. The Bostonians knew of Bernard's lies because William Bollan, agent of his Majesty's Council, had purloined the letters and made them available to the colonists.

The small group discussed the statement at length and how to publicize it.

The tone of their discussion was set early when the "Appeal" disclosed the Bostonians' motivation in publishing Bernard's stolen letters:

> They have however endeavored to extract from these Writings [Bernard's] so far as the Town is concerned in them, to lay before the Public their true Spirit: From whence it will appear how restless Governor Bernard and his Associates have been in their malicious Intrigues to traduce not this Town and Province alone, but the whole British American Continent.

Toward the end of the "Appeal," they wanted to be clear that they still sought unity with Britain. They just needed to say what that would require:

> Their Rights are invaded by these Acts; therefore until they are all repeal'd the Cause of their just Complaints cannot be remove'd: *In short, the Grievances which lie heavily upon us, we shall never think redress'd till every Act pass'd by the British Parliament for the express Purpose of raising Revenue upon us without our Consent, is repealed; till the American Board of Commissioners of Customs is dissolve'd; the Troops recall'd and Things are restored to the State they were in before the late extraordinary Measures of Administration took Place.*

When Otis read the part dealing with the items that needed to become free of the onerous duties, Samuel Adams pointed to the teapot, with a small smile. Lord Hillsborough seemed to want to keep taxing tea.

The small gathering agreed that the contents of the "Appeal" were sound and fair, and that it should be made public to the citizens of Boston and to the world. The conversation had been tiring for all of them, so they adjourned in a subdued mood.

The "Appeal" would be officially endorsed by the Boston Town Council and published in the *Gazette* that fall by Edes and Gill. The document was sent to various men in London, including Members of Parliament, the London Town Council, and one American, Benjamin Franklin, among others. The Americans did not fully anticipate the effect it would have.

* * *

Over the course of the year, the campaign of slander and innuendo against Otis had intensified. The venom being spewed came most intensely from Hutchinson and the Customs officials, notably Messrs. Hutton, Paxton, Burch, and Robinson. That September, Otis had reached the breaking point and ran an advertisement in the *Boston Gazette* that reaffirmed his loyalty to the Crown and urged "Lord Hillsborough, The Board of Trade, and all others whom it may concern...to pay no kind of regard to any of the abusive representations of me...." Otis named the four men and said they were no more worthy of credit than was Governor Bernard. The advertisement stated that Otis had demanded "satisfaction" from the perpetrators, but he had not received a response from them.

The next day, in an effort to receive that satisfaction, Otis went to a coffee house frequented by his adversaries. He was savagely attacked by a gang of red-coated brutes. Later, the *London Chronicle* described what occurred:

> Early on Tuesday evening last a difference arose at the British coffee house in this town between James Otis Esq. and John Robinson Esq. the latter demanding satisfaction for certain expressions in a publication signed by Mr. Otis in the *Boston Gazette* of Monday last. After a proposal on the part of Mr. Otis to decide the controversy by themselves in a separate room, which was consented to by Mr. Robinson, very unexpectedly to Mr. Otis, and while he was rising, Mr. Robinson, in the presence of the public company in the coffee-room, attempted to pull him by the nose, and failing in the attempt, he immediately struck at him with his cane, against which Mr. Otis defended himself, and returned the compliment. A close engagement then ensued, and Mr. Otis, having disarmed his antagonist, several persons in the room fell upon Mr. Otis, some of whom held him while

others struck with cutlasses, canes, and other weapons, and the general cry was "Kill him, kill him!"

A young gentleman, Mr. John Gridley, passing by the room, and feeling Mr. Otis treated in so ungentleman-like and barbarous Manner, and without a friend near him, pressed in, and endeavoring to interpose, was also attacked in the manner Mr. Otis was, by as many as could come near him, and after resolute and manly defense of himself, was at length overpowered, as Mr. Otis had been, by numbers. By this time several others had got into the room, whereupon Mr. Robinson and those who were with him, retired through the back door. Mr. Otis and Mr. Gridley were carried off much wounded, and it is thought that, had not the people come to their assistance, the consequences of this ungenerous assault would have been fatal. The company in the room when Mr. Otis was first attacked consisted chiefly of the officers of the army and the revenue, and it is allowed that both Mr. Otis and Mr. Gridley acquitted themselves with a spirit and resolution becoming Gentlemen of honor.

A witness to the attack, a new customs officer, shouted to the crowd that he would run to the Otis house to let Mrs. Otis know. However, he had no intention to tell the victim's wife and never did. It was the kind of twisted perfidy that the Americans had come to expect from the British minions.

Otis was carried through the streets of Boston, his head throbbing in a sea of pain and struggling to focus as he was taken to the office of Dr. James Lloyd and Dr. Nathaniel Perkins. They were among the most skilled and trusted medical men in the town and served Whigs and Tories alike. Perkins, learned in surgery and pharmacology, attended to Otis with care and compassion. He was a short, thickset man with a pale face that exuded a cheerful and alert air. He could provide the best-known remedies for the array of maladies that afflicted Boston's citizens.

The doctor was skilled at not betraying his feelings of shock, even disgust at the sight of whomever he was about to serve, but the sight of Otis' bleeding head and the sound of his groans alarmed even him. As Otis was gently placed on a nearby cot, he vomited over its side. Perkins' nurse, the efficient Hilda Gutnecht, had left to attend to a matter at home, causing the usually calm doctor to become upset. He barked at the men who had brought Otis to him. He commanded them to take the clean swabs lying on the corner shelf and press the wound gently to stem the trickle of blood streaking down Otis' face.

"What happened?" Perkins asked.

"Otis was attacked by customs commissioners and soldiers at the coffee house," one of the men replied.

"My God, were they trying to kill the poor soul?"

"It would appear" was the response.

"He cannot be moved. He must remain here. Who can tend to him? Does Mrs. Otis know about this?" Perkins asked.

"Yes, she was informed immediately," replied the deceived helper.

The doctor further ministered to Otis, dabbing the awful wound with oils and ointments. The men who had carried Otis to Perkins' office then left, excusing themselves awkwardly and in a distressed state of mind.

Dr. Perkins waited for Ruth Otis and planned what he would tell her: the diagnosis, the prognosis, and the kind of care she might render her husband in his convalescence. He waited. And waited. And waited. Late in the afternoon, his assisting nurse returned, by now fully aware that the famous Otis lay in a serious state in the very office where she worked. Everyone in Boston knew.

"Isn't Mrs. Otis coming?" she asked.

"I am sure she would come if she were told. I will go myself to make sure she knows where he is and to see if she herself is not too distraught at the news to come. Please tend to him, Hilda. I won't be long," Perkins said, with an uncharacteristic tone of urgency.

Perkins reached the Otises' doorstep and greeted Ruth with the serious news, then asked why she had not come to his office.

"Oh, my goodness," she said, turning ashen. "I was never told of this. Will he be all right?"

"It is impossible to know, but you should come to him right now!"

Ruth grabbed her wrap and hurried to Perkins' office, challenged to keep up with the young doctor's pace.

When Ruth and Perkins entered his office, they saw Beth Frothingham in the outer chamber. Nurse Hilda had not allowed her to enter the inner office because she was not an Otis family member.

Perkins understood the situation at once and introduced Ruth to Beth, not sure what would happen next.

"We have met," Ruth said matter-of-factly. Ruth knew all about Beth from various sources, and she had been with her socially on a few occasions. While she felt a tinge of jealousy, the feelings were not deep because her estrangement from her husband was so profound. Ruth felt a kind of relief that Otis had someone who cared for him.

With Perkins' permission, Hilda opened the door and the two women ran to the cot Otis lay on. His breathing was regular, the swabs on his head a dark crimson. Beth required the utmost restraint not to embrace her dear friend. Ruth found it less difficult to restrain herself, but she asked Dr. Perkins if she could touch her husband.

"Yes, of course," he said.

Ruth approached the cot slowly, cautiously and took Otis' cool, limp hand. He did not respond, and she remained but a few minutes by her husband. To Perkins, it seemed Ruth's face became haggard right in front of him. Even her posture changed. She seemed to emanate a blend of distress, compassion, and embarrassment.

"I am sorry, but I must return to my children," she told Perkins. "Please do all you can, Doctor; then bring him back. God bless you." Ruth then hurried out the door.

Beth approached Otis and pulled a stool next to him. She began talking to him softly, knowing he could not hear her, but at the sound of her voice, Otis opened his eyes, his face unable to resist yielding to a tiny smile.

He then lost consciousness again. His breathing became deeper and steadier.

"What is the prognosis, Doctor?" Beth asked.

Perkins said Otis would live through the beating and remain functional.

"Will he return to his normal self?" she asked hopefully.

"I cannot guarantee that, my dear."

Beth pulled a chair next to Otis, shaken to her core. She resolved that he would not endure his recovery alone.

Word spread quickly of the vicious attack. The citizens of Boston supported Otis, briefly renewing his luster as a hero. Bostonians were inflamed by the British bullies. The downward spiral, to which Mercy Otis Warren had referred, continued. Yet even as a victim, Otis remained generous. When the brutal attack came to trial, Otis was awarded a judgment of two thousand pounds sterling, a very considerable sum, to be paid by Robinson. It would have been enough to purchase roughly 300 horses or 400 cows. When Robinson apologized, Otis forgave him, dropped the case, and refused the money. He couldn't help but remember when Robinson "forgave" him for arguing against the Writs of Assistance at the Christmas party.

❦ 15 ❦

October had been an unusually warm month in Boston, and this evening, the air seemed particularly heavy. The Green Dragon was crowded, and the sweat flowed as freely as the ale. Beth Frothingham moved with grace but without her normal zest, and her customers were surprised that she did not banter with them as usual. She moved like a troubled woman, so one patron asked her what was wrong. She found it impossible to be anything but candid. She spoke with barbed bitterness about the attack on Otis. Like him, she was no longer herself.

Beth did not care that nearly everyone in the tavern heard her words, including three of the soldiers who had been with the reprehensible Powell the previous autumn. It had been a year since she had drenched the British officer with beer, but it remained fresh in her mind. The bravado she had shown then was much appreciated by her many friends, but now the sword of Damocles hung over her head. When would it fall? She did not betray her anxiety, and even at her most subdued, she remained a strong and caring friend to scores of her fellow citizens. She spat out epithets about the British, however, and seemed to relish being heard by the Redcoats.

Three soldiers did not take kindly to how Beth had described them and their British compatriots. They had arrived early in the evening and been drinking heavily all night. As the large volume of ale took its effect, their thoughts and conversations became base. The soldiers were sliming their way from apparently honorable gentlemen to vile predators.

"I would like to enter Eve's custom house. I'll wager it is warm and moist there. She jiggles her pratts in ways that harden my sugar stick," said the smallest of the predators.

"You think you can handle her?" the pock-marked predator asked, smirking.

"She might not be a willing prize for any one of us, but she could be a prize for all three of us," the third predator stated. "She will give us satisfaction, if you catch my meaning."

The soldiers' conversation turned from bilious banter to a vile plan. They would show that little wagtail that it was not wise to insult the king's soldiers. They would demand satisfaction in a way that would satisfy them, and put her in her rightful place.

At midnight, after Beth helped clean the tables and sweep the floor, she was ready to make her way home. She left the tavern glowing with the perspiration of an honest evening's work. Tired as she was, she needed to walk to the harbor and relax, reflect, and pray for Otis, who was never far from her thoughts. The solitude and rest that gazing out at the water late at night provided always revived her spirits.

The three predators followed Beth down the largely empty streets. Their focus on their prey overcame their woozy lack of balance. Their hearts beat fast. She was more appetizing in part because she seemed to have lost her spunk, her spirit. Men (if they can be called that) in this state of mind prefer their victims weak, so Beth was perfect for what they wanted to do.

They did not speak as they followed her. She trudged toward the water and then slipped down an empty side street next to a large warehouse. The only sounds were lapping waves on the pier. The moment had arrived for the predators to strike. They ran toward her in a frenzy and grabbed her, the largest of them flinging her to the ground as the other two ripped off their pants and her undergarments with speed and ease. Beth was pinned, on her back, pebbles gouging her sharply and dust entering her mouth and nostrils. She had been catapulted into a dazed state and forced into a grotesque reality that confused her. Was this a nightmare? The men made snorting sounds, and two of them held her arms painfully tight as she squirmed for freedom.

A voice boomed through the night. "Stop this now!" It spoke with the power and authority of God himself. Beth could not fully make out to whom the rescuing voice belonged, but she felt the release of her arms and the disappearance of the man's bodyweight on hers. She heard the sound of fist against flesh, and she felt blood spill on her cheeks, and then there was silence.

Beth looked up to see the face of Crispus Attucks. She observed the slumped bodies of the three soldiers she had been serving ale to all night; only two of them showed evidence of breathing in their unconscious state. The arms of two of them were strangely askew, and the third, the one without signs of breath, was curled into a fetal position. None moved.

"Thank you, Crispus." Still dazed, she could think of nothing else to add. She then reached out to Attucks and sobbed in his arms. He could feel her heaving stomach against his own. He held her tenderly and stroked her hair as a mother might stroke that of an injured child. They stood that way in the Boston night for five minutes, and then he escorted her to her doorstep at Manufactory House and departed. Beth entered her small apartment, hands trembling, barely able to unbutton her blouse. She could not sink into any kind of deep sleep. She kept asking herself, even mumbling the words, "Who are these people?"

* * *

When word got out of the attack on the three British soldiers, their commanders generated a story for John Fleming at the Loyalist-friendly *Boston Chronicle* to run. It described a group of low-life citizens, including several Negros, who jumped the soldiers, first surrounding and then thrashing them.

Several days later, the *Chronicle* ran the story with all the details provided by the "victims." The Loyalist readers were reconfirmed in their impression of those who resisted the British. Such people were wild thugs who would stop at nothing to intimidate and disrespect the men in service of the king. Thank God and thank King George that thousands of British soldiers had come to their town to keep loyal subjects like them safe from the excesses of such hooligans.

When Samuel Adams read the account in the *Chronicle*, he was outraged. He read and heard about everything going on in Boston. He had learned from various sources what really occurred, and the incident was one of many that were never reported accurately. The British soldiers' brutality and arrogance were rampant, yet too often, the written stories that circulated in the town did not reflect that. Adams felt only partial solace in learning what Crispus Attucks had done to the perpetrators. He rarely let himself feel this level of anger. What frustrated him about the attack on Beth was that she did not want to make the facts known. Adams' wife Elizabeth had to explain to him why. No woman is eager to disclose a sexual assault; it infects the victim with a distinctive kind of humiliation. Beth was not alone in enduring this kind of traumatic event, but like her, scores of women wanted to remain silent. So the bogus story being circulated by General Gage and the rest of the British brass would go unrebutted. And Elizabeth Adams made her husband promise not to set the record straight in either public or private conversations. Respect for Beth's dignity demanded that. Adams complied.

* * *

Otis, still in a state of convalescence from the vicious attack, was as frustrated as Adams. He had learned who had assaulted Beth, but he could do nothing about it. Any public legal action would embarrass her; she just wanted to put the experience behind her and move on. However, the men in Beth's life wanted justice; one of those men who felt the outrage and knew who the attackers were was Ebenezer Mackintosh. He had no sense of inhibition to prevent him from providing a private, personal form of justice. Nor did Mackintosh need to tell anyone of his intentions. He told Adams what he was going to do, and Adams tried to dissuade him, as Mackintosh had expected he would. Yet Mackintosh had no fear of reprisal, and for good reason. The shoemaker possessed a unique asset that no other Bostonian had: thousands of loyal followers who would happily retaliate if British authorities harmed their friend and leader. Mackintosh took advantage of that asset over the next two months, causing the predators to regret even more deeply what they had done to Beth.

Otis felt like a broken man. The only enduring sustenance for his spirit might have been the love of his children, of Beth, and possibly of Crispus. His children were still too young for serious, healing conversation; Beth was fragile and still shaken; and that left Crispus, the only one who could be a source of strength, if only there were a way of contacting him.

And if he were contacted, where could they meet? The Otis home, with all of its familiar trappings but with the icy estrangement from Ruth, was no longer an inviting place to meet. Indeed, Otis' home had become a marital morgue. Even the scampering and often loud children could not bring to it the kind of life that he yearned for. And there was divided loyalty among his children to the cause he was fighting for: his older daughter Elizabeth aligned with her mother, and young James and Mary were on their father's side. The political wedge in the family could not be overcome.

Otis felt he needed to meet and talk with Attucks in a safe place, and he needed a way to reach him for an invitation. The answer to both questions had one word: Mackintosh. When Sam Adams made his weekly visit to check on Otis, Adams would be asked to connect with Mackintosh, who, in turn, would contact Attucks. It was a simple plan, and it would work. But it had to wait until Pope's Day was over since planning and carrying out that day, for Mackintosh, was more than a full-time job.

* * *

When Mackintosh, Attucks, and Otis met on a brisk November evening, minor snow flurries were a harbinger of the winter to come. Mackintosh's simple space was cozy with a fire crackling in his spacious fireplace and the smell of a fresh baked apple pie still in the air. The shoemaker had also made flip cocktails for the three of them, adding to the room's pleasing aroma. Attucks and Mackintosh were not certain why they were meeting. Otis needed their strength, but he was not sure how to express that.

They exchanged banter and gossip at the beginning. Mackintosh groaned with feigned exhaustion at trying to control the South End paraders during the recent Pope's Day mayhem. The two men knew they were there for Otis, who had been quiet, so Attucks broke the ice.

"Well, you look pretty good for a battered old man," Attucks said with a smile. "What is on your mind, my friend?"

Otis felt uniquely and totally safe with these two men, sitting in a semicircle facing the fireplace. He was free to say and hear anything, and the two men treated him with respect, not pity.

"I need to feel your strength and to feel hope again," he said. "I am sad and anxious about my addled brain, about my family, about how I can even carry on. You both know I love Beth, and to see her demeaned breaks my heart. Yet I cannot, or will not, enter the world of vengeance. I still believe in our Cause, but I do not know how best to help it. I feel dread at the prospect of the coming bloodshed my sister Mercy predicts. I am growing hopeless. And I get no succor at home, much as I love my children. I know this is a jumble. My apologies. Both of you are strong and know who you are. I am beginning to feel like a stranger to myself. I feel so empty, so at sea." His voice was low and mournful. Pointing to the fireplace, he added, "I'm like that fading ember there that is turning from hot red to gray ash."

The two younger men looked with fondness at him. They glanced at one another. Attucks believed it fell to him to reaffirm what was important, to try to remind Otis of who he truly was.

"James," Attucks said, "you have endured far more than any man should be forced to endure. The coffee house attack was beyond the pale, and yet you remain a man of goodwill. Your family life is enough to sap any man of his faith in other human beings. Your reaction to the daily slanders perpetrated on you could well have turned you to a bitter, shriveled soul, but instead, you remain a man of generous spirit. You are a rock."

"And a true Christian," Mackintosh added. "You have suffered and yet the bitter venom of vengeance has not infected you. Our Savior must be proud." Mackintosh's words sparked in Otis a recollection of his faith, which he too often forgot.

"You both are kind," Otis replied.

"Time will be the judge," Attucks continued, "but I believe you have caused this town to enter into history. My people have lived here thousands of years, and we see the Europeans as invaders, but if the land is to be conquered by outsiders, better that it be governed from within than from a distance. Your Writs of Assistance case set a standard and sent a message, and it may one day be seen as a turning point in history. Today, the people of Boston and those in other colonies salute you; some day, those on other continents may look here to emulate what you have led. Your pronouncements on the equality of all men give heart to people who look like me and raise an expectation of what this emerging new reality can mean."

Mackintosh served them each a large piece of pie and refilled their mugs with flip. Quiet took over the room.

"What you say may or may not be true, Crispus," Otis said, "but I am still here and feel like an old Devon cow about to go out to pasture."

"Enough self-pity, my friend," Attucks replied. "Use your spirit to bless a new day. Encourage the coming of a new order and inspire the skill and boldness of those who can build on your work. Adams and Hancock need your inspiration. You are the sparkle of a glorious wave approaching the shore of freedom. Take satisfaction in that, not self-pity. Be the grand man you truly are!"

"Amen!" said Mackintosh.

Another long pause followed. Otis felt somber but less glum, and both of his admirers smiled softly; affectionate, confident, and pleased to console him.

Otis broke the silence. Turning toward Attucks, he asked with a heavy voice, "If a new nation emerges from all of this, my friend, what do you see for its future? What prospects are there for this glorious freedom you speak of? A freedom built on justice and equality?"

Attucks did not hesitate. "Those in this land could be a light for the world. Men and women here could establish a way of governing that would allow wisdom and righteousness to flourish and curb the worst proclivities in human nature. A new nation would have enormous potential for good, but realizing that potential is far from certain. Think of what it means to create a new nation, what the values and vision and courage of leaders could provide. How many times in the history of civilization has such an opportunity arisen? The full bloom of human potential cannot come to flower as a colony, James. There must be independence. With that independence, there needs to be wisdom, compassion, and leaders with the courage to stand for peace. Men have not often shown the courage to stand for peace, much to the impotent distress of women, but that is possible here. But before there is peace, there will need to be freedom and justice.

"It is possible that a new nation will respect the people and traditions of my mother's ancestors who have occupied these lands for scores of centuries. A new nation, rightly organized and led, could halt the vile slave trafficking that has crushed hundreds of thousands of human beings, and destroyed families. Such a nation could treat all men and women as genuine equals. Peace and freedom could reign supreme here. That is all possible."

Mackintosh rose in a state of excitement and rummaged through the papers on his desk.

"You are reminding me of the Prince of Peace, referred to in Dr. Jonathan Mayhew's sermon of May 23, 1766. Let me read some of it."

Otis smiled to himself as the shoemaker eagerly quoted his old friend, the "radical" Congregational minister, a man like himself, who was willing to stir the pot of resistance:

> And having learnt from the holy scriptures, that wise brave, and virtuous men were always friends of liberty...that the

son of God came down from heaven to make us "free indeed," and that "where the spirit of the Lord is, there is
liberty...."

There was silent appreciation of those words.

Then Otis turned to Attucks and asked, "What stands in the
way of your vision of a new nation arising?"

"Men who prize power and possessions more than they prize
justice and the teachings of your Savior," Attucks replied. "That
said, there are and will be good men and women, and there is
hope."

"How long will it take to form the kind of nation you said was
possible?" Otis asked.

"Ten generations," Attucks replied. "Maybe less, if there are
enough men and women of vision and courage."

The people of Attucks' heritage were possessed of a far grander
sense of the sweep of time than the newcomers from Europe. The
Wampanoag had occupied the land for twelve-thousand years.
And Attucks' Indigenous ancestors understood human weakness
and strength at least as well as the new arrivals, probably better.

With these words of Attucks, both Otis and Mackintosh's faces
sagged and their eyes lost their sparkle. Both men put great stock
in Attucks' thoughts. He seemed to see and understand the future
better than any man they knew.

≈ **16** ≈

Chilly as the Boston weather may have still been in March of 1770, a cauldron was boiling below the town's visible surface. The heat came from a creature that had taken over the streets, the taverns, the docks, and even the churches. Its appetite was enormous and only grew more ravenous as it fed. The creature was created by the poisonous commingling of men in red coats and men in simple trousers and flat-rimmed hats. They could not resist one another; the attraction was too powerful. The creature grew more aroused with every encounter, even with minor slights and offenses, and turned them into meals of righteous violence. The mayhem the creature spawned took many forms: words, facial expressions, crude jokes, as well as muggings, spontaneous fisticuffs, gang beatings, and even rape. Occasionally, it killed, causing it to grow even more hungry and thirsty.

One killing added a massive amount of fuel to the flame of resistance, taking it to an entirely new level. On a cold February night, an angry mob was boisterously harassing customs official Ebenezer Richardson on his way home. As the crowd began to throw stones and sticks at him, Richardson scurried into his house. The house was pelted with rocks, shattering windows. Richardson ran upstairs, grabbed his musket, and fired it through a window, injuring one young person and killing eleven-year-old Christopher Seider with eleven pellets of birdshot to his small torso.

Christopher Seider's funeral was said to be the largest ever seen in America. Samuel Adams helped ensure the maximum of political theater, including covering Christopher's casket with appropriate biblical quotations. Five hundred schoolboys marched in the front of the solemn procession, and thousands followed. None of the participants would forget it. The *Gazette* and Adams would continue to inflame the citizenry and elevate the dead boy to hero status. The tragic killing hung over Boston like a black cloud. Days later, another confrontation further escalated the anger, ill will, and desire to strike out.

At the center of the episode was Samuel Gray, a rope maker and notorious street agitator. He was among the hardest brawlers in

113

Boston. He asked a soldier from the 29th Regiment if he wanted a job. When the soldier said he did, Gray told him he had a privy that needed cleaning. The soldier attacked Gray, and quickly, the battle was joined between the British soldiers and the men who repaired ropes and did other odd jobs. It did not go well for the British.

Adams, Molineux, and others of the Loyal Nine were ready to flame the fire of discontent. Shortly after the Samuel Gray encounter, Adams and his followers appeared to have plastered the streets with forged notices, signed by many of the garrisoned soldiers, stating that the troops intended to attack the townspeople. The idea that soldiers would do this, or that their leaders would permit it, defied belief, but at least one group of people did believe it: a group of small children. On the evening of March 5, a crowd of small boys began throwing snowballs at the British sentry in King Street. Firing small objects at Redcoats was not an unusual occurrence, but this evening was different. The posted threats caused the locals to believe they were in danger. Such a prospect did not cause them to shrink or retreat. Quite the contrary. A crowd formed. Church bells started to ring, alerting all who could hear them that something was amiss.

Crispus Attucks had been dining at a modest victualing house with his whaling friends, all drinking freely of the recently smuggled rum and telling stories and jokes in high humor. The air was thick with smoke and the volume of speech grew louder with every round of drinks. Attucks looked even more imposing than usual; his six-foot frame and muscular body seemed to expand with rum and good company. The two whalers from Rhode Island were in the raucous group and reminded Attucks that some people believed there was still a bounty on him. He laughed contemptuously.

"I am not hiding," he said with a smirk. " Let someone capture me. Would you let that happen, my brothers?"

The assembled men shouted, "No!" seemingly in unison. (Who could tell anymore?)

"Who do you like better," one of the whalers asked, "the Redcoats or the slaveowners?"

Attucks enjoyed the ridiculous question. He had grown up in Framingham on a farm with his father and mother, and the owner had treated his father with respect. His father, the prince from

Africa, was smart, loyal and treated more like an employee than a slave. Others may have viewed him as a slave; the prince never did. Attucks had been sold to Deacon Brown, but he had left the farm in 1750 and chosen not to return. Or to live in fear.

"That is an easy question, my friend," Attucks replied. "I hate the bloody British and particularly those who parade around in red blouses. They are arrogant wagtails." He enjoyed impugning the strutting soldiers' masculinity.

One of those odd and unexpected lulls in conversation took over the cramped room. Suddenly, everyone heard Boston's many church bells start to ring. Something exciting was happening on that frigid March night. Attucks and his friends bolted out of the victualing house, dropping far more currency on the table than they owed.

As word spread throughout the town, the square in front of the Custom House quickly filled up with a turbulent mass of children and angry men who carried clubs, staves, and even pieces of jagged ice. The hot breath of angry men clouded the cold air. John Adams later described it: "the multitude was shouting and huzzahing, and threatening life, the bells ringing, the mob whistling, screaming and rending like an Indian yell, the people from all quarters throwing every species of rubbish they could pick up in the streets." Among those in the taunting crowd, standing in front, were Samuel Gray, the brawling rope-maker; James Caldwell, a ship's mate, and Patrick Carr, an Irishman accustomed to rioting. Crispus Attucks ran to the front row to join them, and like the others, he carried a stave, gesturing threateningly, but he did not attack the armed Redcoats.

Despite the various objects being tossed at the soldiers, they held their fire, using their bayonets to keep the crowd at bay in front of the Custom House. Then a large fragment of brick hit Private Hugh Montgomery and sent him to the ground, leading him to shout, "Fire!" as he took his rifle and fired at the crowd.

Immediately, two bullets hit Crispus Attucks' breast. Attucks was a big target, an easy hit. He crumbled to the ground, looking at his killers with unblinking eyes as he fell. As he lay there, he never shifted his gaze. Crispus Attucks left this mortal world still fearless and defiant. He was joined in death by Gray, Caldwell, and later by Carr. A young bystander, an apprentice named

Samuel Maverick who had not participated in the riot, was the final victim.

The crowd became quiet and dispersed, small groups of men huddling in an odd blend of excitement, fear, and anger. Plans and schemes of revenge flooded out from many mouths, none of which would come to pass. The event was too big to understand and digest.

James Otis was in his home when he learned of the evening's events from John Hancock. The high-spirited Macaroni was embraced and welcomed warmly into the house by Ruth, who was puzzled by Hancock's expression.

"What is wrong, John?" she asked.

"The British have killed four men and a fifth is in grave danger."

By now, Otis was roused from his study and joined the two.

"Who was shot?" he asked urgently.

"Some men you would not know, James," replied Hancock, "and one you know well."

"Who is the one I know?"

"Crispus Attucks. Attucks is dead. Shot in cold blood, or better stated, hot blood."

Otis' brow furrowed as if he were confronted with a complex problem or an impenetrable puzzle.

"What?"

"Attucks is dead," Hancock repeated.

Ruth quickly left the room and went upstairs with no further word. Otis reached out to his friend to avoid falling to the floor, and Hancock held him firmly without speaking. Otis' breath turned into quiet, rhythmic sobs.

"Let's sit down and have something to drink, possibly your best brandy," Hancock suggested, to which Otis quickly agreed.

"Tell me what happened exactly," Otis asked quietly.

Hancock recounted what had occurred, the sequence of spiraling actions that led to the tragedy. Otis' wandering gaze said he was someplace else, yet intermittently struggling to understand what he was being told.

They talked and drank late into the night. As the brandy, flowed Otis opened up to Hancock, recounting the details of a November meeting in Mackintosh's house with Crispus. Hancock was particularly intrigued by what Attucks had said about the ideals they were fighting for, and how the future might look if those ideals were upheld. Hancock was generally familiar with the governance of the Iroquois Confederacy and saw its potential utility if a new government were to be formed, free of British rule. Attucks' vision seemed to resonate deeply with Hancock, but he shared Otis' skepticism of any government being able or willing to plan for future generations. He was disheartened by Attucks' estimate of when the new day of justice and equality would arrive. Three hundred years seemed like an eternity, unfathomable. What struck Hancock most was how deeply Otis believed in Attucks. That Otis seemed to regard the Negro as a serious muse seemed incongruous but intriguing to Hancock.

Finally, when Hancock was in mid-sentence, he noticed Otis slumped in his chair, his fingers holding the stem of the crystal glass, his mouth open, breathing in a slow, barely audible snore. Hancock gently removed the glass from Otis' limp grasp and quietly let himself out.

* * *

Samuel Adams pounced on the bloody tragedy like a hungry lion about to feast. He called a town meeting the next day and gave a rousing speech that added frenzy to the cause and the demand that the British remove all troops from Boston. Those citizens in attendance roared unanimous agreement. Adams and Hancock then led the furious march of Bostonians to the Town House, which overlooked the scene of the bloody incident. They stormed into the same Council Chamber where James Otis had argued the Writs of Assistance case, and the same man sat at the head of the Council Table: Thomas Hutchinson. At Hutchinson's right was Colonel Dalrymple, commander-in-chief of His Majesty's forces in Boston, and twenty-eight councilors wearing "large white wigs, English scarlet cloth cloaks," as John Adams later described them.

The lion and the weasel confronted one another. Samuel Adams, the lion, demanded the removal of all troops from Boston. Hutchinson, the weasel, said he did not have the power to do that. Then the weasel consulted Colonel Dalrymple and proposed one regiment be removed. The lion did not budge. He reminded those present of the anger dwelling in the hearts of fifteen-thousand Bostonians, and the desire some of them felt for immediate and commensurate revenge. The weasel's legs trembled and his face

117

grew pale. Hutchinson eventually promised that both regiments would leave the city, retreating to Castle William. But the work of the lion was far from complete.

Adams needed now to become the lion-tamer; the citizens of Boston and the entire colony had begun to seethe, many wanting revenge. Countrymen as well as city dwellers were beside themselves. However, if violent mayhem were allowed to occur, respect for Boston would evaporate in London, and the likelihood that the king and his ministers would give the Patriots the rights they sought would evaporate as well. The situation confronted Adams with a political balancing act that required he be the grandmaster that he was. He urgently needed a strategy session with Mercy and James Warren, Dr. Joseph Warren, and Hancock to determine how this game needed to be played. James Otis could not be included; he was no longer a rational voice.

Dr. Joseph Warren—no relation to James Warren—was an invaluable replacement for the fading Otis. His slate eyes betrayed his warm and friendly temperament, and the expression on his clean-shaven face seemed to suggest quiet, brilliant amusement. He served Patriots (Whigs) and Loyalists (Tories) alike, and still early in his career, he was esteemed by all.

They met two days after the tragic shooting on a gray and dismal afternoon at James and Mercy Warren's home in Plymouth. A fire burned in their ample fireplace and freshly brewed tea steamed from the small table in the middle of the parlor. Scones just out of the oven were passed to the guests. Adams was eager to summarize the challenges and opportunities they had been given by the tragedy. As he was about to speak, Mercy broke in. She felt deep sadness.

"Samuel," Mercy said, "five people were killed the day before yesterday. Families are grieving, mothers are heartbroken. The downward spiral continues. More hearts will be broken. So before we discuss strategy, can we pray?"

Adams looked down at the floor, appearing to feel guilty. All his attention had been focused on the strategic response to the tragedy, how best to take advantage of what had happened.

"Of course, Mercy. Do you want to lead us?" he asked sheepishly.

A moment of solemn quiet followed, and then Mercy prayed.

"Dear God, please bring comfort and strength to the grieving mothers and fathers of the fallen men and the boy. Embrace them in this, the worst moment of their lives. Bring your loving mercy on all of those who were involved, and forgive the British soldiers who killed our fellow citizens. Let there be justice, but please, let there not be vengeance and more bloodshed. Thank you, Father, for all your blessings, and let the spirit of your Son guide all of our future actions. Amen."

Hancock was moved by the prayer and kept his head lowered after the final words. Adams seemed affected, but he quickly began to create a plan of action. He did not want more violence, but he saw the arc of events moving away from what Mercy said she yearned for. The focus of his concern was how to shape the opinions of those in America and in England, how best to interpret the events.

"We need to accomplish two different and apparently conflicting results. We need the world to understand the brutality of the British and to find ways that this atrocity does not fade from consciousness on our shores. And we need to maintain order and honor the rule of law as it relates to the killers. Regarding the first, we must convey to London that the killing was not justified, and to that end, we need to send our message to the ministers as quickly as possible. We must disabuse them of the idea that we are savages. Regarding the second, we must ensure a fair trial and excellent representation for the red-coated killers."

"So what do we do now, Samuel?" Hancock asked.

"First, we need to name what occurred, and I strongly encourage us to call it the 'Boston Massacre.' The words are powerful and convey that unarmed men were cut down unfairly."

James Warren, the skeptic, shot back, "You think killing a mere four people rises to a 'massacre,' Samuel? I think that is a stretch."

"We need strong language, James," Adams replied. "And we need more. We need a painting or engraving of the scene so the public has this heinous act ingrained in their minds. I will be asking Paul Revere to work on that; he can depict events like this brilliantly."

"And how do you suggest we ensure the soldiers receive outstanding legal representation?" Hancock asked.

"I will ask my brilliant cousin, John, to represent them," said Samuel Adams.

Mercy could not help but gasp. After what the British had done to her brother, her stomach turned at the prospect of the brilliant John Adams defending the killers, but she said nothing.

The *Boston Gazette* of March 12, 1770 described the victims' funeral this way:

> Last Thursday, agreeable to a general Request of the Inhabitants, and by the Consent of Parents and Friends, were carried to their Graves in Succession, the Bodies of Samuel Gray, Samuel Maverick, James Caldwell, and Crispus Attucks, the unhappy Victims who fell in the bloody Massacre of Monday Evening preceding.
>
> On the Occasion most of the Shops in Town were shut, all the Bells were ordered to toll a solemn Peal, as also were those in the neighboring Towns of Charlestown, Roxbury etc.
>
> The Procession began to move between the Hours of 4 and 5 in the Afternoon; two unfortunate Sufferers, viz Mess. James Caldwell and Crispus Attucks, who were Strangers borne from Faneuil-Hall, attended by a numerous Train of Persons of all Ranks; and the other two vis. Mr. Samuel Gray, from the House of Benjamin Gray (Brother) on the North Side of the Exchange, and Mr. Maverick in the Union-Street, each followed by the respective Relations and Friends: the several Hearses forming a junction at King Street, the Theatre of the inhuman Tragedy proceeded from, thence thro' the Main-Street, lengthened by an immense Concourse of People, so numerous as to be obliged to follow in Ranks of six, and brought up by a long Train of Carriages belonging to the principal Gentry of the Town.
>
> The bodies were deposited in a Vault in the middle of the Burying-ground. The aggravated circumstances of Death, the Distress and Sorrow visible in every Countenance, together with the peculiar Solemnity with which the whole funeral was conducted surpasses description.

That dismal, cold, and gray day reported on by the *Gazette* was one of the most mournful in James Otis' life. He joined the throng in the funeral procession, side by side in rows of six, and slogged through the streets of the town. He walked next to Mercy on one side and John Hancock on the other. Mercy and Hancock did their best to cheer up the dear man who was drowning in a sea of sadness. No one in the parade of pathos was chipper; nearly all were silent as they made their way to the burial ground. The bells chimed without stop all over the town and added poignant sounds of mourning. Occasionally, Otis would give forth an odd howl of pain that came from his heart and which he, apparently, could not control, drawing puzzled stares from the nearby citizens. Mercy and Hancock felt embarrassed for him, but the fading star of Boston seemed oblivious to the sounds he was making, not to speak of their effect on others.

Mercy reached out and took hold of her brother's hand. That seemed to calm him. He always knew and never doubted her love. He turned to her and uttered a simple "Thank you!"

Later, as they saw the four "deposited in a Vault," with all the tragic finality that any burial contains, Mercy could feel her brother's hand go limp and she let it go. His head was down and his lips moved as if he were speaking, but no words came out. The large crowd's silence bespoke more than the respectful mourning of four dead men; it suggested the passing of an age of innocent hope in Boston, a hope that things could be worked out with the British rulers. The occasion of honoring the dead was no time for loud protestation or mayhem, but the seeds of far more serious resistance had been planted deep in the consciousness of all but a few citizens. The victims were unarmed; no shot had been fired at the Redcoats, yet four, and later five, would be killed by them. Would there be justice for this atrocity?

The conversation that evening at the Green Dragon was rabid. None of the British soldiers, who would later retreat to their fortress on the nearby island, appeared in the tavern (reflecting a temporary outbreak of common sense on their part). The most heated exchange occurred between Ebenezer Mackintosh and Samuel Adams. It was impossible for the men seated nearby not to hear them.

"I understand that your Cousin John will be representing the imprisoned murderers, Samuel, and that it was your idea. What in blazes are you thinking? These scum deserve no defense, much less one of the town's very best advocates. Whose side are you on? We have worked together, and I have put my neck on the line for you and your cause, and this is the reward?" Mackintosh snarled.

"Calm down, Ebenezer. It is important that we seek justice and not revenge. We need proof of who shot who. There is much that needs to be assessed—"

"Don't tell me to calm down," said Mackintosh. "These Redcoats killed unarmed citizens, and they must pay. In this case, vengeance and justice are one and the same. How can you even hold your head high, Samuel, creating a path to freedom for these killers?"

Part of Samuel's rationale for encouraging his cousin John to represent the soldiers was to avoid hostile cross-examination that could lead jurors to believe the citizens of Boston had incited the violence. He did not disclose this to Mackintosh because he knew it would not convince him. Adams leaned across the table and lowered his voice, gesturing to his companion to lower his as well. In a much softer voice, out of earshot for everyone save Mackintosh, he tried to reassure his compatriot.

"I respect your outrage, Ebenezer, and I feel it, too. But this tragedy has put Boston on center stage among all the colonies and even throughout the civilized world. How we conduct ourselves is of the utmost importance. If we become a vengeful mob, we will be seen as no better than savages, disrespected in the other colonies and across the Atlantic." Then lowering his voice even more, Adams added, "If a new nation emerges from all of this, Ebenezer, it is essential that it be guided by the rule of law. How we conduct ourselves in the coming months could well shape how a new nation is governed."

Mackintosh let Adams' words sink in, and his tightly-wound, slender body visibly relaxed. His face softened, his eyes lost their piercing glare, and he thought of what Attucks had said to him and Otis the preceding November. Perhaps a new nation was emerging, perhaps the conditions Attucks had described could begin to unfold. Yet the four men had been slaughtered and another was near death. The possibly glorious future Attucks had described was still a distant dream. The shoemaker ordered another round for the two of them and remained silent. Adams recounted to him the strategy he thought should be pursued in the coming months and beyond. Most of what Adams said did not register with his smoldering companion. Adams himself felt his own tension dissipate: the shoemaker would not call on his mob of thousands but would grudgingly help maintain order in the town.

* * *

Adams miscalculated the course of the British soldiers' trial and that miscalculation changed the man. Rather than receiving a quick trial, Hutchinson, who was now acting Governor of Massachusetts since Bernard's departure to England, helped delay it until November, a long cooling off period that gave time for the sentiments of Boston citizens to cool as well. It turned out that no Bostonian would serve on the jury; all the jurors were countrymen, far less sympathetic to conviction. John Adams managed to get his co-counsel, Josiah Quincy, to soften his cross-examination, and the two did their jobs brilliantly. Thirty-eight witnesses came forward to make the case that the patriot side had plotted the events and planned the inflammatory attack on the soldiers. Opinion began to switch such that some of Boston's citizens came to be viewed as the perpetrators, not the goaded Redcoats. By the end of the trial, Judge Lynde was moved to say, "I feel myself deeply affected that this affair turns out so much to the disgrace of every person concerned against him (Preston), and so much to the shame of the town in general."

On December 5, only two men were convicted of manslaughter: Hugh Montgomery and Matthew Kilroy (who had experienced an earlier run-in with Samuel Gray). The punishment for killing five Bostonians: each man was branded with an "M" for "murder" on his thumb. Hutchinson and his supporters had slithered out of their problem with virtually no retribution.

By now, many citizens wanted to move on and leave the incident behind. Not so Samuel Adams. The whole experience turned him from a British subject seeking his rights to a Patriot who came to believe that possibly in the future the local militia, not British-rigged judges and juries, would be the hope to resist British military despotism.

Adams' anger burned white hot. He wrote his description of what had happened that fateful day in an article in the *Gazette*, under the name Vindex. He was undaunted by the result of the trial, condemning the jury, reminding the readers of the horrors of March 5, defaming Patrick Carr, who on his deathbed, blamed the citizens for the attack. Adams described the sight of dogs licking

124

the blood on the ground of the victims in King Street, and disparaged any of the witnesses with a contrary view.

His article helped shape public opinion throughout the colony in the direction Adams wished. He coupled that with another masterful move: He caused commemoration of March 5 to be an annual event, with speeches praising the victims and condemning the killers. Adams knew how to keep the pot boiling.

Just as Adams was changing, so was James Otis, and much for the worse. He broke his friends' hearts daily as they saw his actions or heard of them, including an incident in which he took his musket and fired it randomly into the town, possibly with too much rum in him. He was embarrassing himself and potentially endangering others.

Otis had also become an unreliable political ally. Once a shrewd and effective legislator with the country party, now he seemed on occasion to want to placate London and England's local minions. It was clear he could not maintain his prominent role in resistance. Adams had asked Mercy to be the one to tell her brother his role needed to change, but she declined. She could not bear to be alone in giving the news and seeing the heart break of the man she loved so much, the brilliant leader who had been so unguarded and bold in his advocacy, the true Spark. However, she did consent to accompany Samuel Adams when he reluctantly agreed to be the one to say the dreary words of truth that Otis needed to hear.

The Christmas holidays always depressed Adams, a fact he never fully understood. Perhaps it was that they always came with inflated cheer that lasted but a few days. Perhaps it was the dreary season of the longest nights and the shortest days. Or it might have been that he always recalled the poignancy of his loneliness during this season after his first wife had died and before he had married Betsy, a time when two young children, a black slave, and a dog were his only companions in celebrating the birth of Christ.

Adams grieved at what he needed to do and dreaded the meeting with Otis. Their relationship had vacillated over time, but it had been grounded in the deep respect Adams felt toward Otis, who had been a kind of mentor to him early in the last decade. Of late, Adams felt Otis had been too kindly in his attitude toward the British authorities, but he had attributed that to his growing mental instability.

Why am I always the one who must do this sort of thing? Why me? I love and respect Otis, but now I must tell him to leave the leadership of our cause. There has been no better advocate, no better friend, no more eloquent voice for our cause. He is a good man who believes in the goodness of everyone. His heart has been broken in so many ways, and now, I must wrench him from the one domain he has excelled in beyond belief. What will he have left after this?

The meeting occurred at Ruth and James Otis' home in his small office on a morning that ironically dripped with sunshine. A cloud hung over Adams as he had thought carefully about the words to use, how clear and kind the message could be, and how to make sure Otis understood and would acquiesce. While Adams bemoaned that it fell to him to tell Otis his public life needed to end, he knew he had to be the bearer of this news. No other man or woman in the resistance had the standing to do so. Adams was the only man Otis could not ignore. He was like an irresistible force of nature on behalf of the rights of men and women in all the American colonies.

Ruth's greeting of Adams was as cold as the Christmas icicles that hung from the Otis house and her words as pointed as the tips of those winter daggers. Ruth looked at Mercy with muted exasperation.

"Come in. I will get him," she said, turning on her heels and swiftly moving away from her unwanted visitors to call her husband, who had been resting upstairs.

Otis descended with a genial smile, his hair a bit disheveled and his shirt only partially tucked into his gray trousers.

"Samuel, Mercy, what a pleasure to see you. Please, come in. Shall we retire to you-know-where?" he asked with natural, heartfelt graciousness.

They followed Otis into the little office where they had met and strategized so many times. Their earlier meetings had been filled with so much vitality and optimism. They were kindred spirits in the battle for the rights of Americans. They had written pamphlets, articles, and long pronunciamentos together in that little space. Otis' command of the English language was unsurpassed, and he could put into words so many of the thoughts and ideas that the rest of the patriotic conspirators needed to convey to the public.

All that was true, but now Samuel Adams needed to do his duty.

"What brings you both here?" Otis asked brightly.

"We wanted to see how you were," said Adams, "and we need to convey a message as well."

"I am much better; my spirits are good most of the time, and I have not been getting into trouble, at least that I know of," Otis said. "But tell me what the message is and from whom it comes."

"First," Adams replied, "let me honor all you have done, James. You have been the spark and the best voice for the resistance, and you still have the deep affection of the people of this town. You have been attacked physically and verbally, but you have not lost your generous spirit."

"This sounds bad, Samuel," Otis replied. "You are about to deliver some bad news, and I am beginning to feel a bit dizzy. Bear with me, please." Otis lowered his head and stared at the desk in front of him. His breathing had become rapid, and then as the pause continued, his breathing slowed and he said, "Go ahead; tell me the bad news, my beloved sister and my friend."

Adams' eyes became moist and he found himself unable to speak. At first, when he attempted to utter the necessary words, the sounds came out as barely audible squeaks. He stood up from the chair that sat across the desk from Otis and reached out his arms. Otis raised himself from the chair and walked around the desk to embrace his friend, seeming to know now what was coming. He held Adams, whose tears began flowing freely onto Otis' brilliant white shirt. Still, no words could come, and the magnitude of the meeting for Samuel Adams dwarfed any sense of embarrassment any of the three of them might have had.

Otis finally spoke. "I understand, Samuel. My role must now change. My behavior is too erratic, and I have lost my bearings. I am not myself anymore, and I am hurting the cause. That is why you are here, correct?"

Adams nodded, slowly and with some reverence. "Yes, we need your spirit and good wishes, but now you can recede from what is quickly becoming a battleground."

Another long silence. "I have both feared and looked forward to this day, Samuel and dear Mercy. I have known that this could happen, and in my heart, I know it should happen, but it still brings me pain beyond words. The cause has given meaning to my life, and now I must 'recede,' as you put it. What will I do? I will be so alone and without purpose now." Otis groaned.

"There are your children, James," Adams said softly, sensing he was entering ground he might not be well-advised to tread on.

Otis seemed to ignore Adams' attempt to console him. His expression changed from one of consternation to one of peaceful resignation. His mood lightened with surprising speed. Adams knew his friend's temperament was mercurial, but both he and Mercy were surprised to see him shift this quickly. Calmly and with a smile, Otis addressed them.

"Samuel and my dear Mercy, it is up to you and Hancock and Joseph Warren now. I so admire what you have already done. I know we have had our differences. I know we disagreed about non-importation of British goods and the like, and that you have been frustrated and puzzled by my loyalty to the Crown. I admire your tenacity and, for the most part, your judgment. The job ahead is complex and full of danger, but you are equal to it. May I give you some advice and then make a request?"

"Of course, my dear friend," Samuel said, as Mercy nodded.

"My advice is to do what I have not been able to do: maintain perspective and balance as you proceed. Remain close to the lower classes, and people like Mackintosh in particular. Unity in this town is of paramount importance, except for the ardent Loyalists and the Redcoats. Keep it all together, and keep showing your good judgment, both in causing events to happen and reacting to them. You are the heart and the mind of resistance. Keep your balance and keep your faith.

"My request of both of you is that you will keep me apprised of what is happening and give me the opportunity to give you my views. I want to feel like I am still part of this great moment in history. I am already a lonely man, so please let me feel connected to the cause and to you. Will you do that?"

Mercy nodded vigorously, and Adams answered quickly, "Of course we will, James. We will consult with you regularly and value your counsel and support. You will always remain an important part of the spirit of resistance. You must believe that."

Otis turned to his sister. His face now bore an awkward smile, and then he looked at the floor. The conversation was brief and strained. Otis kept looking down, his face bravely trying to hold a smile. When Adams and Mercy departed, they left a house far more barren than when they had arrived.

Whom could Otis trust to carry on the mission with the same spirit he had? Mercy. His thoughts floated back to decades earlier and to his remarkable sister.

Part IV

Lord Have Mercy

⚟ 18 ⚟

Nine-year-old Mercy Otis recalled how she had loved the mid-day meal at the family farm in Barnstable, Massachusetts, that day in 1737. Everyone on the farmstead came together around their large table to eat, joke, and speak as equals. Isaiah, the Negro field hand, and his partner Andrew (who knew what his real Wampanoag name was?) would tell stories, transparently lie to each other, and joke with James Otis, Sr. about how hard they had worked and how superior their skills were. The Otises employed them to be sure, but at lunch, a delightful sense of equality prevailed. Mercy thought nothing of being teased and taught the rudiments of farming by Isaiah and Andrew. They gave her a sense of warm protection, even though she knew nothing of their two races and cultures.

The senior Otis would eat more ravenously than the rest of the family, even more than the men who had been in the fields. Without speaking, his stout frame filled not only his place but seemed to fill the table and even the entire dining room. He was benevolently imposing, possessed of a nature that could not be perturbed, and certainly not intimidated. He was open to all kinds of experiences, which partly explained his many vocations: farmer, lawyer, businessman, and public servant. He had become a true pillar of the Barnstable community.

James Otis, Sr. always felt a bit embarrassed at his lack of a Harvard education, but all who encountered him knew he was possessed of a first-rate intellect. In preparation for Harvard, Otis sent his sons James (Jemmy) and Joseph, at a very early age, to be tutored by his brother-in-law Rev. John Russell, pastor of the West Barnstable church, a learned, gentle, and patient man. Later, when his sons went off to Harvard, James Sr. would feel mixed emotions of pride in them and a faint hint of jealousy. Today, Mercy was feeling that same way because her brothers were being tutored by Rev. Russell. Why couldn't she be tutored too, in both the classics and the great literature of the English language?

Mercy's stomach was in a knot that day she approached her father to ask his permission to join her brothers under the tutelage of Rev. Russell. The lunch table had almost groaned with the weight of turkey, turnips, cornmeal flat bread, and apple pie. Yet Mercy's appetite had nearly vanished. After the servants had cleared the dishes, she approached her father in his study, a place children rarely entered. She was both nervous and excited, eager and on edge. Her heart raced and her skin shimmered, not from the July warmth but from the anticipation.

"What brings you into this room, my daughter?" her father asked, expansively looking over his spectacles with the smallest trace of a smile on his broad face. "Come in, young lady."

Mercy had rehearsed to herself how she would make her case; how she, a girl, could justify studying alongside her brothers, brothers who would grow into men, men who needed a broad and deep education to lead their community, a community complaisant and stable, stable in part because women and men understood their places and roles in the family, the community, and the world.

* * *

She would make her case by asking questions.

"Sit down, Mercy, and tell me what is on your mind," James Otis said, gesturing to the worn, rust-colored sofa to the left of his large, cluttered oak desk.

"I would like to ask you some questions, Father. Is that all right?"

"Of course, go ahead," he replied.

"Did God create all people equal, equal in what they could learn and do?" Mercy knew it might seem an odd question, but even at her early age, she was willing to seem unusual if her curiosity could be satisfied and her sense of what was fair could be advanced. Being a bit odd did not seem to bother her family.

"Well," her father replied, "He made us all equal in some important ways but also distinctive. Everyone has different abilities and traits; that is what makes being human so interesting. For example, you and your brother Jemmy are very different. He may be three years older than you, but you seem to have more common sense. And your mother and I are very different, but we are bound in love." Otis seemed to enjoy and be faintly amused at explaining things to his earnest daughter. Her mind seemed to sparkle with innocent inquisitiveness.

"Did God make men and women equal in intelligence? Are boys smarter than girls?" Mercy continued. She already had a very strong opinion about what the answer should be, but she needed confirmation from her father.

"Of course not, Mercy. You know that. Women do have a certain kind of intelligence that men lack, a kind of understanding of other people's feelings that we men often do not grasp. And men seem handier or at least more interested in making and fixing things. But men and women are fundamentally equal in mental powers," he said.

"Then if they are equal in mental powers, would that mean they are equal in their ability to learn, to be taught important things and learn of faraway worlds?" she asked, getting closer to the final question. At this point, they both knew Mercy was more interested in making a point than seeking the truth.

"Yes, girls can learn just as well as boys," he replied, "but their need to know certain things is different. Men need to learn history and grasp large ideas and principles. Women's needs are not the same. Women need to know how to care for a family, not a simple task."

The conversation was not going exactly in the direction Mercy wanted. An idea for a new question leapt into her mind that she blurted out.

"Does God want men and women to be equally free? Free to learn and grow in their own way?" Mercy had already given that question a great deal of thought.

James Otis, Sr. paused and furrowed his brow. He cleared his throat but did not speak. The room became very quiet, and both could hear the sounds of the dishes being done in the kitchen and the footsteps of servants tidying up the remnants of the lunch.

"Is there something you want to ask me specifically, Mercy? Where are all these questions heading, my dear girl?" he asked, now more matter-of-fact than good-natured.

Mercy paused briefly and then blurted again.

"May I join Jemmy and Joseph and study with Uncle Jonathan? I love to read and learn, and I would love to join my brothers. Please, please, please." Rev. Jonathan Russell was a gentle soul and a scholarly, pious man. She had been imagining the thrill of learning the classics and reading great English literature under his wing. Her heart raced as she waited for the answer.

"Why would you want to do that, Mercy?" Otis asked, and then, as if to interrupt himself, he said, "Why not? If that is what you want to do, young lady, that is what you should do. I will need to talk to your mother about this, so don't mention this until I have, but I think it would be fine, and I believe your mother will, too. But it might just take a little time. She has been through a lot and has much on her mind."

Elation is a tepid word to describe how Mercy felt to hear his words. She nodded when her father told her to keep this to herself, but she so wanted to tell Jemmy. Her older brother was most unconventional in how he viewed his younger sister; he treated her almost as an equal and encouraged her reading, nurtured her curiosity, and supported almost everything she did. Their bond was such that Mercy worked hard to overlook her brother's foibles, the most conspicuous of which was his tendency to lecture her at great length, rather than converse. Yet his good-natured soul was so generous and innocent that Mercy could (sometimes with great effort) accept his somewhat pompous oratory.

Young "Jemmy" Otis trusted his sister totally in their childhood conspiracies, never telling on her, and often defending her behavior to their mother. She could have told Jemmy what their father had agreed to, and she was certain that Jemmy would have kept the confidence, but she believed that God would punish her if she betrayed her father's trust. As well, she believed that in some way it would have been disrespectful of their mother to tell Jemmy.

As soon as Mercy left her father's den, light on her feet, feeling a whole new world beginning to open up to her, Jemmy stopped her at the foot of the stairs and asked what she had been talking to their father about.

"Oh, I was telling him he should pay Isaiah and Andrew more for all the work they do." It was an odd response, but Mercy thought she said it with enough assurance that Jemmy would believe it.

"What possible basis of comparison do you have to suggest that to father?" Jemmy asked, reasonably.

"I don't know; it just seems fair to pay them more," Mercy replied. Then Jemmy changed the subject rapidly, as he was wont to do.

"Let's play some Ring Taw, Sis," he suggested. Mercy quickly agreed, feeling that shooting marbles in the dirt sounded singularly appropriate for the moment; she needed something to bring her back down to earth.

"Fine idea, my brother. Be prepared to be humiliated, again," Mercy replied, gently shoving his chest.

As the two played between the house and the rickety shed in the shade of the buttonwood tree on the dusty ground, Mercy wondered how their father would broach the subject of her being tutored by Uncle John. Their mother kept her own counsel and could be hard to interpret. Mercy always felt she should be closer to her mother; she believed a mother and daughter should have a special bond, but Mercy never felt it. Mary Allyne Otis was a good woman from a good family, and she never complained. She would go on to give birth thirteen times, only to see six of her children die. The weight she carried was so different from that of their father: his weight seemed to reflect power and well-being, and her weight seemed to signify a constant burden she carried, made more painful by the tragedy of child loss.

Mercy had expected a longer wait for the verdict from her mother. That night, after their family dinner of roasted chicken, corn, and Johnny cake, Mrs. Otis took her daughter aside. Her face did not give a clue as to what she was going to say; it had the same expression Mercy would see when she was told to do a chore.

"Mercy, my dear, your father has told me what you want to do," she began, shaking her head. "I know you have an inquiring and restless mind, but why do you want such a formal education? You will make a wonderful wife someday, and you already have shown such gifts in needlepoint and embroidery. But home-making is not simple, and you still have much to learn. Your father, bless his heart, does not fully grasp what we women must do to keep a household together, so he thinks it would be fine for you to study under your uncle. But I just have to ask 'Why?'" Her voice had a tinge of disapproval, but also genuine curiosity.

"Mother, you know me better than anyone in the world," Mercy replied. "I am curious and love to learn. I hope it does not sound immodest, but I think I am as bright as Jemmy, and joining him in this would deepen our bond. I am sure as a mother you would want that. I would be so happy if you said 'Yes'; it would mean everything to me."

"Well, I will not stand in your way," replied Mrs. Otis with a bemused smile. "We need more joy in our home, so you should do it. Now go help with the dishes."

At that moment, Mercy believed it was the happiest day of her young life. After she had finished drying the tableware and silverware, she climbed the stairs of the high double house with its gambrel roof, still light-headed. Behind the closed door of her parents' bedroom, she heard her mother's muffled sobs. It was not the first time she had heard them, not the first time she felt a poignant ambivalence about wanting to comfort her, knowing it was not her place to intrude, but also wanting to help relieve her mother's pain. Mercy never dared knock on that door. She could only imagine what was going on in her mother's heart. Was Mercy part of her pain? Did her youth and joy magnify her mother's anguish or reduce it? Dutiful and often cheerful in the presence of her family, but occasionally in a pond of sorrow by herself, Mary Otis remained a mystery. Mercy's joy continued, but it was tinged with confused sadness at her mother's plight. Mercy took refuge where she often did, in her books. It seemed fitting that this time Mercy would open the Holy Bible to find both solace and inspiration.

She read Psalm 107: 1, 8:

> "Oh give thanks to the LORD, for he is good, for his faithful love endures forever!"
>
> "Let them praise the LORD for his great love, for his wonderful things he has done for them."

Indeed, Mercy would then go on to study with her brothers under their uncle, the Reverend John Russell. She adored it, and thrived as she entered into a world of ancient Roman history, Classical literature, and the finest writings in English. She bathed in the genius of Pope, Dryden, Milton, and Shakespeare. Added to that was the gift of doing it with Jemmy, and talking about what they were learning, often deep into the night. They immersed themselves in the great literary works they read, and their minds were set ablaze by learning about the cruel tyranny perpetrated by Roman despots.

Mercy knew she would never attend Harvard and that Jemmy would. He needed to learn Latin and Greek, and she was not permitted to, yet the love of their mother tongue and the lessons learned from ancient history were bequeathed to them both with equal intensity. As a woman, Mercy's path did not seem destined to be one of public leadership, which Harvard groomed men to do, yet the more she learned, the more she felt sure of herself intellectually. More importantly, she knew she was loved and respected by the person she trusted and adored above all others, her older brother.

In what seemed like a few years, Mercy would see Jemmy graduate from Harvard and meet someone who would change her life forever.

It was not a short trip from West Barnstable to Cambridge, and the horses were a bit ill-tempered, possibly because of the sweltering summer heat. They seemed to resent being prodded on by Ichabod, their driver; if the horses only knew him as a person and not one wielding the whip, they would have appreciated that he was a gentle and humble soul. Even though the horses were in a bad mood, Mercy was thrilled, in part to get out of Barnstable and in part to see Harvard. Her world was getting bigger.

As the carriage approached the Harvard Yard, Mercy was surprised by the large and motley crowd swarming on the grass and in the cobblestone streets. The graduation ceremony was not simply an in-grown event of the privileged, but a community celebration, a celebration that was raucous with flowing (if often discordant) music and massive quantities of beer and wine. Jemmy seemed amused by the whole scene and greeted a few of his classmates, but he did not linger with them. He stayed close to his family. His mother and father exuded a mixture of pride and a trace of bewilderment at the chaotic scene.

Mercy rather enjoyed the incongruity of seeing the Harvard Overseers (a mixture of the members of the General Court of the Bay Colony and six clergy representing the six communities surrounding Cambridge) mingling in the same throng as townspeople, be they dock workers, merchants, ropers, tailors, or sailors.

Before the official commencement procession started, Jemmy waved across the teeming mix of humanity to a younger man. He returned the greeting with a radiant smile that evoked in Mercy strange and unexpected feelings. Her first emotion was one of relief that Jemmy had a friend who exuded such warmth toward her brother, since Jemmy had few if any close friends she knew of. She had been disconcerted by that apparent void in his life. The stranger's smile calmed her. The other sentiment aroused in her was a visceral attraction to a young man whose beaming face suggested such good humor, vitality, and confidence. The effect of the fleeting encounter was to make her feel relaxed, and even festive.

Mercy's mind kept flitting to the young stranger throughout the seemingly interminable graduation ceremony. Speeches were delivered in English, Greek, and Latin, and the whole proceeding was not so much an event to honor knowledge and wisdom as an occasion for cocky young men to show their intellectual plumage, like young peacocks. Mercy was feeling increasingly self-conscious from the unladylike perspiration discoloring her gray dress. She hoped that in the drunken swarm, nobody would notice.

"Incredibly, insufferably boring, isn't it?" were the unexpected words that interrupted her private thoughts. The words came from the same young stranger who had smiled at Jemmy before the proceedings had commenced. The young man standing next to Mercy had a solid frame and a handsome, if somewhat enigmatic, face. His hair was light brown, and his expression was an interesting blend of skepticism and benevolence.

"I am sorry for being so rude," said the young man. "Let me introduce myself. My name is James Warren, a fellow student of your brother's."

Mercy, eager to reply, said, "You are not rude at all, and I am—"

"I know who you are," said James Warren. "You are Mercy. Jemmy talks about you all the time."

❖ 19 ❖

On a warm June day in 1770, Mercy Otis Warren sat at her desk in the family's study, a room she shared with her husband on alternate days of the week, and a place that enabled her to create plays and poems without the interruption of children. She had been putting the final touches on her play, *The Adulateur*, which skewered the lieutenant governor as effectively as any political assault would do. She had brought to the play several characters, including the sinister Rapatio, a thinly veiled Thomas Hutchinson, and Brutus, who personified her brother, Jemmy. Other roles included Junius, Cassius, Dupe, Bagshot, and Meagre. "Servia" was Massachusetts. Mercy would test the words and phrases she had written on her dear husband.

James Warren remained infatuated with Mercy and smitten by her use of the English language. When she called him into the study, James seemed eager to hear what she had written.

"How do you like this one, James?" Mercy asked. "It's spoken by Junius in Act II:

> 'The inhuman soldiers stamp the hostile ground,
> His garments stain'd with blood
> The streets of Servia sweat with human gore
> Oh, Brutus, I'm on fire—hand me my sword
> And give me to the foe—
> And if we die—let's die like men
> And bravely fall expiring on the foe—
> That man dies well who sheds his blood for freedom.'

"Those truly are fighting words, my dear," James replied. "Well said. I really like 'The streets of Servia sweat with human gore.' Brings back the massacre nicely."

"Let me try two more on you," Mercy said. "One from Rapatio and one from Brutus, all right?"

"More than all right; I can't wait," Warren said.

> Rapatio.
> 'What say my friends? Shall patriots, grov'ling patriots
> Thus thwart our schemes? Push back the plan of action!

140

And make it thus recoil? Mistaken wretches!
Unthinking fools! They work their own destruction.
Let them amuse themselves with thoughts of freedom,
And bask amid the sunshine of an hour;—
They hover over the secret precipice—
The leap is death. Come, cunning be my guide,
Beleagur'd with hell—Come all those hateful passions,
That rouse the mind to action.'

"I love 'Come, cunning be my guide.' That is magnificent!" James exclaimed. "Truly describes Hutchinson, but sadly for him, he's not cunning enough. Well done, my love. Now give me Brutus."

"This is longer, so try to pay attention, a challenge for you I know," Mercy said with a smile. "These are the final lines of the play." Mercy read with great enthusiasm:

Brutus
'Yes, the wish'd for period
May soon arrive, when murders, blood, and carnage,
Shall crimson all the streets; when this poor country
Shall loose her richest blood, forbid it heaven!
And may these monsters find their glories fade,
Crush'd in the ruins they themselves have made
While thou my country, shall again revive
Shake off misfortune, and thro' ages live
See thro' the waste a ray of virtue gleame,
Dispell the shades and brighten all the scene
Wak'd into life the blooming forest glows,
And all the desert blossoms as a role,
From distant lands see virtuous millions fly
To happier climates, and a milder sky.
While on the mind successive pleasures pour
'Till time expires, and ages are no more.'

Mercy finished reading. Part of her motivation was to have Brutus (James Otis) give eloquent voice to the cause, even as, in his current, real life, he was now challenged to be consistently coherent.

"What do you think, my husband?" Mercy asked.

James hesitated, which disconcerted her. She had labored hard to find just the right words, and she was proud of the balance between the necessary violence of the confrontation described at the top of Brutus' remarks and the hopeful, radiant future that lay ahead for "my country" so earnestly described in the lower part. Like all authors, she felt vulnerable in hearing someone else's thoughts about her work, but she had never felt dangerously exposed with her own husband before.

"What is wrong?" she asked.

"The words are brilliant, the ideas elegantly put forward," James replied. "What I am puzzled by is the tone, not just of this but the whole piece. It seems so bellicose. Several years ago when we were meeting with Adams and Hancock, you decried the coming battle, the loss of life, the bloodshed that would be part of what you called the 'downward spiral.' You had brought a woman's sensibility to the conflict that was looming. Now, in this play, you seem almost eager for the fight. And if I didn't know you had written it, I would have said a man had. It is defiant and aggressive. Don't misunderstand me; I think the play is a first-rate indictment of our British overlords, but I am concerned about your own frame of mind. Puzzled, mainly. Does this make any sense to you?"

Mercy needed to absorb these thoughts. James was forcing her to an unexpected introspection when all she had wanted was his reaction to the lines she had written. As she was thinking, their two oldest sons, James and Winslow, entered the study, brimming with energy and the need for permission. James was tall and sinewy with the sharp features of his mother and Winslow shorter, and far more muscular, taking after his father in expression and mannerisms.

"Mother," said James, "can we go down to the wharfs?"

"Mr. Hancock," explained Winslow, "told us we could board one of his ships and get a preliminary lesson in sailing and the workings of the ship."

"Please! Can we?" they asked in unison. The distraction calmed both James and Mercy.

"Yes," Mercy replied, "but be home for dinner, and pay close attention to what you are taught. We will want to hear what you learned."

The boys bounded out of the room, leaving James and Mercy in a kind of limbo that had been created by James' observation and question.

"Remember, James," Mercy finally said, "this play is anonymous, so no one other than you will be sure of its author. The tone is very male, and I did that intentionally, to draw attention away from speculation about me. As to the gory language, I have long since reconciled myself to war. War is inevitable, and I want the Patriots who see or read *The Adulateur* to feel the pride and the passion that fighting for rights and respect require. Hutchinson needs to be stripped bare of any legitimacy, and I hope this play will help. His departure is coming, and the sooner the better. And, I must confess, it is deeply satisfying to mock a person like Hutchinson; mockery emasculates. And there is no good response to this kind of mockery."

"And to be honest," she added with fervor, "the fact that Hutchinson and his ilk have destroyed my brother has hardened my resolve. James Otis needs to be vindicated, no matter what."

"Are you motivated by justice or revenge?" James asked, looking solemnly at her. "Revenge is bad for the soul; we have talked about this. You cannot let Hutchinson or anyone else erode your soul."

"It is both justice and revenge, dear husband," Mercy replied. "How would you feel if your brother were brought to a condition like mine has been? Would you be a saint and forgive Hutchinson?"

"Hutchinson has always been in an untenable position," said James, "serving two masters: one in London and another in Boston. Hutchinson is a literate man who has lost his wife and is struggling to raise a family and govern a town that is often unruly. Hutchinson is a Harvard man, too, someone with a shared pedigree and education. As for your dear brother, Jemmy showed signs of mental instability long before Robinson's attack, even before Hutchinson's campaign to slander him. Hutchinson did not caused Jemmy's insanity, but he has preyed upon it and made it worse."

Mercy glared at her husband in a way she never had before; the look made her feel like a stranger to herself. She believed there are times when unswerving loyalty to family should trump all else. Beholding her husband's puzzled face quickly calmed her down, however. She bridled at his words and adored the man. How could she not adore him?

Mercy remembered their courtship with clarity as if it had been the preceding week. And so did he. It had seemed like forever for both of them before they finally agreed to marry. They each knew the other was the deepest, truest friend of their heart. When they were courting, the distance between Plymouth and Barnstable only made their hearts grow fonder. When they did come together, his actual presence always had the beautifully strange effect of eliciting in Mercy feelings of both calm and excitement. They had each ripened nicely, he at twenty-eight and she at twenty-six. Their wedding day remained imprinted indelibly in both of their memories and souls.

That November day in Barnstable had been unnaturally and luxuriously warm, as if Nature were opening her arms to their union. The guests in the Otis home were few; their respective family members and a few close friends. Mercy's brothers were animated, and James and his much younger brother Samuel seemed mischievously happy and fun. Her brother James had gently mocked the way Mercy and her betrothed had announced their intentions by issuing banns that they attached to the West Barnstable Meeting House. He knew they would exchange their vows in the family house and not a church, believing as they did that marriage was a civil contract more than a religious sacrament. That decision was not a simple one: they shared the belief that they were entering a sacred union. After considerable discussion, they reached a common conclusion that their familiar home would be as inviting to the Almighty as West Barnstable Meeting House would ever be.

The paterfamilias, James Otis, Sr., had grown very fond of young James Warren, his soon-to-be son-in-law. Otis Sr. had been to Plymouth, Warren's hometown, and knew his father. Bringing James Warren into the Otis family (for that is how he saw it) seemed natural. He acted like the "Colonel," commanding in a good-natured way, frequently sizing up James with a faint smile and a twinkle in his eye.

"Let's get on with it!" Otis Sr. exclaimed, instantly quieting the small crowd. Mercy's stomach had been churning throughout the morning, and even the sight of her beloved James did not cause it to calm. They quickly made their way into the parlor in front of the mantle, and a reverent hush overtook the house.

As the skinny, old magistrate (whose name they both had forgotten) prepared to have them take their vows, James took Mercy's hand and her churning insides instantly settled down. She was overcome with such joy that she had great difficulty speaking. James' gaze remained solid and confident. They were quickly officially married, and the Otis home began to hum again with contentment and fun. The food that followed, complete with the bridal cakes and tasty sack posset, provided a sweet relief, although Mercy's appetite was still miniscule. After the psalm was sung to the newlyweds, the loving hive of family and friends indulged in a charivari, teasing them as the pair retired to the bridal chamber.

* * *

Mercy's thoughts returned to her play. She strategized with her husband on how to ensure wide circulation while avoiding detection as the author. Mercy believed to her core that Thomas Hutchinson was worthy of her scorn; he was weak and he had helped ruin her brother.

As the text of *The Adulateur* was circulated throughout Boston, the desired effect was achieved. An increasing number of Bostonians grew to see Hutchinson and his cronies as contemptuous of them and their rights.

In Mercy's hands, the pen was, if not mightier than the sword, at least equal to it in power.

Part V

Tea For Two

<h1 style="text-align:center">≈ 20 ≈</h1>

Late June of 1773 brought a familiar sweltering heat and suffocating mugginess to Boston that left its residents short-fused. What Samuel Adams was about to present to his colleagues in the Massachusetts House of Representatives would do nothing to induce a cheery or forgiving attitude. The noose around the neck of his enemy, Thomas Hutchinson, was about to become tighter. The matter to be considered was of such importance and sensitivity that the members cleared the galleries of the House; only the lawmakers could be present for this. Juiciest of all, Adams was about to present a revelation. Nothing whets the appetite of a politician like a revelation.

The source of what would be revealed was London-based Benjamin Franklin. Some Americans questioned where Mr. Franklin's loyalties lay. Franklin and Adams had an on-again, off-again relationship; in 1770, Adams had opposed the brilliant bon vivant for the job of representing the colonies in London, for various reasons. Franklin loved to hobnob with powerful leaders, and it did not sit well with residents of Boston that Franklin had befriended Lord Hillsborough, visiting him as he did at the lord's lovely estate in Ireland.

Hillsborough had deeply angered many people in Boston in 1771 when he changed the way the Governor of Massachusetts was compensated. Instead of having the Massachusetts legislature pay the governor's salary, Hillsborough persuaded British leaders to have London pay it, thus loosening the bonds between Bostonians and the colony's governor. The power of the purse was jealously prized by local leaders; taking it away created yet a deeper wedge between Boston and London. Resistance to this further elevated Adams' standing in the town. Adams argued vehemently that this change would overturn the necessary checks and balances of the provincial constitution, freeing the governor from any control by the people.

Franklin knew he had some fence-mending to do in his home colony across the Atlantic. What Franklin was to provide Adams would prove to be the beginning of Hutchinson's undoing.

Further demonstrating his deviousness, Hutchinson had secretly sent a series of letters to Thomas Whately, a former member of Parliament, and the enterprising Franklin had come into possession of them. The letters contained some views that Hutchinson would never have wanted Bostonians to see. One phrase Adams pounced on, like a hungry lion on its crippled prey, was Hutchinson's statement that "there must be an abridgment of what is called English Liberty," a phrase that did not sit well with citizens of Boston, coming as it did from a man who frequently urged Parliament to assert its sovereignty over the American colonies.

Franklin had sent the letters to Adams with the clear stipulation that only a limited number of people should see them, namely John and Samuel Adams, James Bowdoin, Thomas Cushing, Charles Chauncy, and Samuel Cooper. That a wise and sophisticated man like Benjamin Franklin would think such a group could keep a secret defies belief. More than that, he knew how much Adams hated Hutchinson. Franklin had to have known that he had just thrown red meat to the lion.

Adams laid down the terms for use of the information he was to give them, and the House agreed. Adams read excerpts to his colleagues. Hancock then rose to say that "some body in the Common" had given him a manuscript that appeared to be a copy of the Hutchinson letters that Adams had. It was then moved that the two sets of letters be compared and, if identical, the Clerk of the House should attest to them and prepare them for publication.

Adams' actions kept the charade alive. To adhere to the letter of Franklin's stipulation, Adams circulated copies of the actual Hutchinson letters that Franklin had sent to the group; he bled the letters for every possible negative interpretation of Hutchinson's motivations that they could be seen to contain. He saw to it that they were distributed throughout Boston, and the entire colony. With the help of the Sons of Liberty, the other colonies in America would also see them. Adams' incessant and effective attack on Hutchinson ate away at Hutchinson's credibility like a toxic acid. Adams was helped by the Boston Committee of Correspondence, which saw Hutchinson's letters as part of a larger plot against New England, conceived of by its "malicious and invidious enemies."

Even citizens in the countryside, his base of support, began to turn on Hutchinson. Samuel Adams was regaining his footing in the public swirl of resistance politics, continuing to use friendly media like the *Boston Gazette* to wage a constant, sophisticated assault on the governor.

The assault was having a deepening effect on Hutchinson, who had spent years aspiring to be the governor. Since he had achieved his goal in 1771, his life had become miserable. By the summer of 1773, he desperately wanted a leave of absence. Knowing he was despised throughout the town, Hutchinson walked the streets of Boston with less frequency and more caution. Being hated in a small town is a curse and the word was out that Hutchinson wanted to escape. Even the swarm of British soldiers that infested the town seemed to view him with contempt.

John Hancock encountered the dreary Hutchinson as the governor sat alone in the Green Dragon on a warm evening in early July. Hutchinson was relieved to be joined by the ever-cheerful and wealthy Hancock, a man open to the company of a wide range of people, no matter their views. Hancock had reconciled with Samuel Adams and was squarely on the side of resistance, but he felt compassion for the forlorn Hutchinson.

"You look very sad, Thomas. What is wrong?" Hancock asked.

"What is right would be a better question," Hutchinson replied, inviting Hancock to join him with a welcoming gesture.

"I should think you would be on top of the world, Thomas. You are the governor, living in a vibrant beautiful city, with children who are ascending in the world of commerce. You are a success, by many standards," Hancock replied, knowing how falsely the words rang.

"One detail you neglected, John," Hutchinson replied. "I am loathed by a vast majority of my fellow citizens. You have never experienced that feeling. Ever since the *Liberty* affair, you have been adored."

"May I give you some advice, Thomas?" Hancock asked.

"Yes, absolutely," the governor replied.

"Ask London for a leave of absence so you can regroup and rethink your strategies," Hancock said. "We all need a break from time to time, and you have been under a great deal of strain."

"Interesting that you suggest that, John. I sent a letter yesterday to the prime minister requesting exactly that. The last straw has been the reaction in this town to the Tea Act."

"Yes, Thomas, the Tea Act might very well be the last straw," Hancock replied cryptically. "Now, let's order a brew." He looked over to Beth Frothingham and raised two fingers, knowing she would bring them the best, most expensive libation available.

Beth turned her back on the two men and did not serve them. Hancock understood and felt foolish for having beckoned her; she was loyal to James Otis and the cause and despised Hutchinson.

"The little wagtail is ignoring us, John," Hutchinson said.

"Beth is a good woman with a fine mind and a wonderful temperament, Thomas," Hancock said. "Now if you will excuse me, I must take my leave. Good day, Governor." Hancock rose and slowly walked out of the Green Dragon. From that time on, there would not be even feigned cordiality between the two men.

Yet Hutchinson's role in the coming storm was not yet complete. His faulty judgment would soon be tested again, this time in the case of unwanted tea in Boston.

21

Ah, tea! For the Americans, tea had become an important part of life, not just another beverage and certainly not something as mundane as a mere staple. The serving of tea was familiar and social within a family and within different social circles in Boston; it brought people together in intimate ways. It also connected Americans to the world, a world in which they were growing to believe they had a special role. While they maintained a keen sense of identification with their British ancestors and even with contemporaries, they sensed something in their resistance had larger meaning. Tea bespoke gentility, manners, a sense of rooted custom, even a sense of proper values, but using it as a political weapon did not sit well with the citizens of Boston.

Leave it to the leaders in London to turn an innocent and unifying libation into a political and commercial enterprise that would further alienate the Americans. Leave it to Samuel Adams to turn the prospect of cheap tea into a sinister plot by the British overlords to further erode the rights of Americans. And leave it to Thomas Hutchinson to find himself once again on the defensive, reviled by the citizens of Boston. The elements to the story are these:

The East India Company had a very influential role with Parliament, and had large excesses of tea in their warehouses. It persuaded Parliament to pass the Tea Act, which provided rebates to the sellers of tea to Americans, further deflating the prices of tea. The Tea Act also enabled the East India Company to determine local sellers (consignees), another corrupting influence of the de facto monopoly. Most objectionable to Adams was perpetuating a duty on tea that went back to the Townshend Act; he saw cheap tea as an inducement to the colonists to wink an eye at the tax. Most objectionable to the local merchants who sold tea were the grossly discounted East India Company tea prices with which they could not compete. The many smugglers of tea shared the same objection as well. (In 1771, Hutchinson had estimated that 83 percent of tea in Boston was smuggled in.)

What Bostonians found most vexing, and which added fuel to the fire of Boston resistance, was that Governor Hutchinson's sons were two of the specially designated consignees of the East India Company tea. The crowd of resisters resented Thomas and Elisha Hutchinson for flagrantly ignoring the non-importation agreements in the late 1760s; it was only natural the Sons of Liberty sought to stigmatize them. The Hutchinson sons, like their father, came to see how despised they had become.

All of this happened within the context of Boston losing some credibility in the eyes of other cities like New York and Philadelphia because Boston merchants had not been adequately supportive of non-importation of British products. Boston patriots needed to show their primacy as resisters to the overlords in England. In late October, when the ships loaded with 1,700 chests of tea set sail from England, many in Boston were eager to send them back as full as when they arrived. Patriot leaders in Philadelphia and New York were similarly adamant.

At the same time the tea-laden ships were departing England, James and Mercy Otis Warren convened a small meeting to discuss strategy. This meant another trek to their home in Plymouth for Samuel Adams and John Hancock. They also invited Dr. Joseph Warren because of his emerging leadership in colonial affairs as well as his close ties to the Sons of Liberty. They were motivated in part to provide a larger perspective for Adams, who had seemed to go beyond the pale in his rhetoric and actions surrounding the Tea Act. William Molineux wanted to join the small group, but it was felt he was too "volatile" to discuss strategy dispassionately. Sheer hatred of the local British officials and of Governor Hutchinson was not a needed ingredient to forming a winning strategy. There needed to be cool reasoning and smart tactics. Dr. Joseph Warren filled the bill to provide the brilliant mind they sought. He had become a welcome addition to the group.

Hancock started the conversation as he took a generous sip of the Madeira port. "I am getting confused, there are so many Warrens here," he said, chuckling. "When your brother was at these gatherings, Mercy, there were too many Jameses and now a gaggle of Warrens."

Everyone looked at the young Dr. Warren. His youthful, handsome, somewhat feminine face exuded intelligence and composure, his receding hairline suggesting that the ample forehead was needed to cover a very large brain.

"Mercy thought that since we seem to be headed for war, we needed more Warrens," James Warren lamely joked. The others looked at their host with expressions of feigned pity.

"Why are we here, dear hosts?" Adams asked a bit brusquely, always on task, always pushing.

"We need a plan, and then we need you and Joseph to persuade the Sons of Liberty to execute it," Mercy replied.

Joseph Warren jumped in. "There is a fundamental strategic question: Should we respond to the coming ships full of tea in a way that promotes calm or enthusiastic resistance? When that question is answered, all the rest of our conversation will be about tactics."

"Well, you certainly get right down to it, Joseph. Does everyone agree we should decide this first?" Hancock asked.

Adams felt his control of the discussion slipping away; until now, it had always been he who had guided conversations on strategy. Yet he agreed with Joseph Warren and appreciated his directness. Now Adams needed to persuade the group of his plan. Before he had a chance to respond to the doctor, Mercy interjected her views, which were based in part on plausible rumors.

"We all know," Mercy said, "that if the ships go past Castle William and come into the harbor, British law requires that the tea be unloaded, the duties paid, and there is no turning back. When in port, they have twenty days in which to make payment to the Customs office in King Street. If the ships remain outside of the harbor, they can still return to England with no fuss. I am told our compatriots in New York and Philadelphia are demanding such return trips. We could pursue that path and avoid havoc here."

Then Joseph Warren outlined a strategy, a bold and ingenious one, that could solve a number of problems.

"First, we must resist and do so with the greatest possible publicity and peaceful force. The conflict needs to occur; the opposition to the duties on tea must be clear and emphatic. To allow the ships to return to England still full of tea, with no show of outrage on our part, leaves the question of our rights unanswered. Even the East India Company wanted to eliminate the tax, but the great Prime Minister Lord North has said "No." He will not relent on the principle of Parliament's primacy of taxing power. I recommend we mobilize the Sons of Liberty, possibly a mass meeting at the Liberty Tree, and inspire them to action. Then we visit the consignees of the East India Company to let them know of the dire consequences that accepting and selling the tea will cause. We start with Hutchinson's sons. We can help them remember what happened to those who tried to enforce the Stamp Act. We can get them to relinquish their right to sell tea with the same kind of persuasion." The implied intimidation of Joseph Warren's plan seemed incongruous; as a doctor, he did not seem to be a man inclined to violence, yet his words made sense.

"I like where you are going with this, Joseph," said Adams. "We fully engage the Sons and remind them and all of Boston what the stakes are. I doubt that the money-grubbing Hutchinson will yield to this pressure, but we win either way—if they do yield and agree not to sell East India Company tea, they look weak, as do the British overlords. If they refuse to give up their right to sell the tainted tea, they further inflame our citizens. It remains on us to remind our fellow Bostonians what the stakes are. So full engagement of the Sons is essential. I have one question," Adams said, looking at all of them with intensity.

"What is that, Samuel?" Hancock asked.

"How do we ensure," asked Adams, "that the coming ships sail all the way to port and yet avert the unloading of tea and payment of the duties? For the full righteous fury of the cause to be unleashed, it is essential that the ships enter the harbor. If our public is primed sufficiently, we can be assured of a melee when they try to unload the ships and levy the duties. But if they do bring the tea to port, the British will be within their rights to enforce existing law and require acceptance of the tea and the payment of the duties. How do we deal with this conundrum?"

"If Hutchinson agrees," said Mercy, "the tea could be sent back to England, and our plan will not work. There would be none of the commotion we are trying to create. The only way this works is if Hutchinson refuses the return of the tea."

"I know Hutchinson," said Adams. "He lacks the wisdom to send the tea back. It is always a possibility, but we should proceed with our plan and assume continued stupidity on the part of our governor. So, what should we do?"

Joseph Warren, calm and brilliant, was quick to answer. "The ships will come into port. They will languish there; the tea remains aboard untouched for days. We shall convene the body of people concerned with this, for economic or political reasons, and find ways to keep them engaged and motivated. We shall then ask Rotch, the ship's owner, to seek Hutchinson's permission to return the ships to England with the tea on board. He will refuse, just as Samuel predicts. The evening before the last of the twenty days the shipment can remain unloaded, your Mohawks will board the ships. The Sons of Liberty will provide us all the Mohawks we need, Samuel. The Mohawks will unload the tea and place it where tea likes to be placed: in water. Many of the chests they say are coming from London will find their home in Boston Harbor."

"No duties, no grossly cheap tea," said Mercy, "and we thereby send a strong message to other colonies and to London that things must change, and that once again Boston is leading the way. But how do we make sure the captains take the ships to port?"

"I will take care of that," Adams replied. The silence that hung in the air reflected a simple fact: They did not really want to know what Adams had in mind.

"How," Mercy then asked, "do we make sure our country friends outside of town stand with us? We can't repeat the mistakes we made in response to the massacre. We need them with us this time."

"I have a plan for that, too, Mercy. We will handle this through the committees of correspondence. We will bring our country cousins to join us at Faneuil Hall when the tea ships are at the edge of the harbor. Our neighbors from nearby towns will be part of the solution. We will be united this time," Adams assured everyone.

As the little group disbanded, they knew a new echelon of resistance was about to be reached. They felt the tingle of anticipation that comes with smart and daring plans, the results of which cannot possibly be known, except by the Almighty.

* * *

When the first ship, the *Dartmouth*, anchored below Castle William, its captain, James Hall, was summoned to the Green Dragon to meet with Samuel Adams, Joseph Warren, and several other active members of the committee of correspondence, many of whom were also Sons of Liberty. According to those assembled, Captain Hall said he felt confident crossing the Atlantic Ocean but very nervous about the meeting he had agreed to join. "Men can be much more treacherous than oceans," he stated.

156

The men seated themselves at a table for eight and ordered drinks in an atmosphere of bonhomie for all of them, except the captain.

"How was the trip, James?" Doctor Warren asked, trying to put Hall at ease.

"Cold and slow but without incident. The weather is always savage this time of year, but if you respect the ocean, it is almost always cooperative. All Mother Nature asks of us is respect and understanding." Hall tried to sound relaxed, but his stomach was churning like a turbulent sea.

"That is all we ask of our British rulers," Warren replied, "respect and understanding." This remark elicited cool, subdued chuckles from his colleagues who had experienced neither from the British.

Samuel Adams then spoke, forgoing more small talk.

"Many of us are concerned about some of the cargo you have brought in your whaling vessel, James. The tea has put us in a quandary. Our message—our request—to you is simple. We want you to bring the *Dartmouth* to one of the wharfs. Beyond that, we have no other requests. After that, our communications will be with the ship's owner. John Rotch is a fine man, and we feel good about reasoning with him," Adams said, trying to sound reasonable and calm.

"I understand, Samuel. I understand," Hall replied.

"The last thing we want is violence, James," said Adams, "but I would be remiss if I failed to tell you that some of our fellow citizens have spoken of tarring and feathering people they view as opponents. It does happen. We do not condone that, of course. We just want cooperation, 'respect, and understanding.' But feelings are running very strong, as I think you know."

"I am very aware of that, Samuel. I appreciate your taking the time to apprise me of the sentiments of our fellow citizens, but I know. I am an American and simply a captain trying to do my job. I would much rather transport whale spermaceti to England than bring tea to our shores."

Everyone at the table understood and felt compassion for the *Dartmouth*'s captain. Hall had no more interest in becoming entangled in a political mess than Samuel Adams had in disentangling it. As well, Francis Rotch, the young owner of the *Dartmouth*, was equally unhappy to find himself mired in the controversy. His family and that of John Hancock had engaged in a trade war with one another on the appropriate price of whale oil the decade before, which was one reason many Bostonians did not feel warmly toward Rotch. As well, the Rotches, who were Nantucket Quakers, did not embrace the campaign against Parliament.

Yet Francis Rotch showed some mettle when he agreed to appear in front of a massive crowd, possibly 5,000 citizens, in the Old South Church.

Samuel Adams and his little team had been busy planning and bringing together diverse people, inflaming some, inspiring others, but above all communicating, cajoling, and calling on his fellow citizens to show visible protest. He had made sure the North End Caucus was fully committed so that civic leaders like William Molineux and Paul Revere were on board, and on the South End, the boisterous followers of Ebenezer Mackintosh were in the fold. The Boston Committee of Correspondence engaged in spirited dialogue (as they might describe it) with the various potential consignees of the coming tea, men like Richard Clarke and Hutchinson's sons, who needed to be dissuaded from accepting and selling the tea. The town's selectmen tried to mediate to no avail. As expected, most attempts to dissuade the greedy consignees from accepting the tea failed.

Hutchinson had sought support for his side from the upper body of the legislature, the Council, but they protested taxation without representation, further isolating the governor. He had retreated to his estate in Milton, seven miles away. Adams continued to execute their plan, which included working hand in glove with the *Boston Gazette* editors, Edes and Gille. The two men enjoyed using their paper to keep the pot of resistance boiling. The little band of patriotic conspirators had done their work so well that many Bostonians began to believe that drinking any tea at all, for the moment, was a form of perfidy.

Mercy Otis Warren was one of a very few women who found her way to the large gathering of protest on November 29. The day was gray and cold, and the Old South Church was unusually chilly. The gathering was an unofficial one, which had the benefit of allowing any decisions coming out of it to be extra-legal. Samuel Adams, Joseph Warren, and the Sons of Liberty were among the leaders who convened it, and they had made a point of reaching out to leaders from outside of Boston in the nearby towns and countryside.

Early in the meeting, Samuel Adams pushed three resolutions forward: first, the tea should be returned to England; second, nobody on these shores should pay the duties on it; and third, the tea should be returned in the same vessel that brought it. Enthusiasm for these measures grew as the day wore on and rum was furtively consumed. All the resolutions passed unanimously. Anyone standing in the way of these ideas would have been viewed with scorn. None dared to try.

The mass of men threatened Rotch with "peril" if he unloaded the tea, but Rotch had few good options. The *Dartmouth* could not return to England with the tea unless he had approval from the governor, and the governor would not provide that without the clearance of the Custom House officials. If Rotch broke the law, he would lose the freight charges he had earned for shipping the tea and could have his ship seized by the authorities. Still, he wanted to remain in the good graces of the citizens of Boston.

Meanwhile, the Adams team was carrying out another part of their plan, this one focused on ensuring that the tea was not unloaded clandestinely by their adversaries. They appointed twenty-five men whom they disingenuously termed "Assistants to the Captain and Ship's Crew to take Care that the Tea was not smuggled out of the Ship or the Ship removed out of their Power." Pretending to protect the *Dartmouth* from potentially unruly Boston crowds, they were really keeping it from the merchants who wanted to sell it. By 9 p.m., the "Assistants" had boarded boats at the wharves and rowed out to guard the *Dartmouth*.

The twenty-day clock was ticking, moving toward December 16. As he had been at the beginning of that fateful period, Rotch found himself at center stage at the end of it. If Samuel Adams was the lion and Hutchinson the weasel, young Rotch showed the zigzagging behavior of a squirrel in the middle of a busy street, changing directions frantically to avoid the carriages. He told some men he would send the tea back to England, then told others he had said that under duress.

Rotch's vacillating prompted yet another meeting of concerned citizens in the Old South Meeting House on December 14 to pressure him further. The largest gathering yet, it attracted men from the surrounding towns and countryside. Once again, Rotch told the group he had been forced to say he would return the tea.

Josiah Quincy, who had been John Adams' co-counsel in defending the British soldiers of the massacre, tried to moderate the heated debate. While he was a leader in the Sons of Liberty, many in Boston remembered Quincy's defense of the indefensible, the murderous soldiers. He suggested a way to mitigate the economic damage that would occur to Rotch if the law were violated and Rotch lost his ship. He suggested that townspeople should chip in to pay for the cost of the loss of the *Dartmouth*, offering fifty guineas himself. There were no other takers for this feeble idea.

After more heated pressure, Rotch agreed to request a clearance for the *Dartmouth* from the port's collector, Richard Harrison. Samuel Adams led a delegation of ten to join Rotch in that mission. But Harrison was no fan of the Sons of Liberty, having been attacked by their kind in the wake of the seizure of Hancock's ship, the *Liberty*, in 1768. Harrison consulted with Robert Hallowell, the Boston comptroller, who had also been a victim of mob violence, in his case the 1765 riots following the Stamp Act.

As expected, Harrison told Rotch he had no authority to provide clearance for an illegal voyage.

December 16 finally arrived, the last day to act before the authorities could force compliance with the law, force the unloading of the tea, and force the payment of duties. Most galling of all for the Patriots was that some of the revenue from those duties would pay the salaries of Hutchinson and other civil officials. Once again, thousands of people gathered that morning at the Old South Meeting House, many walking or riding for miles in the muck caused by the cold rain. When told of Harrison's decision, the announcement elicited jeers from all assembled. There was only one man remaining who could override Harrison's decision: Thomas Hutchinson. The seething Body instructed Rotch to ask the governor for permission to return the ship and the tea to England. Rotch would need to ride the seven miles to Hutchinson's estate in the town of Milton, in the cold, wet, and dismal weather, and return with the governor's decision. It needed to occur immediately. Rotch agreed to try. What would Hutchinson decide?

22

Samuel Adams and his team of resisters were confident that Hutchinson would do the ill-advised thing, but they still felt a queasy uncertainty. They were on edge from the moment Rotch mounted his horse for his trip to Milton and the governor's estate. Edes and Gille had recently published a letter in the *Boston Gazette* from a citizen of Philadelphia that they hoped would goad the town of Boston to action:

> Our Tea Consignees have all resigned, and you need not fear; the Tea will not be landed here or at New York. All that we fear is that you will shrink in Boston.

The last sentence of that letter had the desired effect on the citizens of Boston. All of the colonies were watching them; the other colonies seemed to think Boston might be losing its resolve and willingness to be on the cutting edge of resistance. Some of the colonies thought Boston was weak on non-importation. Did the town still have the spine and spirit to resist?

The excitement at the Old South Meeting House was not limited to the thousands assembled there. That afternoon and evening, the entire town of Boston was abuzz with anticipation. Many people in homes and shops were preparing to respond to the governor's actions and to the plan of the leaders at the Old South Meeting House. Small groups of Patriots came together all over town: from under the boughs of the Liberty Tree on the South End to Copp's Hill on the North, in carpenter and cabinet-makers shops, at the Green Dragon and other taverns, in parlors, in warehouses, even in churches. In the Long Room above the *Gazette*'s printing press, Benjamin Edes' son kept the punch bowl full for the Mohawks who had assembled there in anticipation of the evening's events. Many in the town were thinking of Griffin's Wharf and what might happen there that night.

Adams and his team had identified dozens of men who could do what needed to be done. The men had all agreed to disguise themselves as Indians and swear an oath of secrecy to protect one another's identity. They were craftsmen, traders, merchants, and a wide array of townspeople more than willing to be of service. Young blacksmiths, roper apprentices, and other journeymen eagerly engaged in the project, so long as their masters permitted it. One man who did not need permission from anyone was a man recently released from debtor prison: Ebenezer Mackintosh. The shoemaker had hidden his Indian blanket and charcoal behind the Green Dragon, where he was drinking and chatting with Beth Frothingham. Mackintosh appeared haggard; his face was ashen, and the black stubble on his gaunt face betrayed a neglect to his grooming that suggested rock bottom spirits. Beth seemed concerned.

"Ebenezer, you look sad, not well," she said with characteristic candor and compassion.

"I have been better, my dear," he replied, trying to appear lighthearted. "I need to pay more attention to my finances, and I am losing followers. I may be losing the confidence of the Sons of Liberty, as well. I fear they think I lack self-control. The only efforts that give me meaning are those supporting the resistance, events like what will be occurring tonight. I have recruited many of my "chickens" from the South End to help dispose of the tea, if that should become necessary. I cannot wait."

"I envy you, Ebenezer. I wish I could join you. I have an idea I hope you will consider," Beth said, her blue eyes twinkling.

"Pray tell, what is your idea?" Mackintosh asked.

When Beth told him, he quickly agreed to do it, should he be working on Griffin's Wharf that evening. Mackintosh then asked about Otis.

"Since the Resolution of Thanks from the town he received three years ago, he has been despondent," she replied, "and as you know well, he is erratic and unbalanced."

Mackintosh felt unsure how much to ask Beth about Otis. Had she and Otis remained close? Had they been intimate? He could not bring himself to ask these questions. He did, however, better understand how a man comes to feel estranged, lonely, and ashamed. Mackintosh confessed his own feelings of shame and his sense of being betrayed by his social "betters." Men who had used him in the past to rally thousands in protest now treated him like a pariah. Mackintosh said he remained deeply committed to the cause, however, and even thrilled at the prospect of continuing to play a role in the public protest.

Beth listened patiently and looked at the shoemaker with respect and compassion. She knew what he had done for the cause, still believed he had special qualities, and told him so. She acknowledged that Mackintosh was a man destined to be used and unappreciated, yet he remained a Patriot.

Her words were a balm to Mackintosh's soul. Color came back to his face and his eyes regained the light Beth had seen years before. His slouch vanished; he felt his spine stiffen.

"God bless you, young lady," Mackintosh said, reaching for his pocket to pay for his ale. Beth stopped him.

"This is on me," she said. "I just ask you to do what I encouraged you to do; that is far more than recompense for a free beer, my good man." He expressed his gratitude and left the tavern.

When Beth recounted to Samuel Adams the whole conversation with Mackintosh at the Green Dragon, it made him feel at once sheepish and grateful that Mackintosh would continue to lead the protest. Would there need to be continued protest? That would depend on what kind of response Hutchinson had given Rotch, the beleaguered owner of the *Dartmouth*.

Word came to the Old South Meeting House that Rotch was close, returning from the meeting with the governor and soon to deliver Hutchinson's verdict. The swarm of Bostonians were in a near-frenzy of anticipation. When Rotch entered the hall, his slumping body told them what they needed to know. Hutchinson had said "no" without equivocation. The explosion of disapproving shouts could be heard blocks away from the Meeting House.

"Will you send the tea back to England anyway?" the crowd asked.

"No," Rotch said. It would ruin him.

"Will you unload the tea?" the crowd asked.

Rotch said "no," the consignees would not take it (although it was unclear if that was true).

Rotch could not move in any direction. And the following day, the customs officials were scheduled to seize his ship. There was nothing he could do. The assembled mass treated him with respect and understanding and even voted approval of his conduct.

As the proceedings were finally concluding, a contingent of the Body had already slipped out of the hall to join the other

Mohawks who were prepared for the next step. The prominent men who had convened the meeting and presided over it were careful not to join the throng about to converge on Griffin's Wharf. Unnoticed, Mercy joined the mass of men and women headed for the harbor.

A calm darkness settled early on the harbor that chilly December night. The moon was but a thin sliver, yet there were so many lanterns in the jostling crowd on the wharf that the scene took on the hue of a strange kind of daylight. The convergence on Griffin's Wharf was orderly, reflecting the careful planning that Adams and his colleagues had undertaken. Men with smudged faces, wearing Indian blankets, walked briskly, with calm focus, onto the wharf and then onto the three ships. The Mohawks were led by eighteen men who acted with clarity of purpose. Each of the three ships was visited by fifty men who, at the outset, mimicked the sounds of real Mohawks, both in chants and whoops. They boisterously contrived nonsensical words for all to hear. Although no rational person would take these men for real Indians, the disguise did serve a real purpose—it would provide just enough cover to protect the men from legal prosecution. The disguise also gave permission to unleash in some men a kind of wild energy and enthusiasm that proved infectious.

Still, the whole episode was done with its own unique decorum. The captains and mates were politely asked to turn over the necessary keys, candles, hoisting tackle, and ropes needed to remove the tea, and all of them acquiesced. The Mohawks were respectfully implored to spare the other cargo and be gentle with fragile items, and the Mohawks happily and carefully complied.

The massive crowd of spectators provided an easy target for the British guns on the nearby warships, so there was some trepidation at the beginning. The teeming mass clearly provided the Mohawks with both moral support and actual protection from British gunfire. The massacre was still fresh in everybody's mind. If the British tried to use deadly force again, it was sure to turn the large mass of Patriots into an angry and unforgiving mob. The British had the guns, but the Americans had the people. Admiral John Montagu observed the activities from his ship, but he did not act. He understood he could have stopped the Mohawks in their tracks if he had been asked to intervene. (He later commented, "If they had, I could easily have prevented the execution of this plan but must have endangered the Lives of many innocent People by firing upon the Town.") The British leaders in charge that night had a brief outbreak of good sense.

A significant number of the Mohawks were men well-acquainted with ships in one way or another, and their deep familiarity with such vessels proved invaluable in this mission. They knew how to find and handle cargo. Mackintosh was not in this category, but his past actions had gained him the respect of the tough men who worked on the wharfs of Boston. The shoemaker had gathered his "chickens," as he strangely called his men from the South End, and they joined the mixed assembly in undertaking the tasks at hand. Early in the assault, Mackintosh remembered what Beth had asked him to do: start a one word chant of O T I S, which his followers did for ten minutes in an otherwise strangely quiet night.

The work itself required great strength and effort: Each crate of tea weighed hundreds of pounds, and there were hundreds of crates. Early in the evening, the men were very quiet, almost solemn in this endeavor. The sound of hatchets cracking open the crates of tea punctuated the stillness.

The men sequentially emptied the ships of tea, starting with the *Dartmouth*. It was three hours of strenuous and well-coordinated work. Except for some strained backs and raw hands, there were no serious injuries. Because it was low tide, the tea itself was close to the surface, and in some cases, youngsters needed to be used to tip some protruding crates into the shallow harbor. They destroyed 342 chests of tea weighing 92,000 pounds. As the various Mohawks left the ships and walked off of Griffin's Wharf, the enthusiastic crowd cheered them, patted their backs, and reveled in the mood of defiant celebration.

John Adams later said of the Tea Party: "This is the most magnificent Movement of all. There is Dignity, a Majesty, a Sublimity in this last Effort of the Patriots that I greatly admire. This Destruction of the Tea is so bold, so daring, so firm, intrepid and inflexible, and it must have important Consequences and so lasting that I cannot but consider it as an Epoch in History."

Hutchinson later said of the event: "This is the boldest stroke which has yet been struck in America. The body of people had gone too far to recede...and open and general revolt must be the consequence."

The news of the occurrences in Boston arrived in London by means of John Hancock's ship *Hayley* on January 19, 1774 when it landed in Dover. The full meaning of the tea's destruction was quickly understood by those in London, both supporters and foes of the American colonies. Benjamin Franklin explained the extent and nature of the British rulers' reaction. King George simply said, "I am much hurt that the instigation of bad men hath again drawn the people of Boston to take such unjustifiable steps; but I trust by degrees tea will find its way there."

The king greatly underestimated the scope of the town's resistance. His ministers and minions were far less sanguine and forgiving. The powers in London, including the prime minister, Lord North, grappled with exactly what to do. Just as the planners of the Tea Party had calculated, the British rulers determined that the idea of bringing the Mohawks to justice would be fruitless. Apparently, some thought was given to prosecuting James Warren, Samuel Adams, John Hancock, and Thomas Cushing for treason, but Solicitor General Alexander Wedderburn felt there was insufficient evidence to convict them, although he believed treasonable offenses had occurred.

America's man in London, Benjamin Franklin, could no longer be the moderating influence who had helped the British leaders soften their responses to the past "offenses." After Franklin confessed to purloining the letters from Hutchinson, the tide of goodwill turned strongly against him in the corridors of power. He was publicly derided and stripped of one of his duties, deputy postmaster general of North America, a job at which he had excelled.

Lord North and his ministers were eager beyond words to respond to the tea's destruction, to punish Boston. As Lord Chancellor Apsley said, it was desirable "to mark out Boston and separate that town from the rest of (the) Delinquents." Some, like Lord Dartmouth, believed that even the other colonies in America would see the necessity of punishing Boston. Lord Chief Justice Mansfield gave voice to these men's sentiments that Parliament would "temporize no longer." It was almost as if the very manhood of the British leaders had been mocked. Lord North himself was virtually frothing at the mouth.

After all that had occurred in the preceding decade, it is hard to understand why the British leaders thought the proud citizens of

Boston would cower. Once again, blustering, powerful men showed an absence of good judgment. It was as if Lord North and his ministers had met, not in Cabinet but in a tavern, and drunk excessively from the twin potion of power and revenge. They hurled out one idea after another, all to show the Americans who were the rulers and who were the ruled. The essence of their anger could have been expressed like this:

"Let's shut down all commerce into Boston Harbor, except maybe food and arms for our men, until they pay for the tea and admit guilt!" Lord Dartmouth declared.

"They have too much self-government. They shouldn't select who is in the council; we should. And they shouldn't select juries; our people should. Same with judges, in times of crisis," bellowed Lord Chief Justice Mansfield. "And move the capital out of Boston to Salem! Limit all these blasted town meetings to once a year; they just incite the rabble!"

"And our fine soldiers should be billeted wherever the governor wants, like taverns or vacant houses," Lord North cried out, "and if one of our officials is tried for a capital offense, let the governor change the venue of the trial to give our people a fair chance!"

All these ideas were passed into law—the Boston Port Bill; the Massachusetts Government Bill; and the Administration of Justice Act, among others. Known as the Coercive Acts, the Americans called them "Intolerable Acts." There was opposition to the English overlords in England, as well, but the voices of men like Edmund Burke and Isaac Barré were ignored. Burke said, "An Englishman is the unfittest person on earth to argue another Englishman into slavery."

The day the Boston Port Act went into effect, June 1, 1774, Thomas Hutchinson slithered out of Boston bound for England. The unhappy tenure of his failed governorship was over. While he received some accolades from wealthy merchants, a vast majority of Bostonians were happy to see him go. Samuel Adams' relentless campaign against Hutchinson had succeeded. As the church bells tolled in the town of Boston, some said they were bells of mourning for the closing of the port, but others heard a peel of celebration heralding the departure of Hutchinson. The man who would replace him had been approached and enlisted the preceding February.

The man called upon to enforce the Intolerable Acts was a general, Thomas Gage (who had been a comrade-in arms with George Washington during the French-Indian Wars). He would serve a dual role as the colony's new governor and military commander. There could be no more obvious and ominous signal from the British of their ultimate intent. Attempts to govern with the consent of the governed were now finished. The iron hand of British rule was about to show the unruly Americans who was who.

The British rulers decided that everyone in and near Boston needed to be taught a lesson. Lord North, General Gage, and Gage's seasoned troops would be the teachers.

Part VI

Secrets and Blood

≈ **23** ≈

The downward spiral Mercy Otis Warren had predicted was accelerating like a comet headed for Earth, the sparks sure to light up the American sky.

In the following months, Bostonians were on edge, more attuned than ever to the many British acts of brutality and the government's use of arbitrary power. Every other man seemed to wear a red coat. The soldiers would stop shopkeepers and dockworkers alike, for no good reason other than to strut their power. Mercy had become defensive and angry. Such was her frame of mind when she received a note from her sister-in-law. Ruth seemed surprisingly eager to meet after years of cool estrangement. Mercy agreed but insisted she visit the Otis home, so she could take her leave if the conversation turned in the wrong direction.

On a cool September morning, Mercy approached what had been her brother's home, a place where James Otis spent less and less time; a frosty abode to Mercy even at the height of summer. Yet Ruth exuded warm hospitality when she opened the door.

"Thank you for meeting with me, Mercy." Ruth spoke slowly, calmly, with a serenity Mercy found interesting and attractive. "I know we have grown distant from one another, which I regret." Ruth's cadence and tone suggested she had practiced reciting the exact words. "I wanted to meet for two reasons: to connect with you again and to ask your advice."

After a long pause, Mercy said, "I am happy to renew our friendship, Ruth. And what advice might you need?"

Ruth handed Mercy a cup of tea. Then placing her own teacup on its saucer, she stood, then kneeled in front of Mercy, a bizarre and totally unexpected posture from a stately, dignified woman, as if she were engaging in some kind of sacred act.

"I have prayed and thought, and thought and prayed. I have prayed to our Lord for guidance and inspiration. He keeps telling me I need to find a better way to connect with my husband. Despite his derangement, I want to make amends, even with our differences. I just can't live like this anymore."

170

"Is there something more, Ruth?" Mercy asked, genuinely curious.

"It is just wrong for a husband and wife to be like this," Ruth replied. "We should be able to reach out to one another. We have failed our children by failing to do that. I want them to know their father and I can still exhibit warmth toward one another. The feeling has taken me over. I think it would be best if I asked his forgiveness, Mercy, even though I do not feel I have done anything really wrong."

"Have you talked to your husband, Ruth?" Mercy asked. "Have you asked this of him?"

"No, I have not. That raises the second thing I ask of you, Mercy. I need your advice. How should I approach your brother. What should I do?" Ruth was begging for answers.

Mercy shook her head and remained silent. No appropriate words came to her mind, a mind that could use words more masterfully than anyone else could in Boston. Finally, she spoke.

"You have been an unwitting accomplice to the likes of Robinson, Bernard, Hutchinson, and many others," Mercy said, feeling her gorge rise. "It is very difficult for me to look beyond that. Hutchinson has done all he could to malign my brother, and often with sheer lies. Do you disavow these evil men?"

Now Ruth created the silence. Her delay suggested she still sided with the likes of Hutchinson. She was asking herself how honest she should be about how very difficult it had been to live with Otis. He had become a man whose primary love was resistance rather than his wife. He ignored her needs, rarely truly listened. He was a good man but one who had ignored his wife and made no serious effort to understand her. They lived in different worlds.

"Yes, we are very different people, but we loved each other once. I really cannot say more, Mercy," Ruth replied. "What is your advice?"

Mercy responded in a soft voice. "His challenges and demons are legion already. He may lack the resilience to make amends. So my advice is to go to him and tell him the things you have just told me. Know that there may be no reconciliation, but try to convey respect to him and some degree of affection. If you can summon up some love, that is his best balm. Try to maintain your dignity and protect his when you talk to him. Give your marriage a kind of loving eulogy. Honor the period when it was good."

Ruth nodded her head without comment. Then Mercy added, "And I have a suggestion that might provide some measure of healing for him, a way that could soften his heart toward you, if you are up to doing this."

"What is it?"

Mercy proposed a course of action that could quietly help the resistance, and Ruth listened intently. Mercy then rose, stretched her arms out, embraced Ruth, and said, with a softened heart, "Now go forth and sin no more, my child." Ruth bowed, another strange gesture for her, and bid her sister-in-law farewell. Mercy walked out the door, believing the cause had a new and unexpected ally.

Ruth was to follow Mercy's suggestion the following year, a year of the utmost consequence.

24

March 5, 1775 was the fifth anniversary of the Boston Massacre, and once again, Samuel Adams had planned and orchestrated the commemorating event with care. Since March 5 fell on a Sunday that year, the service at the Old South Meeting House was held the following day. This year's speaker would be the young Dr. Joseph Warren, nearly twenty years Adams' junior. The respected doctor had cared for Whigs and Tories, Patriots and Loyalists, alike. He had already garnered admiration from many quarters of the town. A good number of women were in the crowd as well, possibly moved by the fact that the handsome Dr. Warren had lost his beloved wife Betsy two years before, making him an appealing widower, albeit one with four young children.

One group was not as enamored of the young doctor: the powers in London and their local servants in Boston. At the first meeting of the Continental Congress in Philadelphia in September of 1774, Paul Revere delivered copies of the *Suffolk Resolves*. It was viewed as a radical manifesto by Loyalists. It denounced the Coercive Acts, sanctioned civil disobedience, and announced the calling of a Provincial Congress in Concord, a proposed extralegal government. And it ominously required the local militias to renounce loyalty to the existing British government and to "acquaint themselves with the art of war." Remarkably, all the colonies approved the document and it was accepted unanimously, although there were unspoken misgivings.

The author of the *Suffolk Resolves* was Dr. Joseph Warren.

That may have explained the larger than usual attendance by British soldiers. Dr. Warren's speech was given when a thick British bravado was in the air, a display of false courage that rarely ends well. Before the March 5 event, General Gage himself had reputedly said that if there was a single man of the King's troops killed in any of their towns, he would burn it to the ground, a statement that circulated widely and further inflamed the British soldiers and the citizens of Massachusetts. The Redcoats who assembled in the meetinghouse to listen to the young doctor lacked any spirit of respectful solemnity. Indeed, they exuded belligerence, made more intense because Samuel Adams was the moderator. The British had grown to hate him with a passion.

The meetinghouse was crammed to the walls. On the Patriot side, the core stalwarts included John Hancock, Dr. Benjamin Church, William Cooper, and James and Mercy Warren. James Otis and Beth Frothingham stood in the back of the hall, near Ebenezer Mackintosh, engrossed. The crowd pulsated with patriot fervor but remained controlled. The speech's content would change that.

After introductory comments, Dr. Warren took the stage and stated modestly that his remarks would never be able to equal in eloquence those of the previous year's speakers, including John Hancock, but "with sincerity, equal to theirs, I mourn over my bleeding country." Prompted and encouraged by Adams and Hancock to remind the audience of the Wrongs perpetrated by the British and the Savagery of the Massacre itself, Dr. Warren recalled for the assembled the bleeding red in the white snow of March 5, 1770. "The baleful images of terror crowd around me, and discontented ghosts with hollow groans, appear to solemnize the anniversary of the fifth of March," he said. (He refrained from waving the bloody shirt that had been a prop at earlier anniversary events.)

These were not words of reconciliation. The British officers frequently interrupted Warren and even laughed at his comments, eliciting strong and angry shouts from the assembled crowd. Warren would go on to claim that Independence was not the aim of him or his allies, adding, "However difficult the combat, you will never decline it when freedom is the prize."

When Samuel Adams followed Warren to suggest the appointment of the following year's speaker at the massacre anniversary event, his words were even more excessive and inflammatory, including the phrase "Bloody Massacre." The British soldiers bellowed out "Fie! Fie!" in the loudest possible voices they had. Those in the distant balconies heard "Fire! Fire!" and believing the building was ablaze, according to one later Tory report, they "bounced out of the windows, and swarmed downs the gutters, like rats into the streets."

The confusion was magnified by the coincidental appearance of a British regiment of regulars beating their drums, which some patriots took to be a signal of an imminent attack, causing them to scurry for cover. Calm was eventually restored, for which Samuel Adams argued that his allied Whigs, not the Redcoats, deserved the credit. Indeed, the "moderator" indicated that if the civilians had so desired, no British officer would have been left alive. Tensions persisted in the streets, however, and taunts and heckling between the patriots and the British were rampant. As James Otis and Beth strolled away from the meetinghouse, a gaggle of British regulars strutted toward them. Otis had not been seen in public for months.

"So, who let you out, Otis? Aren't you supposed to be out in the country where no one can see you? We thought you had been removed from town for our protection!" one of the soldiers shouted. The men circled Otis and Beth, jeering and laughing.

"Ignore their jibes, Beth; they are buffoons," Otis said. The Redcoats crowded closer to the couple, blocking their path.

"Excuse me, sir, but let us pass," Otis said with simple gentility. The soldiers stood fast, sneering. Unbeknownst to the soldiers, a fast-gathering crowd of townspeople had formed, converging from both ends of Milk Street. The familiar voice of Ebenezer Mackintosh boomed forth, "Is there some kind of problem, gentlemen?" The soldiers were surrounded by nearly one hundred unarmed men who moved confidently toward the armed soldiers. Then Mackintosh, a man who felt he had nothing left to lose, brashly added, "Are you going to shoot us, too? Go ahead; you know you can get away with murder, you spineless squeeze crabs!"

There was a startled silence. Then two of the soldiers grabbed their rifles, but they were interrupted when the largest of them, the only officer, shouted "No!" He added, "We will deal with these people, and many others, in a more suitable way later."

"What is that supposed to mean?" Mackintosh asked.

The large British officer did not answer; he smirked and told his men to move on.

Otis and Beth made their way to the Manufactory House and Beth's apartment. She worked to cheer him up; Otis had frequently endured being mocked by British soldiers and even some provincial Loyalists, and it always dampened his spirits. His friendship with Beth was one of the few sources of succor to him.

Otis' wife got her support and stimulation from a very different source. Ruth Cunningham Otis had always had an easy time with the British officials and some of their wives. Inspired by her earlier conversation with Mercy, she continued to cultivate a new friend, Margaret Gage, the governor's wife.

Ruth enjoyed being with Margaret for tea, a weekly ritual they looked forward to every Monday afternoon. The two women had met at a Merrywell party and taken to one another like long-lost sisters. They spent that evening at Merrywell's laughing and gossiping before and after dinner, just the two of them. Margaret was equal to Ruth in sheer beauty, her lush brown hair and eyes and her well-proportioned stature were attractive to anyone in her presence. Her face conveyed a pensive spirit when it was not laughing or slyly smirking at Ruth's wit. The move to Boston had been difficult for her. After her vibrant social life in New York, Boston seemed boring, dull. Margaret was grateful for her new friend Ruth, whose adult companionship also provided relief from the Gage's seven children.

"Ruth, I feel like I have finally found someone I can confide in," said Margaret, sipping her tea that Monday afternoon, "someone I can trust. Being American-born, I have never felt fully accepted by the English, and being married to Thomas Gage, I know that many Bostonians look askance at me."

"My dear woman," Ruth replied, "I could write a book about being looked askance at. My husband and his strange behavior have made people look at him with puzzlement and me with pity."

"How is your husband, Ruth?" Margaret asked. "It is such a shame; he is reputed to be such a brilliant man, and now he is deranged. You must be a saint to live with this, and to raise your children and carry on with dignity." She spoke like a woman who had very recently arrived in Boston, unaware that the Otises had not lived together for years.

"It has been the challenge of my life, Margaret," Ruth said, her eyes downcast. "His politics have driven a deep and hopeless wedge in our family. Two of my children have turned against me. The oldest, dear Elizabeth, is my only real child, I am afraid."

"We both belong in England, Ruth," Margaret replied. "People are more tolerant there, more civilized. They are our people."

The words were poignant for Ruth to hear, because, like Margaret, she was American-born, yet her heart had always resided in England. But because her husband was the man he was, the idea of moving there had never been worth a mention. The agreement she had made with Mercy during their unusual visit, coupled with her desire to bridge the gulf with her husband, were taking Ruth down a new path even she did not fully understand. Although she had rejected the kind of resistance her husband had embraced, she was on the threshold of serving the Patriots' cause, and most significantly at that. Just how and when that would occur was not yet clear, but she sensed Margaret Gage might be part of the answer.

"I am so thankful for our friendship, Margaret. Words cannot express my gratitude," Ruth said, walking over to her friend and bending over to embrace her.

"No, I am the lucky one, dear Ruth," Margaret said with conviction.

Margaret expressed her appreciation of having a woman friend who reminded her of her own softness of spirit, her aversion to the kind of violence General Gage had been forced to engage with and might be part of again. Margaret's husband increasingly cursed Samuel Adams and John Hancock; the general could and would forgive everyone else, he had told his wife repeatedly, but never those two. Margaret told Ruth this, not knowing of her real fondness for Hancock, a fondness that could even move her to help Hancock's cause.

Ruth now had a pathway to learning the thinking of the most powerful man in Boston and, indeed, the entire colony. Her new role in extracting information from such a trusting woman as Margaret Gage infused her with guilt, yet it injected her with a ripple of excitement. Ruth also was concerned that no harm should come to John Hancock, one of the few "patriots" with whom she felt a deep kinship. If General Gage was bent on getting Hancock, Ruth needed to know.

Thomas Gage was a man with considerable experience and four thousand troops in Boston. He had been selected to subdue Boston once and for all. His face exuded more calm stability than daring, with its drooping brown eyes, high forehead, long angular nose, and rounded chin. Yet if Gage did not look like a hero, England was the most powerful nation on Earth. It was rich with well-trained professional soldiers and equipment that was unsurpassed. The recent French-Indian War ensured an ample number of battle-hardened men. Britain knew how to fight, and the leaders in London wanted action. General Gage had been awaiting instructions from London in response to a report he had sent describing the situation in Boston. Finally on April 16, the HMS *Falcon* sailed into Boston Harbor with the instructions Gage needed.

Lord Dartmouth summarized the sentiments of Lord North, his Cabinet, and King George III. "The King's Dignity, and the Honor and Safety of the Empire, require that, in such a Situation, Force should be repelled by Force."

Gage also had information that provided him with a concrete mission: a rebel informant had told the British of a large cache of arms in Concord. Gage had already sent out expeditions to gather intelligence about towns in the countryside, notably a misadventure in Salem. The episode in Salem was instructive, and had greatly embarrassed the British overlords.

On February 25, Gage had 240 men sail from Boston to Marblehead and then march to Salem to find a cache of cannon barrels. When he reached the town, the people of Salem impeded him and his troops, preventing them from crossing a key bridge. Captain Alexander Leslie, the British leader, found himself stymied at every turn. His brief verbal exchange with the local militia leader, Captain Felt, said it all:

Captain Leslie: "By God I will not be defeated!"

Captain Felt: "You must acknowledge that you have been already baffled."

Then Captain Leslie proclaimed that he was on the King's Highway and could not be stopped from crossing the drawbridge. An unflappable old man named James Barr replied, "It is not the King's Highway; it is a road built by the owners of the lots on the other side, and no king, country, or town has anything to do with it."

In the end, Captain Leslie's choice was either to fire on the unruly Americans or take his troops back to Boston. He did not want another "massacre." He chose the latter course of action.

The Redcoats learned two things that day: a strong spirit of resistance was growing throughout the land, and local militias could be activated very quickly in the rural communities. Gage was feeling truly squeezed, from impatient leaders in London and the impatient soldiers under his command, some of whom had just been humiliated. He believed the time for a show of force had now arrived.

The use of that power would be focused on acquiring the armaments hidden in Concord and intimidating anyone standing between the Redcoats and those arms.

Secrecy was of paramount importance for an effective execution of his planned assault. Gage prided himself on his ability to control the flow of information. Only three men knew of the plan, and all were totally trustworthy. And Gage had mentioned it briefly to his wife, Margaret. Margaret, in turn, had told only one person, and only after procuring a solemn vow that this information would remain completely confidential. If Margaret Gage could not trust Ruth Otis, whom could she possibly trust?

Joseph Warren had a very unexpected and fateful encounter in his office shortly after Ruth met with Margaret Gage. On April 17, Ruth made an unlikely visit to the doctor's office, but it was not for medical help. Dr. Warren had become the mastermind of the Patriots' efforts to learn of British military intentions. Warren's brilliance and trustworthiness, combined with his ardent commitment to the Cause, made him the perfect leader for this kind of work. But he insisted on providing medical care for British and Americans alike.

Dr. Warren had been caring for a low-level customs official who had been tarred and feathered by the unruly men who had come to resist, and even hate, the British occupiers. The ruthless pouring of the hot pine tar would create blisters on the victim's skin and required salve and ointment to help heal the pour soul who had been attacked. When he saw the beautiful, perfectly groomed Mrs. Otis in the waiting room, Dr. Warren was surprised and intrigued. He finished with his patient and signaled her into his office, ahead of other patients who had been waiting much longer than Ruth, the wealthy Loyalist.

"What brings you here, Ruth?" he asked. "What ails you?"

"Nothing ails me, Joseph," she replied softly, followed by a brief, awkward silence. Her throat became constricted and, suddenly, her mouth was as dry as dust.

"I have information that you might find interesting," she replied. "But you must tell no one your source. I am deadly serious, Joseph. And I understand you have every reason to disbelieve me. I will tell you my source and what I know if you give me your solemn word that you will not tell a soul where you heard this. You must go to your grave without disclosing this. Can you make that promise, Joseph?"

Warren had been skeptical, even incredulous, but this unexpected meeting had taken on an air of such bizarreness that the doctor believed what Ruth was going to disclose might actually be true. He agreed to her request. The sincerity on his face, and his reputation, caused her to believe him.

"I have befriended Margaret Gage, a fine woman," Ruth said. "She has told me something that might be helpful to your cause, much as I still disagree with that cause. My sister-in-law, Mercy, is the reason I am here. I feel odd to be here, but I am driven to tell you this, Joseph."

"Please, Ruth, what is it?" the doctor asked, thinking of the patients in his waiting room and eager to make this meeting brief and productive.

"Late tomorrow, the British will send a large expedition of men to Lexington and Concord to purloin the armaments that have been hidden there by the rebels and their militia. There will be multiple groups, descending from different directions. Their overwhelming force is designed to intimidate the locals as well as grab the muskets and powder and all the other things. They expect that their forces will be so large that the so-called Patriots are unlikely to resist," Ruth said with a strangely dazed monotone. "And might I add that General Gage is targeting two men in particular."

"Who might they be? No, let me guess: Samuel Adams and John Hancock," the doctor said. Ruth simply nodded.

"Why are you telling me this, Ruth, and why should I believe you?" Dr. Warren asked. "Indeed, why should I not believe this is a ruse that your Loyalist friends and the Redcoats have come up with? How can I possibly trust you, Ruth, after all you have said you believe?"

"Well, Margaret Gage trusts me, Joseph. But you don't have to." Ruth turned toward the door and left without a farewell.

Joseph Warren needed no time to decide; he believed Ruth and he knew he needed to act quickly. Patriots from Boston to Concord needed to know what Ruth had told him. He needed to connect with Revere and Dawes at once.

As Ruth made her way home, she was debating with herself whether she should tell her husband what she had done. Of course, he would be surprised and grateful, but his behavior had become so erratic that she was not sure Otis would believe her or what he would do with the information. The justification for her hesitancy was confirmed when she entered their house. Otis was pacing the floor in the entryway and fuming.

"You probably knew this, Ruth, but I just learned that Elizabeth plans to marry that Brown fellow. 'Captain Brown' as he insists on being called, the arrogant prig. How can she do this to me?" Otis bellowed, following Ruth into their spacious parlor.

Ruth had always liked the young British soldier, finding him very attractive, and she had actively encouraged her oldest daughter to marry him. She knew Otis hated the man and felt deeply estranged from Elizabeth, but Ruth felt Brown was "perfect" for her Loyalist daughter.

Turning to her husband with a look of exasperation and sad resolve, she said, "Excuse me, James, but she is not doing it to you; she is doing it for herself and her future. The marriage will occur, and I hope you will at least consider a path of quiet acceptance. If not for her, do so for Mary and Jemmy. We do not need more turmoil in this house. We have come to a modicum of goodwill and civility, and raging against Elizabeth's future husband can only upset everyone. There is really nothing you can do."

Otis had become all too accustomed to having decisions made without his advice and consent. This was just a more poignant reminder of his impotence in the family. He sputtered incoherently, but he did so more quietly. The lava of his fury gradually cooled, and he withdrew once again into that lonely empty room of his soul.

Then James Otis III, seventeen, bounded into the room, causing his father's spirits to come back to life. Young Jemmy had filled out to a powerful, compact young man, attractive to other young men for his energy and bonhomie (now lacking in his father) and attractive to young women because of his innocent charm. For Otis, Jemmy's total loyalty to himself and complete commitment to the cause provided him with a slender lifeline of hope and spirit.

The younger Otis walked past his mother, slapped his father on the back, and made his way to the kitchen, not noticing he had just walked past yet another painful exchange between his parents. Ruth loved her son, but she was at a loss how to bridge the political chasm that had rent the family asunder. Jemmy's expressions of affection rang hollow to Ruth, and his father did little to try to help his son connect with his mother. Otis wallowed in the righteousness of the cause—in Ruth's mind, a form of moral preening he could not see and would not understand.

The warm unthinking trust that should bind a family had long since been dissolved. If Ruth were to tell her son what she had told Dr. Warren, might it have moved the family in a new direction? Perhaps, but she knew if she disclosed that meeting to Jemmy, all of Boston would likely know within a day, and the number of her remaining Loyalist friends would dwindle even more.

Ruth would consider telling Otis and Jemmy what she had done at another time. And of what consequence was it anyway?

25

A new vibration had come into Massachusetts in April of 1775, one that not only buzzed with the bees of spring and rebirth of the lush greenery that adorned the various small communities of the colony, but a vibration of alert excitement among the farmers and townspeople. Lexington was now at the center of a subtle, seismic shimmer. By outward appearances, familiar landmarks provided a sense of reassuring continuity, such as Lexington Green with its thick grass giving off the special fragrance that comes from a recent rain. But April 18 in Lexington would be anything but calm.

Samuel Adams and John Hancock had been in the area of Concord for the meeting of the Provincial Congress. They were staying in the home of Jonas Clarke, Lexington's Congregational minister, a place Hancock knew well; Clarke had succeeded Hancock's grandfather in the pulpit. It was from that very house that Hancock's uncle Thomas had taken him away from Lexington and into the world of Boston business. The white two-story house looked almost directly down the road toward the Green. The prominent place was easy to find for the messenger dispatched from the Black Horse Tavern by Eldridge Gerry, a fellow patriot. The note, which arrived that evening at eight o'clock, was a warning that reported the arrival of Major Mitchell of the advance patrol, a man who had been given verbal orders to capture both Hancock and Adams. As Reverend Clarke recalled:

> Mr. Hancock in particular had been, more than once, personally insulted, by some officers of the troops, in Boston; it was not without some just grounds supposed, that under the cover of darkness sudden arrest, if not assassination might be attempted.

Samuel Adams was even more reviled by the British than Hancock. Adams had been the butt of British ridicule and intimidation for years, a common refrain being that Adams could not bear to look at hemp rope because it suggested the prospect of him hanging from it one day.

On this momentous night, Hancock and Adams were marked men, yet neither acted as if they really believed that.

Hancock wrote a confident, reassuring note back to Gerry. Both he and Hancock seemed calm, ensconced in the home of the respected Reverend Clarke. The Clarke home was full that night; in addition to the minister and his wife, Lucy, there was Hancock's fiancée, Dorothy "Dolly" Quincy, and his beloved Aunt Lydia, both of whom had fled the British-occupied Boston on April 7. They felt somewhat reassured by the presence of nine members of the Lexington militia who surrounded the house to protect them from a possible visit by Major Mitchell and his small band of regulars.

Before retiring for the evening, Adams and Hancock engaged in friendly banter, trying to calm the nerves of the others and themselves, trying to take their minds off of what might occur that evening. Their conviviality covered up a past between the two that had been occasionally troubled. Three years earlier, Hancock had proposed an inquiry into Boston finances designed to embarrass Adams, who oversaw the town's lotteries. But the petty differences of the two had deeply worried their friends, who ultimately succeeded in reconciling the two.

"Well, John, it looks like you are going to be a commoner like the rest of us. Since Boston is now fully occupied by the British and the assets of the House of Hancock reside there, where is your wealth now?" Adams asked cheerfully.

The unflappable Hancock smiled at Adams and first pointed to his heart, then his head, and then stretched out his arms expansively. "My wealth is everywhere, dear Samuel. Were you not so blind, you would understand that yours is, too," Hancock said radiantly.

The chatter continued against the backdrop of the crackling fire and knitting needles chiming. As they all became drowsy, shortly before midnight, everyone in the Clarke home retired to their respective rooms. They would not have the opportunity to fall into a deep slumber because as they lay between sleep and wakefulness, everyone in the house heard a horse galloping down the road from the Lexington Green. They could hear a harsh exchange of words between the militia's Sergeant William Munroe and the new arrival, and then a loud knocking on the front door.

When Reverend Clarke leaned out of the bedroom window to inquire who was at the front steps, Hancock's head appeared at another window and said in an unruffled tone, " Come in, Revere; we are not afraid of you."

Paul Revere had already had a long night riding out of Boston and warning those on the path to Lexington and Concord of the gathering swarm of British regulars who were on the way. Shortly after Revere's arrival, he was joined by William Dawes, the other herald of British regulars in the countryside. Dawes had slipped across the Boston Neck before the British sealed it off. Joseph Warren had stressed the need to find, and warn, Adams and Hancock, and Revere knew where to look. While Revere was a meticulous craftsman and silversmith who was unrushed in creating excellent artwork and silver gems, tonight allowed no time. This avid Son of Liberty now had a simple mission: let the patriots in the countryside know of the advancing regulars, and keep Adams and Hancock safe.

"They are closing in quickly, and you two are the primary human targets, as I hope you know," Revere said, barely acknowledging the startled Clarkes who observed the visitor in their flowing nightgowns.

"Gerry has told us of Mitchell and his regulars, but they are likely on their way to Concord now," Hancock said.

"You two must leave and make yourselves scarce. Gage wants you, and he has been under enormous pressure from London to take you out of circulation. You are not safe," Revere said, sending shivers down the spine of Hancock's fiancée, Dolly Quincy.

"We will depart in due course," Adams answered, trying to sound calm.

Revere looked at the two men with consternation. "I don't think you realize the stakes, gentlemen. They now see us not as mere upstarts, but as the enemy. Prime Minister North, Lord Dartmouth, and the King himself have placed targets on your backs," Revere said. Mrs. Clarke emitted a sound that was a blend of groan and sigh, and Dolly Quincy's complexion became even more pallid. With that, Revere made his way to the door and went into the clear, cold night to continue his ride of alarm and warning. The ride took several unexpected turns.

The moonlight was very bright, near its apex, and Revere and Dawes rode into the hamlet of Lincoln on their way to Concord, joined by Dr. Samuel Prescott of Concord, who had been out wooing Lydia Mulliken of Lexington. Suddenly, two and then six British soldiers emerged from the shadows of the trees. While Dawes and Prescott escaped, Revere was arrested. He was joined by several other prisoners the British had nabbed. Soon Major Mitchell himself joined the other Redcoats, his anger as visible as the steam coming off his horses.

"Tell us what you know," Mitchell demanded, his pistol pointed at Revere's head. Revere calmly told the soldiers of all the communities he had warned that evening and that soon hundreds of patriots would be ready for whatever might present itself. Mitchell pushed for details that Revere cheerfully provided. To the ears of Mitchell and his men, Revere's words seemed to swagger and strut, not tiptoe, out of his mouth. Then Mitchell commanded his prisoner to mount his horse and gave the steed's reins to another Redcoat so Revere could not bolt to freedom.

As they approached Lexington, the small party heard the boom of a signal gun breaking the crisp air. "What does that mean?" Mitchell barked to Revere.

Revere shrugged his shoulders. "Everyone in the countryside knows you are coming and they are in a state of full preparedness," the silversmith replied without emotion.

Then the bell of the Meeting House in Lexington penetrated the silence, prompting one of the other prisoners to say to Mitchell, "The bells are ringing, the town's alarmed, and you're all dead men."

Sensing that he might well be in serious danger, Mitchell let all the prisoners free, except Revere. He then had Revere swap horses with one of the British soldiers so Revere was stuck with a fat, slow steed. After asking Revere the distance to Concord, Mitchell and his crew raced past the meeting house and galloped on, leaving Revere in the middle of the road near Lexington Green Revere was still uncertain if other possible regulars could be lying in wait for him, so instead of crossing Lexington Green, he circled north past the cemetery, back to Reverend Clarke's house.

Revere was astounded to find John Hancock and Samuel Adams still in the parlor, chatting away in the Clarke home. These men appeared to be foolishly deluded; they were in real danger, but they remained in the house. Neither had experience in war, yet there sat Hancock blithely describing his coming transformation into a warrior.

"I am qualified to go into battle if need be," Hancock said, cleaning his pistol and polishing his sword. " Remember, I have served as the captain of the First Corps of Cadets in our town. I know how to lead." The remark was absurd; the Corps of Cadets was an honorific group with no military responsibility or knowledge. It was trotted out for special civic occasions in Boston. It had even led General Gage into Boston after the new governor had landed at the port. The vast self-confidence that Hancock had gained through business and political activity clouded any semblance of judgment he had regarding his military skills.

"You are a damned fool, John," Revere said, to which Adams added, "A true understatement." Adams provided the needed perspective to dissuade Hancock from seeking his own military engagement by adding, " Our role is a larger role in history; our value lies well beyond the grit of military work, John. Your skills are required in the larger world, and the cause cannot afford to lose you." The flattering truth had its desired effect. Finally, Hancock and Adams agreed to flee to a safe house away from Lexington and north. Leaving his fiancée Dolly was not easy for Hancock, but he knew she would be safer at Reverend Clarke's house than if she traveled with him.

Still bathed in radiant moonlight, Lexington remained in a state of quiet uncertainty, in that netherworld of time between three and dawn. The Americans had been roused from their beds, fully aware this moment would come. Trudging dutifully from farms and tiny hamlets as well as Lexington itself, they came, composed, alert. Their boots were wet with dew, and the night air still carried the faint remembrance of a colder season, with its bracing, clean, clear quality. Revere had seen no evidence of Redcoats in his scouting on the road to Concord, and so the local militia disbanded, but they were told by their captain, John Parker, to remain ready to respond if the town were to be visited by the unwelcome British.

Parker, forty-six, was a tall man with a large head and a high, wide brow, a man hardened in battle in the French-Indian War, a man respected by the seventy men in his militia who had elected him captain. (He did not disclose it, but he was dying of tuberculosis.) His men had assembled in the dead of night, still with the thought of discussing and "consulting," never intending to initiate a battle. Indeed, the militias throughout Massachusetts had been explicitly instructed to show the utmost restraint to maintain the confidence of Americans in other colonies. If the men of the Bay Colony were to precipitate needless violence, the moral leadership of Massachusetts would have evaporated.

The British regulars making their way toward Lexington and Concord were not under similar pressure to restrain themselves.

The advance party, led by Major John Pitcairn, fifty-three, arrived in Lexington exhausted and surly from the long trek from Boston, some still drenched from wading in the Charles River. They were following orders; they needed to secure the armaments in Concord and search the surrounding area for American munitions. Pitcairn, a Scotsman by origin, had arrived from England with the six hundred Redcoats who were quartered in Boston the previous year. His men were billeted all over the town, often very unwelcome by their neighbors. The soldiers felt disrespected by the other British soldiers, as well: Pitcairn's marines were men of the Navy and not the Army, and while the marines believed themselves to be superior, they felt the disdain of their compatriots. Pitcairn, a man of medium stature and an effeminate face that belied his toughness, did not think fondly of the Americans. He had penned these words after the patriots had placed the tea in the Boston Harbor:

> Orders are anxiously expected from England to chastise these very bad people. The General had some of the Great Wigs, as they are called here, with him two days ago, when he took that opportunity of telling them, and swore to it by the living God, that if there was a single man of the King's troops killed in any of their towns, he would burn it to the ground. What fools you are, said he, to pretend to resist the power of Great Britain; she maintained last war three hundred thousand men, and will do the same now rather than suffer the ungrateful people of this country to continue their rebellion. This behavior of the General's gives great satisfaction to the friends of the Government. I am satisfied that one effective campaign, a smart action, and burning of two or three of their towns, will set everything to rights. Nothing now, I am afraid, but this will ever convince these foolish, bad people that England is in earnest.

After militia, Captain Parker dismissed his men, and a number of them went to Buckman's Tavern, the popular gathering place for the "foolish, bad" Americans who lived in the vicinity of Lexington. The men in the Lexington Militia often drank there after training drills on the adjacent Green. This evening, the large fireplace crackled, warming the spacious tap room and adding to the sense of calm familiarity. The men were careful not to overindulge that evening because each understood the need for sobriety and control. Paul Revere had come to the tavern to help retrieve a trunk of valuable papers belonging to John Hancock that was stored upstairs, but the visit was cut short. A man burst into the tavern to announce the regulars were less than half a mile away and closing in fast. All the men scrambled out of Buckman's Tavern.

The eastern sky was beginning to lighten when Captain Parker commanded nineteen-year-old William Diamond to begin beating a loud roll on his drum to summon all the men in earshot to assemble on the Green. Major Pitcairn heard the drum and halted his troops so they could load their muskets. To Pitcairn, a man who had been a marine for nearly thirty years, the sound of such drums could only mean one thing: a looming battle.

Captain Parker ordered his men to populate the Bedford Road side of the Lexington Green triangle and thus allow the British to take the road on the left side that led to Concord. Parker and his men could observe the British from across the Green. Other stray men and women looked at the events from different perspectives; some from near the Buckman Tavern, some near the home of Nathan Monroe, whose house was near the road to Concord. The early morning light made it challenging to make out the figures exactly, and Pitcairn believed the scattered men and women could well be armed rebels. The dim light may have also explained why a contingent of one hundred of his regulars proceeded the wrong way, on to Bedford Road, which alarmed Pitcairn even more. The simple march to Concord was unraveling.

Pitcairn's alarm was mirrored by Parker, the Patriot, who saw the soldiers advancing now from both directions, apparently in a strategy to surround the militia. Then Pitcairn galloped across the line of British infantry that had turned off onto the Bedford Road. Now facing the militia, he felt compelled to bellow, "Lay down your arms, you damned rebels, and disperse!" It seemed now to the Americans that a sea of Redcoats was rolling toward them, some brandishing swords, with several officers racing toward the militia at full tilt. The thunder of the horses' hooves shook the earth.

Several British officers yelled, "Fire, by God! Fire!"

Parker yelled at his men to disperse, and they did, fleeing in different directions.

The alert citizens of Lexington were accustomed to the sound of muskets firing; the militia practiced regularly on the Lexington Green. So the men, women, and children made no mistake when they heard the familiar loud bang. But the sounds of British pistols were new to them. It was clear that someone in the chaos of the early day had fired his musket, and then a crackling of successive reports sounded out.

Eight members of the militia lay dead, including Captain Parker's aging cousin Jonas, who had also been run through with a bayonet. They lay at a considerable distance from one another. Their names were Jonas Parker, Jonathan Harrington, Isaac Muzzy, Robert Munroe, Samuel Hadley, John Brown, Asahel Porter, and Caleb Harrington.

On the British side, one infantryman was wounded in the leg and Major Pitcairn's horse was nicked in two places.

The painful birth of the new Nation had begun.

As John Hancock and Samuel Adams were distancing themselves from Lexington, they too heard the pop of gunfire. Adams turned to his companion and said, "Oh, what a glorious morning this is!"

Hancock, inhaling deeply and believing Adams was discussing the weather, said, "I agree!" Adams smiled to himself and did not tell Hancock why he thought it was a "glorious morning." All of Samuel Adams' relentless work of resistance had come to fruition. There would be no turning back now.

As the sun rose over the Eastern horizon and the orchestra of crows, chickadees, robins, goldfinches, and grackles were squawking and chirping to celebrate the new day, and the quiet mist rose from the Green, all those in Lexington were in a state of anxious curiosity and dreadful excitement. Even before the loved ones of the eight dead Americans were to learn of their family tragedies, a new understanding of reality had come to the town. That understanding would ripple out quickly to the surrounding countryside and to Boston, and then throughout all the colonies, up and down the coast and across the Atlantic.

Reverend Jonas Clarke turned to his family, and to Dolly Quincy and Hancock's Aunt Lydia, all still in their nightgowns and feeling confused and fearful, all milling around the parlor. The reverend proclaimed, almost as if from the pulpit, "Everything has changed. From this remarkable day will an important era begin for both America and Britain. God help us all!"

Epilogue

In June of 1775, at age fifty, the "flame of Fire" was still burning. James Otis had recently moved in to live with Mercy and her family. He was less and less rooted in reality. The news of Lexington and Concord forced him to see there was no turning back from armed resistance. Mercy and her brother sat in the drawing room, sipping tea and reflecting.

"James, look what you have wrought," said Mercy. "All hell is breaking loose. Who knew that this would actually happen, back in 1761?"

"You knew, Mercy. You have been telling us all along about the downward spiral," Otis replied with affection.

"Do you believe that it is worth it, James?" she asked. "Tearing families like yours apart, the bitterness and anger, the death. Is this worth it?"

Otis knew Mercy's question was empty. She had been writing poems and plays about liberty and justice for years, stating clearly that these ideals were absolutely worth dying for.

Yet they also both knew that their sons could soon be engaged in the conflict.

"As Crispus told me before the Writs case, if you are not free, you are not fully human. The price for liberty is exorbitant but must be paid," Otis said solemnly.

Otis retired to the small bedroom the Warrens had given him. Suddenly, a stream of Minutemen and militia raced by the house. Rumors had circulated that the British were about to march out en masse to seize both Bunker Hill and Breed's Hill in Charlestown in order to gain a favorable position to control the Boston Harbor. The men who were racing by the Warren home indicated that those hills were under siege. Otis was overcome with the drive to join the fight. Once again, he was not fully in control of himself.

Unbeknownst to Mercy, her brother slipped out of the house and followed the stream of much younger men. He stopped at a nearby farmhouse and borrowed a musket, and then raced to catch up. As he made his way past the men in the rear, one of them shouted, "Who is that fat old man, and how could he possibly be of use?" The answer came fast and emphatic from the militia captain: "That is James Otis, the hero. Show him the respect he deserves, young man." And word spread that Otis had joined them, eliciting compassionate head shakes and quiet smiles.

Otis joined the combatants for several hours. He saw several of his young comrades die or become wounded. One had his arm blown off cleanly and another his head split in two. Later reports stated that Otis had run into a hail of bullets, all of which miraculously missed him. As midnight approached, his energy was totally spent and he trudged slowly back to the Warrens, exhausted but unscathed.

Mercy greeted her brother with a blend of relief and the kind of protective anger a mother feels toward a wayward child who had finally found his way home.

As Otis trudged through the front door. he was met with an unexpected greeting from his sister.

"What do you think you are doing, Jemmy? Why didn't you tell me where you were going and what you were doing? You look terrible. You are panting like a dog. This is not acceptable!"

The frost in the air came from his sister, not the cool night outside. It confused Otis.

"I went to join the patriots to try to do my part. I was trying to help the cause as best I could. Why are you acting this way?"

Mercy sighed, shook her head, and remained silent. Otis was genuinely surprised not to receive a warm welcome.

"I'm going to bed, " he said with an unusually harsh tone. His sister lowered her head and sighed again, this time more deeply.

Her brother's wild unpredictability was becoming unacceptable. With everything else happening in her family's life, Mercy needed to find a way to rid them of the chaos her brother created. It was a painful decision that she had agonized over for several years. Finally, she had to tell her beloved brother he could no longer stay with them.

In 1781, some noble souls came to the rescue: the Osgood family of Andover.

The Osgood brothers included Jacob, Isaac, and Samuel. Samuel was a Harvard man, having studied theology. Samuel Osgood's handsome face emanated confidence and clarity; it seemed to say about the man "I know who I am and do not need to impress you." He was a compassionate soul who, like many of his contemporaries, fought fiercely at Lexington and Concord and in the Siege of Boston. His valor and ability caused him to be promoted to colonel. When he left the army in 1776, he was named to the Massachusetts Board of War by the Provincial Congress. His quiet and effective leadership led him to be elected to represent Massachusetts in the Continental Congress from 1782 to 1784.

Osgood had always respected James Otis, so inviting him to his beautiful, spacious farm seemed natural. Osgood's wife, Martha, had died three years before, and they had no children. Perhaps Osgood wanted some company, so inviting the brilliant hero of Boston's 1760s seemed like a good idea. The presence of his calm host had a salutary effect on Otis. His periods of lucidity seemed to have been lasting longer and longer. It reached the point of such apparent progress that in early April of 1783, John Hancock extended an invitation to Otis and Osgood for dinner, and the two men happily accepted.

The twenty-mile trip from Andover to Boston seemed to fly by for Osgood as Otis regaled him with stories of the sixties and lessons from the Ancients. The carriage was solid and the horse strong so Osgood could focus clearly and comfortably on his friend and his stories. There was little opportunity for Osgood to speak (which he did not resent at all). Otis' humor was such that even the driver of the carriage would laugh out loud at the jokes and quips of the famous patriot.

As they approached the Hancock mansion on Beacon Hill, Osgood, a wealthy man himself, was impressed. The mansion had belonged to Hancock's Uncle Thomas. Built of square-cut granite blocks and trimmed at each corner with brownstone quoins, it had two large windows at either side of the grand entrance, permitting a breathtaking view of Boston Common, as well as the city, the harbor, and the surrounding countryside. The house had fifty-three windows with the best crown glass from London. Hancock's love of landscaping was reflected in a variety of shade trees and elegant gardens, with many plants coming from English nurseries. The inside was equally spacious and elegant.

Osgood turned to Otis and said, "Remind me, James. We are not in a monarchy, correct? Once we are independent of British rule, is this what all Americans have to look forward to?" He pointed toward the Hancock mansion.

"Guaranteed," Otis said, smiling back at his friend.

Hancock had planned the small dinner party carefully. This was not like earlier parties; everyone who was invited to join Hancock and Dolly, and Otis and Osgood, were sympathetic to James Otis, the guest of honor: Samuel and Elizabeth Adams; Samuel and Elizabeth Otis; and, of course, Mercy Otis Warren and her husband James.

As they nibbled on the skewered chicken appetizer and Brie cheese, a strange blend of celebration and trepidation was in the air. The tide had turned in the war itself; the Battle of Yorktown had ensured the American victory, and American spirits were high. Yet all the guests knew of Otis' derangement and periodic bouts with melancholy. They did not know which James Otis would present himself that evening. Osgood had consulted with Hancock about the seating arrangement, insisting James Otis be flanked by Mercy and Osgood, two people who had loved and protected the patriot. John and Dolly Hancock anchored each end of the elegantly set table. The meal was simple, consisting of mutton, carrots, and whipped potatoes accompanied by the finest Bordeaux wine that money could buy.

"Thank you, Hancocks, for inviting us to such a wonderful feast," James Warren said. "Victory and celebration are in the air, and Mercy and I can think of no one we would rather spend the evening with than you two and this lovely group."

"You are most welcome, James. We are charmed and honored to have you here. We are particularly honored to have James Otis, the Patriot, with us. Let me toast the man responsible for the beginning of resistance. Here is to you, James Otis," Hancock replied. They all raised their glasses, clinked them, and shouted, "Here, here!" Otis smiled and blushed. He was at a loss for words, and after an awkward pause, the group broke into three separate conversations. Mercy's sister-in-law, Elizabeth Otis, a young, slender, brown-haired woman with a gentle regal air, sat directly across from Mercy. She felt compelled to express her condolences to both Otis and Mercy.

"I am so sorry for the sacrifice your family has had to make, for the awful loss you have had to endure," she said. "It must be so hard to carry on."

Otis and Mercy thanked her and acknowledged the pain they felt. They each carried a definite sense of responsibility for what had befallen their sons. Otis' oldest son had been killed, and Mercy's had sustained a crippling wound to his leg. Had the resistance not reached the point of war, both of the young men would have been alive, with years of prosperity and good fortune likely awaiting them. Mercy's face had taken on a new expression of subdued sadness. As for her brother, his derangement made it difficult to ascertain the depths of pain he was experiencing, but the loss of his son might have triggered a sense of guilt and emptiness whenever he thought of young Jemmy.

Elizabeth and Mercy were both eager to turn their attention elsewhere, so they began to listen in on the conversation between Samuel Otis, John Hancock, and Samuel Adams. It had not taken the three men long to begin debating the best form of government that the nearly independent nation should adopt.

Samuel Otis, fifteen years younger than his brother James, was an affable, almost handsome man with penetrating eyes and a naturally elegant bearing. He started the discussion.

"I say this only partially in jest: I believe George Washington should be our king. He is the one who has brought all the colonies together, bringing order out of the chaos of local militias. We need a strong central government that can unite us all. We need our first national leader to be above politics, and to set an example for all of us."

Hancock must have heard these words of praise for Washington with a mixture of disdain and reluctant agreement. Washington lacked the polish and pedigree that the five Harvard men at the table had, but it was certainly true he had unified the colonies and, more importantly, led them to victory. Hancock still recalled with good-natured envy how the Continental Congress had selected Washington, and not himself, to be commander-in-chief of the patriot forces. Hancock's natural generosity and good sense led him to remain silent. Samuel Adams was the one to take the bait Samuel Otis had dangled.

"Of course, the idea of rejecting one king and creating a new one is ludicrous. But I disagree with your more serious point. We do not need a strong centralized government. That leads to the very kind of tyranny our British overlords have tried to force us to accept. Power is a corrupting force and needs to be shared and exercised at the local level. Our friends like Jefferson from the southern colonies are right about that. A strong central government will create a new kind of monarchy, but with another name," Adams concluded, nearly shouting.

"Amen to that, Mr. Adams," Mercy chimed in. As the conversation became more spirited, James Otis became more subdued, his head leaning down, almost as if he were in prayer.

Samuel Otis persisted. "How can we defend the new nation if we are a bunch of scattered colonies, each fending for itself? How can we ensure uniform rights and build a prosperous nation financially if we are but a group of pathetic fiefdoms?" he asked.

"We want the people to be powerful, not the government," Mercy stated, perhaps too loudly.

"That is a false dichotomy, my dear sister," said Samuel Otis. "We can have both."

James Otis began to mutter to himself, using words that were unintelligible. The rest of the group tried to ignore this, hoping he would stop, hoping at least that he could remain silent, hoping he felt their love and residual respect.

Hancock wanted to turn the table talk back to James Otis and continue a celebration of his role and his triumphs.

"James, your words twenty years ago at the Writs of Assistance trial woke up all of Boston. You showed us all that with Reason and Fervor we could resist tyranny. Your words and your arguments rippled across the colonies and across the Atlantic. You and Mr. Adams here have opened our eyes and reminded us of what was of the utmost importance: our rights and our freedom." Hancock's words caused murmurs of agreement.

Samuel Adams continued the praise, saying, "You and Mercy have used words as tools and as weapons; tools to show us where we are and need to go, and weapons to give us heart to fight fiercely." Adams went on to recall details of the sixties that exalted a number of patriots, and with James Otis at the center of the effective acts of resistance. Adams' words elicited head nods and smiles from the guests.

Otis then looked at Hancock and Adams with a blank stare of incomprehension. He stood up so quickly he almost lost his balance and began to shout in Latin, reciting Virgil and Cicero, and using his whole body for histrionic effect. He moved quickly around the dining room, pounding on the end tables for effect, never lapsing into English. His face became red and began to glow with sweat, and the volume of his words increased with each passing minute. His brother Samuel and James Warren rose simultaneously and approached Otis. He pushed them aside and continued. Hancock and Adams rose to help, but to no avail. The tragic rant just grew louder.

"Jemmy, stop this now!" Mercy shouted at the top of her lungs. "Stop!" She approached her brother, getting dangerously close to him, literally face to face. A final time she said, in a much softer tone, "Stop," and then he did. Otis lowered his head like a guilty child and walked out of the dining room into the long hall, to the front door, and out of the house. Osgood and Samuel Otis raced after him, across Hancock's manicured lawn, finally reaching and subduing him. Otis and his brother Samuel held one another under the pall of utmost pain, and Otis sobbed on his brother's shoulder.

A deep sense of sad embarrassment fell over the rest of the guests. When James Otis returned to the table, the conversation became safely banal, and he retreated to his state of impassive silence. When the guests had finished the dessert of Alma Pudding, Otis turned to Osgood and said, "We must return to the farm now!" to which Hancock objected. "No, stay here for the night and you can return tomorrow. It is not wise to travel at night." James Otis persisted adamantly, relentlessly that they return.

Before departing, Otis approached Mercy for a private word. "I hope when God Almighty, in his Providence, shall take me out of time into eternity, it will be by a flash of lightning!"

Mercy nodded and beheld her brother with compassionate understanding. James Otis had been in a living Hell. "We love and respect you, Jemmy, and feel such sorrow for your torment," she replied. They embraced and Otis joined Osgood. Samuel Otis insisted he join the two men for the long, dark, cold return to Andover, his own horse trailing the carriage on the dreary trip back.

The three arrived at the Osgood farm in the dead of night, With almost no strength left, Otis found a new wellspring of energy: deranged rage. He proceeded to his boxes of letters, papers, speeches, essays, articles—everything he had written; took the documents outside to the burn pit and destroyed all of them. History would be forever cheated, deprived of Otis' full story. Exhausted, he collapsed onto his bed for an instantaneous and deep sleep. Otis had always been an early riser, but of late, he had slept longer and longer. The day after the Hancock party, he awoke at noon, surprised at the hour. He had the drugged sensation that intense sleep can sometimes cause. Another surprise was the envelope at the foot of his bed.

Beth Frothingham had written to him every month ever since he had left Boston. She had married Paul Cooper, a man worthy of this remarkable woman. (Cooper was a wainwright and had actually repaired the very carriage the men had used the previous night.) Otis had loved reading Beth's words and remained impressed at her incredible penmanship. The platonic love she felt for him leapt out from every page, a love encouraged by her husband. Jemmy had so few things to nourish his soul, and Beth's letters led the small list.

> Dearest James,
>
> I have been thinking of you more often than usual over the past month. When I am not cleaning up after Jacob and Willy and trying to keep them from harm's way, my mind flashes to you. I will treasure forever the sessions and times we had together. I probably have told you many times, but the memory of your pure soul and kind heart remain with me daily and have helped me through the difficult times in Boston. Just remembering that we are all part of a much bigger cause, and that we are on the threshold of a whole new day for our colony and our land, gives me courage and hope. When I think of who embodied that courage and hope, I think of you. Your spirit has "infected" our whole family.
>
> The British remnants who remain in our town are still obnoxious, and when the last of them leaves our shores, it will not be soon enough. At the Green Dragon, they remain arrogant pigs. (I know that sounds uncharitable, but if you knew what they do and say to me, you would understand.) Still, work is otherwise going well and our two boys make it both more challenging and more necessary (we need the money). Paul always tells me to greet you, so please know he sends his very best as well.
>
> I hope you do not find it inappropriate, but I wanted to tell you that this is what I pray for you each day:
>
> Dear God, please love and protect James, and let him know how much You love him and how much he is loved by your other servants here on Earth. Let him know that he

is not alone, even if many of his days are solitary. Please give him peace and let him have his wishes come true and his needs be met. Pour down Your love from heaven and take him into Your loving arms as You see fit and in the manner You most wish to do. Thank You dear Lord for allowing James to be in my life and in the lives of countless patriots. Bless this man forever.

Amen.

Thinking of you always. Paul and I are wondering if we might visit you this summer; I would love to have you meet our boys.

Love,
Beth

Otis could not suppress a smile as he read the letter and the prayer. What a blessing to have had this woman in his life. What a balm in a world of quiet, incessant torture. Sweet Beth was aware of the demons that drove Otis, yet cheerfully remained in his life, providing him one of his very few points of light. Beth consciously ignored many of Otis' flaws and shortcomings, including his sad inability to forgive his older daughter, Elizabeth, who had married a British soldier (injured seriously at Bunker Hill) and moved to England. In his Last Will and Testament, written that March, Otis left Elizabeth one shilling, a token of the scorn he felt toward his older daughter.

While Elizabeth never sought reconciliation, Ruth wanted it. She felt the need to make amends with her husband. Ruth had spent the years during the Boston occupation and the Boston siege a changed woman, not in her loyalty to the Crown but in her openness to those with opposing views. Ruth had changed in just the manner Francis Merrywell had suggested, with only one piece of unfinished business. She still had not summoned the courage to visit her husband. After much soul-searching, Ruth decided to make the long trek from Boston to Osgood's Andover farm, a trip much overdue. She would do it at the beginning of June.

The Friday afternoon of May 23 saw a number of guests at the Osgood farm. The air had been heavy, the humidity oppressive. The guests and family were waiting out a thunderstorm, grateful for the cool air it was delivering. Otis was regaling several young and restless children with stories as he stood near the front door of the simple, lovely house, holding his cane in one hand and standing against the post of the door. The animated story he was telling was interrupted by a single thunderous, deafening explosion and a blinding flash of lightning. The lightning struck the chimney, followed a rafter of the roof that rested on the upright timbers, and reached the doorpost Otis was leaning on. James Otis died instantly, falling into the arms of Samuel Osgood. The other guests were untouched. No mark could be found on Otis' face, and his lips had assumed the subtlest of smiles, the familiar shape that his mouth had formed throughout his life of brilliant oratory and earnest conversation.

The *Boston Gazette* of May 26, 1783 described it this way:

> We hear from Andover last Friday Evening the House of Mr. Isaac Osgood was set on fire and much shattered by Lightning, by which Hon. James Otis, Esq., of this Town, leaning upon his Cane at the front Door, was instantly killed. Several Persons were in the House at the Time, some of whom were violently affected by the shock, but immediately recovering, ran to Mr. Otis' support; but he expired without a groan. The Friends and Acquaintances of the Deceased are informed his Funeral is to be To-Morrow from his House near County Court House. Freemasons are to precede the Corps.

A large and growing cortege of mourners made the trip from Andover to Boston and on to the Old Granary Burying Ground. Ruth Cunningham Otis insisted the remains of her husband be interred in the Cunningham tomb. She had never reached him in time to seek and receive reconciliation, but she would lay next to him for eternity in Boston's most prominent cemetery.

On June 7, 1783, *The New-Hampshire Gazette* published the following commemorative ode by Thomas Dawes on Otis' death:

On the DEATH of the Honourable James Otis, Esq.

Then OTIS rose, and first in patriot fame,

To listening crowds resistance dared proclaim,

From soul to soul the great idea ran,

The fire of freedom flew from man to man.

His pen, like Sydney's made the doctrines known;

His tongue like Tully's shook a tyrant's throne.

From men like OTIS Independence grew

From such beginnings empire rose to view.

Long after he had left the Presidency, John Adams said of James Otis:

> I have been young, and now am old, and I solemnly say I have never known a man whose love of country was more ardent or sincere, never one who suffered so much, never one whose service for any 10 years of his life were so important and essential to the cause of his country, as those of Mr. Otis from 1760 to 1770.

In his death by lightning, James Otis' wish had been granted and his torment had ceased. The "flame of Fire" described by John Adams had been put out, but the cause James Otis and his fellow Patriots fought for was not extinguished. It is a cause that will never cease to require the brave, consistent vigilance of Americans, a cause that is, and always will be, infused in the lifeblood of all citizens, however long ago or recently they may have arrived on these shores.

What Happened to the Historical Characters?

Dr. Joseph Warren died valiantly at the Battle of Bunker Hill in 1775. He could easily have avoided service and the danger of combat, but he chose not to.

Otis' son, **James Otis III**, died in a British naval prison in 1776 as a sailor fighting for the Patriot cause.

Ruth Cunningham Otis continued to live in Boston and died at age sixty.

Daughter **Elizabeth Otis** married Captain Brown and moved permanently to England.

Daughter **Mary Otis** married Captain Benjamin Lincoln, who died at twenty-eight, leaving her to raise her two children alone.

Mercy Otis Warren wrote the first history of the American Revolution, *History of the Rise, Progress, and Termination of the American Revolution* (1805). She was an Anti-Federalist who opposed the expansion of power of the national government.

James Warren was George Washington's paymaster in the Continental Army. After the war, he, like his wife Mercy, was a vocal and prominent Anti-Federalist.

John Hancock and **Samuel Adams** signed the Declaration of Independence and successively became Governors of Massachusetts. The scope of their work was provincial, not national.

General Gage and Margaret Gage moved back to England.

Customs Officer John Robinson moved back to England.

Governor Thomas Hutchinson finished his days in England in depressed obscurity.

Benjamin Edes continued publishing the *Boston Gazette* until 1798. He died at seventy-one.

John Gill severed ties with Edes after the evacuation of Boston and died at fifty-three.

Ebenezer Mackintosh walked to New Hampshire and married. He died poor and uncelebrated.

William Molineux died in 1774. The cause of his death was not clear.

John Adams became the second President of the United States.

Samuel Otis was a quartermaster in the Continental Army. He was the first Secretary of the United States Senate. He held the Bible when George Washington was sworn in as President.

Samuel Osgood served in the Massachusetts and New York legislatures. His New York City home served as the first Presidential Mansion. He was the first President of what is now Citibank.

Paul Revere served as a militia officer in the war and then returned to his silversmith trade, expanding it with work in iron casting, as well as bronze bell and cannon casting.

Crispus Attucks embodies the unrealized dream of a potentially greater nation. Half Native, half African, the fact that he was the first to die in the Revolution is some kind of sign, divine challenge, and light shining on how this country must change if it is to realize its stated ideals.

Lessons Learned

If you treat me as an enemy long enough, I will become your enemy.

Then. Benjamin Franklin summed it up best as the British contemplated a major show of force in Boston. He said, "you will not find a rebellion there, but you may cause one." And they most certainly did. The British triggered animosity in countless, very personal ways. Abuse such as impressing Americans into the British Navy was one irritant, as was the high-handed use of the Writs of Assistance. Smaller insults and incursions into daily life also occurred when the mass of British soldiers came to occupy Boston in 1768, looking for lodging and displacing local people, as well as strutting into familiar taverns like the Green Dragon in the full regalia of their red coats. The politics of resentment is an eternal force, and bullies often sow the seeds of their own demise.

Now. New pathways to understanding and goodwill need to be created in our fractured society, whether it is between police and blacks; urban and rural; labor and business; Christians, Jews, and Muslims; North and South, or any other of a host of divisions. Must we keep treating one another like enemies? Can't we try to find ways to understand and respect one another? Initiatives like Braver Angels bring people with opposing political views together to truly listen to one another. Local efforts like the Twin Cities Regional Council of Mayors serves a similar purpose. There will always be conflict in politics, and that can be healthy, but treating others as enemies is toxic and is slowly killing our body politic.

Smart leadership is essential, but success can only come with a broad cross-section.

Then. The Harvard-educated leaders needed people like the humble shoemaker Ebenezer Mackintosh and his loyal followers to advance their cause. Trust-building across class lines was essential.

Now. A challenge for Democrats has been the apparent disconnect between liberal elites and what had been an important part of the base of the party: workers and the working poor. That party has not communicated and acted effectively on behalf of people who have lost their jobs or are otherwise living on the edge financially.

To make lasting change, public opinion needs to be forefront at all times.

Then. Samual Adams called the hasty, unplanned killing of five citizens by British soldiers on March 5 of 1770 the "Boston Massacre." That brilliant move caused ill will to fester among Bostonians long after the event, as did the annual commemorations of the "Massacre."

Now. Starting in 1980 with President Ronald Reagan, Republicans have seized the initiative in the domain of shaping public opinion. Democrats have done much for the American people, but they have found it challenging to communicate their past successes or their vision for the future. That failure has enabled Republicans to define Democrats in effective and negative ways.

Riots and mobs are useful to get the attention of the powers that be, but there are limits.

Then. Bostonians were always walking the tightrope between excess and civility, and when the British felt some kind of line had been crossed, they felt the need to rattle their swords. When protests became too violent and protracted, the British crackdown of 1768 occurred.

Now. There was widespread vandalism throughout the United States after the murder of George Floyd, much done by people with no interest in social justice. On the other hand, respectful and energetic demonstrations following that murder have been important forces for positive change. The January 6 invasion of the US Capitol was hideous and frightening, but thankfully served no purpose to advance any toxic cause. The mob had gone way too far. Many rioters of the January 6 insurrection were convicted of crimes, reaffirming the rule of law.

Acts of public defiance require careful strategic thinking.

Then. Risk-taking needs to be well-calculated and the effects of planned actions need to be shrewdly considered. And it helps to guess right. The planners of the Boston Tea Party thought through possible and likely outcomes with great care, and they saw their actions in a larger context.

Now. Whether the issue is human rights, climate change, or anything else, the best acts of defiance are part of a larger strategy with a finely tuned sense of public relations and clear ideas on changing public policy. If the actions are not strategic, they can be self-defeating. The shining examples of doing it right were the civil rights leaders in the 1950s and 1960s. They were able to defy bad laws bravely and brilliantly, to powerful effect.

Mocking the powerful with well-chosen words can seriously erode respect for those leaders.

Then. Mercy Otis Warren's thinly veiled poems and plays undercut Governor Thomas Hutchinson and inflamed Bostonians in ways the government was unable to fight. By mocking powerful figures, using their actual weaknesses, no easy response is possible.

Now. Certain television channels and social media are sources of effective mockery. Today, however, the humor tends to lock people into their polarized camps. How much the shrinking group of true independents can be influenced is an open question. Using satire in ways that can move them could be part of a communication strategy that wins elections.

Nothing is inevitable.

Then. The American war with Great Britain could have been avoided if the British had been willing to give Americans the same rights as English citizens. Even short of that, the British could have played their cards better to appease the Americans. Failing to do that, coupled with the macho need to strut their power, British actions led to the armed conflict that occurred.

Now. How Americans and their leaders will reorder priorities and change the culture after COVID-19, George Floyd, and the January 6 invasion of the US Capitol is an open question. The door is open to significant social and economic improvement. Creative solutions to climate change, racial and income inequity, and education reform are possible. On the other hand, voter suppression, polarized political hatreds, and the perverse effects of big money in campaigning and governing could continue. Neither progress nor decay is inevitable.

Ideas and ideals have great power when articulated and acted on.

Then. It has been said, "There is nothing more powerful than an idea whose time has come." The ideas and ideals that animated the drive for resistance, and then independence, gave the patriots a deep sense of shared purpose and the heady sense that they were fighting for something way beyond themselves, something truly historic. That feeling elicits courage and shared sacrifice among people of all walks of life. It did then and it can now.

Now. For the good of the nation, leaders today would be well-served by remembering and articulating the high ideals that led to Revolution and the formation of a new nation. Concepts like truth, justice, equity, opportunity, and God-given rights need to honored in word and in deed. Efforts to show that we are being led by these ideals can help America to become more unified.

What might those leaders tell us today?

The grand concepts that we identify with Jefferson, Madison, Hamilton, and the others were all developed well before the American Revolution and the Declaration of Independence. James Otis proclaimed many of those ideals as early as 1764 in "The Rights of the British Colonies Asserted and Proved."

Here are five excerpts from that document. Otis' real words are in italics and after each one there are encouraging words to today's America, as if these five patriots could join us now. *Listen to a rendition of James Otis, Samuel Adams, John Hancock, Mercy Otis Warren, and Crispus Attucks.*

On the source of the right to freedom.

"There can be no prescription old enough to supersede the law of nature, and the grant of God almighty; who has given all men a natural right to be free."

James Otis: Remember that although God has given you those rights, tyrants can take them away. Tyranny can take blatant or subtle forms. Beware of demagogues who corrode the rule of law and eventually your freedom. Use that freedom well and not just for yourself but for everyone. The people I lived with in Boston opened a new chapter of history in the 1760s. You can write another new chapter that expands true freedom for all.

On where the power must reside.

"...supreme absolute power is originally and ultimately in the people...."

Samuel Adams: As you look at power in our country, do you really think it still resides with the people? If it did, why would your elected leaders act so differently from what the people say they want when they are polled on climate change, abortion, early childhood education, gun control, fair taxes, and many more issues? Please work to make the people's will supreme and cut the role of massive money in governing. Honor the importance of all our citizens to improve the nation at the grassroots level. The American spirit is still alive, and everyone must join in to help.

On the purpose of government.

"The end of government being the good of mankind...it is above all things to provide for the security, the quiet and happy enjoyment of life, liberty and property...."

John Hancock: I was wealthy and helped finance the Revolution, which was for the rights of all the citizens throughout the provinces of America. You are all in this together. The inequality of wealth in America today dwarfs the differences we had in Boston, and you are much the worse for it. Make your leaders be true to the words they love so much: life, liberty, and the pursuit of happiness. Bring those words to life for all Americans. You can do it, so do it!

On the need for principled opposition, on occasion.

"Whenever their administrators, in any of those forms, deviate from truth, justice and equity, they verge toward tyranny and are to be opposed, and if they prove incorrigible, they will be deposed by the people, if the people are not rendered too abject."

Mercy Otis Warren: For all of the indignities and outrages we suffered in Boston, we did not engage in self-pity. We kept pushing for our rights until we reached that momentous crossroads. You are at another crossroad. Too many of your current and past politicians have made a mockery of Truth. They must be opposed. Join those who are already fighting for economic justice, human rights, and environmental protection. Make "good trouble," as the late John Lewis put it. Move our great nation to its finest destiny. All citizens are needed for this great adventure. Act.

On one of America's two grave stains.

"Slavery is so vile and miserable an estate of man, and so directly opposite to the generous temper and courage of our nation, it's hard to be conceived that an Englishman, much less a gentleman, should plead for it...."

Crispus Attucks: The fabled Founders failed miserably to protect our nation from the poisonous evil of slavery. The vicious racism too rampant in America since the Revolution has, through the generations, made a mockery of the highfalutin phrases of the Declaration of Independence. The disgrace of how Indigenous people have been treated is America's other stain. To protect the Earth, you must honor the values of those who have lived here for thousands of years. We must treat one another and the earth with respect.

It is time for all Americans to come together and be true to our highest ideals. If our forebears in America broke from England over these ideals, why cannot we take the responsibility of seeing them fulfilled? We can and we must.

A Final Note

Whether Loyalists like Ruth Otis or Patriots like Mercy Otis Warren, women played major roles in the brewing conflict. Yet women were denied decision-making power. Male energy on both sides of the Atlantic drove the two sides to war. As I wrote the book, I would occasionally wonder how this might have developed differently if women had run the show then. When England sent in thousands of soldiers to Boston in 1768, their leaders wanted to show the upstart Americans who was the dominant power. Once that occurred, the men in America shifted and became first opponents and then enemies. My own view is that if women could gain at least equality in governing nations, including the most powerful ones, the tendency toward festering animosity and then to war would be greatly reduced.

Acknowledgments

I would like to thank the following for their support and assistance in the creation of this book.

Family. The family I grew up in was deeply interested in history. That family enabled me to go to Harvard and major in American history; both sister Emily and brother Pock majored in it. My current expanded family has been very supportive of this effort to understand and explain James Otis the Patriot and some of the key people and events of his time. Some family members have given me invaluable feedback.

Professional supporters. David Unowsky, past owner of the Hungry Mind Bookstore, has given me great advice, guidance, and support. Tyler Tichelaar, outstanding author and editor, has been crucial in making this book the best it can be. Patricia Francisco, celebrated author, reviewed and advised me in ways that truly elevated the book's quality.

Friends. Various friends have taken the time to read the manuscript at various stages of its development. While some may have been too kind in their responses, they have also provided ideas and reactions that helped shape the book.

Sources. A wide variety of books, be they biographies or general histories, have enabled me to learn about this fascinating time in history and get a sense of the personalities of the key players in pre-Revolutionary Boston. Electronic journals have also been very helpful. Google has been an indispensable "partner." It is an amazing tool for checking and rechecking historical accuracy.

The times we live in. In recent years, the urgency of reaffirming democratic norms and the need to appreciate fully the source of our democracy have given me added motivation to write this book. I hope in some small way the book will help the reader more deeply appreciate the importance of the ideals that are the foundation to how America can thrive, now, and into the future.

About the Author

Todd Otis was born in 1945 and lives in Minneapolis with his partner, Ren. He is the father of Philip, Katharine, and Madeline, and stepfather of Josh and Heather. He is the proud grandfather of eight amazing grandchildren. He was educated at the St. Paul Academy and earned an AB from Harvard College and an MS in Journalism from Columbia University. He is an indirect descendant of James Otis the Patriot.

Todd's public service includes being a volunteer in the Peace Corps, Senegal, as well as serving as a Minnesota State Representative from 1979 to 1990, after which he consulted and advocated for support of environmental and educational reforms. The last twenty years of his working life were dedicated to improving the early care and education of Minnesota's youngest citizens.

Today, Todd serves on several boards. He is also the author of *A Review of Nuclear Energy in the United States: Hidden Power* (Praeger, 1981). He enjoys being with his family and friends, reading, writing, playing tennis, watching Minnesota sports teams, and traveling with Ren Dewar.